SLAP SHOT AT LOVE

SLAP SHOT SERIES
BOOK 1

A.K. ISAACS

To Jess.

SLAP SHOT AT LOVE

AUTHOR'S NOTE

Dearest Reader,

While this book is mostly light and fun, I want to give you a heads-up that it contains social anxiety representation, including an on-page panic attack.

It also includes the discussion of an off-page attempted date rape that takes place before the story begins.

I worked very hard to handle both of these things with the care and thoughtfulness they deserve. As a reader, I always appreciate knowing about sensitive issues that may come up in a story, so I wanted to mention it.

I hope you enjoy spending some time with Cassie and Caleb! Please be sure to take care of yourself.

All my love,

A.K. Isaacs

CALEB

PREFACE

The first time I noticed Cassie Flowers was right around the moment her fist connected with my face. I mean, I was asking for it. Like, I had literally asked her to try to hit me. I just hadn't expected someone roughly half my size to be able to. Multiple times. But I never made the mistake of not noticing Cassie ever again, that's for sure.

I blame Thomas King. After all, he was the one who kept bragging about how much boxing classes were helping his mobility on the ice. He just neglected to mention that he only ever hit a bag. He wasn't out there sparring with experienced fighters. I should have known since we all generally liked to leave that to our team's enforcer.

But since we had a long break between games, I figured I might as well give the whole boxing thing a try. Which was how I found myself waiting outside the office of the highly intimidating club owner, Anthony, overhearing a very annoyed woman trying to avoid me at all costs.

"I'm sorry, but you cannot expect me to spar with a professional hockey player. That's insane!" she said.

I rubbed my sweaty hands on my thighs, trying to keep them from trembling. I couldn't spar with this woman with shaky hands, after all. Meeting new people might make me nervous, but sparring with this woman definitely didn't.

"Cassie, when I asked for your help with a VIP, you seemed excited," Anthony said in a gruff voice.

"I was! That was before you told me I'm supposed to fight a guy who's wearing a no-contact jersey in practice because he's injured. What if I hurt him?" she asked in a whisper as if she was genuinely concerned, and it made me chuckle to myself under my breath.

"You're not going to hurt him," Anthony said. "And he knows what he's getting into."

I did not, in fact, know what I was getting into.

She made some unrecognizable grumbles, followed by, "Fine, but I will not be held responsible if the Blizzards don't make it to the playoffs this year."

So she knew who I was, and she knew we were on the verge of not making the playoffs because of all our injuries this season… I stored both things in the back of my brain for later because after a few more grumbles I couldn't quite make out, the tiny, feisty woman emerged from the office with her hands on her hips and a grimace spread across her face. Her long, brown hair was pulled into a loose braid that fell over her shoulder, and her cheeks were slightly red, presumably from her previous workout. Or maybe they were red because of the fury she was about to unleash on me. It was still unclear. All I knew was that this little woman in leggings and a sports bra should not have been worried about hurting me.

"So," she said, crossing her arms across her chest. "I guess you want me to hit you?"

"No, I want you to *try* to hit me," I said with a smirk.

I followed the dumb joke with a wink that even I knew

was cheesy and stupid (and I rarely know how to interact with people, let alone gorgeous women who are inexplicably refusing to take a swing at me.)

She did not like the wink. And she showed just how much she didn't like it right around the time she fought me better than any player I'd been annoyed with enough to fight in a game. I wound up with a black eye and a very bruised ego, but I did somehow get my best friend out of the horrible encounter, so it's pretty much a draw in my mind.

CHAPTER 1
CASSIE
TWO-ISH YEARS LATER

've always loved school. I guess that's why I became a teacher. Which is probably why the first week back at school is my favorite time of the year. New school supplies, setting up my teacher planner, meeting my new students and reconnecting with my fellow teachers, I love all of it. Most people wouldn't guess that I love much of anything, I suppose. Caleb tells me I tend to come across as a bit of a hardass. But I really do have a soft spot for new beginnings and making sure that each of my students is given the best possible opportunity to succeed.

I'm on recess duty for the whole seventh grade, and so far this week, it's been easy going. I know it's only day four of the school year, but the air is crisp, the sun is shining, and I'm feeling like nothing can get in the way of a great school year.

And, of course—presumably as payback for something I did in a past life—that's the moment I hear the chant break out.

"Fight! Fight! Fight!"

It's coming from clear across the playground, so I sprint toward the crowd of twelve-year-olds forming by the swing set, hoping that the increased cardio I did over the summer gets me there before something too horrible happens. When I reach the circle of kids, I'm reminded that I'm unfortunately around their same height, but I somehow manage to weasel my way between a couple of giggling girls.

"Hey!" I shout.

"You're such a loser," a tiny kid says to the much larger kid towering over him. "No wonder your dad died. It was probably from embarrassment."

The big kid's face turns a color of red usually reserved for cartoon characters as he swings his arm back. I know from my experience at the boxing club that what he's about to do will cause a lot of damage to the small kid's face if I don't stop this.

"Hey!" I shout again. "That's enough!"

The big kid, Ralph, who isn't in my class but I know of because his dad died last year, looks over at me. His face turns from red to white in an instant as he lowers his arm.

"I'm sorry, I..." he starts.

"Save it for Principal Meyers," I say. "Both of you, come with me."

Ralph approaches me, his head hanging low.

"But..." the small kid starts to protest.

I level him with my best do-not-fuck-with-me teacher stare, and he files in behind Ralph. Neither of them says a word on the walk to the principal's office, so I use the time to gather my thoughts about what the hell just happened. Violence is never an answer. Even I know that, and I spend most of my free time smashing my fist into a two-hundred-pound bag of sand. But mocking a kid whose dad just died and using that death to do so is beyond cruel. Both kids deserve to be punished, but I have a feeling Principal Meyers won't see it that way.

"Hi Karla," I say to the office receptionist. "I need to speak with Principal Meyers right away."

Karla, the sweetest old lady there ever was, nods with a smile at the entrance to the principal's inner office.

"You two take a seat out here. And don't you dare give Karla any trouble," I say sternly.

"Yes, Mrs. Flowers," says Ralph.

The small kid just rolls his eyes. Charming.

I enter the office, and Principal Meyers already seems distracted. "I heard about what happened," he says without looking up from his computer. "You can spare me the details. I have a busy day."

How did he hear about it? It just happened.

"Well, sir, I think it's a bit more nuanced than what you might have heard..."

At the same time, he says, "Ralph is suspended, of course."

"Sir, I'm not sure that's necessary. Normally, punishment for fighting is just a lot of detention."

"But punishment for instigating a fight is suspension," he says, still reading something on his screen.

"I don't think Ralph was the instigator. He seemed to be reacting when I got there. And a suspension would go on his permanent record."

"So, you didn't even see the fight start?" He's looking at me now, but it's like I'm the dumbest person alive, and it makes my heart clench in the worst way. It makes me wish I was at the boxing club.

"Well, no. But..." I start to explain the context of what I *did* see happen, but his hand shoots up in an effort to shush me.

"Ralph gets suspended. Devon gets one detention. You can send them in now," he says, dismissing me before quickly turning back to whatever's so goddamn interesting on his computer.

I slowly exit the room and see Ralph sitting quietly in the corner and Devon standing across from him, smirking. Whatever Devon said must have been hurtful because Ralph's cheeks are stained with tears. Karla might be sweet, but her child-management skills could use some work, I guess.

I hesitate for just a moment. I try to get up the guts to fight with my principal. To take a stand and help Ralph out. I know he shouldn't have threatened to hit Devon, but that kid's clearly a little shit, and Ralph has been through a lot. Aren't we all allowed a mistake or two before things wind up on the records that get sent to colleges?

But I need this job. It's in a great district, which is hard to find in the Denver area. It pays better than any other district I got an offer from out of college, and I can already barely afford my shitty little apartment. Principal Meyers doesn't take kindly to pushback. I can't risk it.

So, I grit my teeth, take a deep breath, and say, "You can both go into the office now."

They both file in, and I turn to Karla. "Are you good if I head out now? We just need to call Ralph's mom, and I could use a walk before my next class."

"Of course, sweetie. I'll make the call right now. Enjoy your walk."

I nod and turn out of the room. Once I've grabbed my phone and headphones from my empty classroom, I head out the front door of the school and take off in a run. I'm not exactly in the best clothes for it, but I need to blow off some steam if I'm going to be the teacher kids like Ralph deserve this afternoon.

About ten minutes into my run, my phone buzzes. I pause to catch my breath, and a smile inadvertently dances across my lips when I see the text.

Caleb: Are we still on for boxing class tonight, Daisy?

Caleb has always called me flower names because my last name is Flowers. It would drive me nuts if anyone else did it, but with Caleb, it kinda makes me feel warm and cozy for some reason.

Cassie: Yes, I definitely need it. Principal Meyers is at it again.

After hitting send on my reply, I'm careful to add an eye-roll emoji so Caleb doesn't get too worried since he has a tendency to do that. I turn to head back to school, feeling a little bit better about the outlook of the second half of my day. At least I get to see Caleb.

CHAPTER 2
CALEB

My wristshot is horrible.

Okay, that's a lie. It isn't horrible. But it does need work. That's why I'm at the first optional skate of the pre-season way later than everyone else who decided to stop by. It's just me and the ice and a bunch of pucks that have frustratingly not made their way into the net at the speed and angle I want them to. Well, there's also a reporter from a local podcast here snapping some photos and, presumably, tweeting. But I'm trying to ignore him.

Too bad I can't. Because I know why he's still here, and it's not just to get some content on a website. It's me. I promised him at our last game of the playoffs last season that I'd sit down with him at the beginning of the pre-season and do an on-camera interview. I guess part of me hoped he'd have forgotten by now. But he clearly hasn't, and now I know I'm using my wrister as an excuse not to go over there.

I smash another puck into the net and pretend I'm satisfied with how it went in. Really, I'm never satisfied, but especially not right now because my hands are all sweaty and shaky inside my gloves. Our reserved ice time is almost up, and that means I have to talk to him. I can't just walk away like he hasn't been patiently waiting for me for hours. He's actually a pretty decent guy. His coverage of the team is fair, and he always treats us with respect. When we do interviews for his column, he even lets me redo my answers when I stumble all over my words.

But this is going to be different. It's on camera for the outlet's website and YouTube channel. Immediately, hockey fans across the world will have access to my mumbley, bumbley words and red cheeks. Some people find it endearing. Others, not so much. Either way, I hate it, and I can't seem to get any better.

As I send one last puck to the back of the net, the clock ticks, signaling three o'clock. My excuses are officially nonexistent, and I have to do this. I skate over to the entrance of the ice nearest to him and open the door.

"Hey, Peter," I say, hoping the fear doesn't come through in my voice. He's a shorter guy with spiky hair and a hoodie. He shouldn't be so intimidating. And yet, here we are.

"Caleb, great to see you. You look good out there."

I know he means it because he's always honest, and that calms me a bit. I lean my stick against the boards and peel off my gloves.

"Thanks," I say with a shrug.

"Listen," he starts. "I know it's the first day back, but I'd love to get that interview done before the season starts. I think it'll help set the tone for the kind of season we're all hoping the team will have. Especially if they hear it from you."

I know I have to do things like this for the team, but that doesn't keep my heartbeat from speeding up in my chest.

"Totally," I say, my voice only shaking a small amount in

comparison to my hands. "Why don't I get changed, and we can meet outside?"

"Perfect," he says with a nod. "See you out there."

I hobble to the practice facility dressing room in my skates. Once I'm in the dressing room, I start to peel my practice gear off. Once I'm slightly less bulky, I retrieve my phone from my bag and fire off a text to Cassie.

Caleb: I have to do an interview before I can get to the gym, so I'll get there right on time. Sorry.

Three dots appear instantaneously.

Cassie: Make it up to me with mozzarella sticks after.

Cassie: And don't forget to breathe.

I can feel a small smile on my face as I read the second message. Sometimes, it feels like Cassie is the only person who understands my weird, panicky reactions to other people. When we first met, the shock of her being able to beat me up somehow tore down my walls, and suddenly, we were friends. All it took was a basket of mozzarella sticks (for our hunger) and a bag of frozen peas (for my eye) to bring us together.

When I first saw her, I saw a beautiful spitfire of a woman. But now that I know her, I see so much more than that. Sometimes, it's overwhelming how amazing she is. She's so much more than her pretty-but-icy exterior. She knows exactly what people need to hear when they need to hear it. She cares so much about her students. She's the best person I know.

Which is why I really wanted to talk to her before class. I know she's upset about something that happened at school today, and I want to be able to fix it. When something is wrong for her, the world feels like it shifts on its axis, and I've decided that it's on me to fix all earth-tilting matters to the best of my ability.

I step into the shower and try my best to take Cassie's advice. *Breathe.* I repeat to myself over and over again as I work to steady my heartbeat and my hands. I hear the word in her voice, I realize, and I think that's part of why it almost works.

I say *almost* because eventually, I have to get out of the shower, put on some clothes, and meet Peter outside. I keep saying it as I walk down the hall toward the exit. *Breathe. Breathe. Breathe.* But eventually, it stops helping, and by the time I walk out the door, I'm all shaky again.

"Caleb!" Peter hollers from across the parking lot with a wave. I lightly jog over to meet him and notice he doesn't have his camera set up or even a phone on a tripod. When I reach him, he has an apologetic look on his face. "I'm so sorry. I don't know if you've looked at your phone in the past two minutes, but Dallas just traded Lek to Quebec for a fifth-round draft pick. I need to go to the office and write this up. Can we reschedule?"

Oh, thank goodness.

I try not to look relieved as I say, "Yes, of course."

"Any comment on the trade?"

"Lek is a great wing. Good move by Quebec. Gives them some needed depth," I say because it's true.

What I don't say is that the move was moronic for Dallas, even though that's also true.

"Thanks, Caleb. I'll see you soon," says Peter before ducking into his Subaru hatchback.

I pull out my phone to see if maybe he didn't mention something Dallas got in the trade. But no, he was right, and so I was. Moronic. I click on my text thread with Cassie.

Caleb: Crisis averted. Trade news. See you soon.

I make my way to my SUV and put on an audiobook for the short drive to our boxing gym. I love reading, but I don't get a lot of time for it during the season, so audiobooks it is. As I let the words flow into my brain, almost all the fear about the interview slips away. Soon, it'll just me me, Cassie, and a basket of mozzarella sticks.

CHAPTER 3
CASSIE

My fist connects with the bag, and it goes flying. I throw a hook, and it ricochets in the other direction as a huff of air leaves my body. I feel the anger of the day seething out of me, one hit after another, drawing it from the depths of my stomach and into the black hole that is the heavy bag. I decided a long time ago that my anger isn't a problem here. This is where I go when it's in danger of boiling over the top, when I'm so close to losing my cool that my chest is constantly tight, and I'm too close to saying words I won't remember but will definitely regret.

"Cassie!" Caleb hollers from the bag beside me. He sounds a bit annoyed, like maybe he's been trying to get my attention for a while.

"Huh?" I turn to face him as the bell dings, indicating the end of the round.

I bounce between my feet to keep my heart rate up and slowly work my way over to him.

"Are you okay?" he asks, a concerned frown on his face.

"Yeah," I lie.

I turn away from him to get a sip of my water, hoping he can't tell I'm basically seeing red every time I hit the bag tonight. This is why I can't be in a relationship. I'm incapable of letting people help me.

"That's not true, and you know it!" he yells after me as I skillfully let the water pour from my gloved hands into my mouth.

"I'm just upset about something from school today. We can talk about it at the bar."

I'm saved by the bell as it dings, signaling the beginning of the next round.

"Okay," he says, taking a ready stance at his bag. "But this isn't over."

I know it isn't over because Caleb would never let me be this mad without trying to fix it. Neither of us can stand to see the other one struggling. It's why I reminded him to breathe before his interview today, and it's why he's going to force me to talk about my feelings over a basket of fried cheese later. The problem is, I don't know what my feelings are. I know I'm mad about Principal Meyers, and I know I want to help Ralph. Except the only way I know how to help the kid involves asking Caleb for something I know he won't want to give.

We've been sticking to regular boxing in this class, but it's our final round of the day, which means that it's freestyle time. I get to throw in some kickboxing for fun in the last minute or so of the round. I prep my right foot on the ground behind me and round my leg up to the top of the bag, grunting as I make an impact. Here, I'm a warrior. Here, I'm in control. Here, I'm going to make loud noises and turn red in the face and be as ugly as I damn well please, thank you very much.

Next, I slam my left knee into the bag and prepare for one

final kick. It's my last chance to let out my anger, to decide what I'm going to do. It's my last opportunity to leave it all here, in the place where it's safe. I wind up my leg and let it fly. My foot connects perfectly with the bag, and it rebounds away from me. But I'm not ready to be done, even with the impending bell coming in a few seconds. I let my left hand smash into the bag in a hook, and my right responds with an uppercut. I keep drilling uppercuts until the bell rings and the music stops. I don't stop until Anthony dings the bell again, signaling that I really need to be done so he can set up for the next class. I finally let my hands fall to my sides and heave a loud sigh, my head falling back as I prepared to whine for more time.

But then I see Caleb. He's leaning against the lockers in the corner, as far as he can possibly be from other people. I instantly know that he's worried about people trying to talk to him. And just like that, a switch flips. Suddenly, I'm not what matters. My anger isn't what controls me. Now, it's something else entirely. I don't have a word for it, but it's this nagging sense that he needs me. As my heart rate steadies, I walk toward him. The anger evaporates from my body when our eyes connect, his crinkling at the sides from his grin.

"Ready for some melted cheese and to tell me what on earth is going on?" he asks.

No, I think. It's not that I don't want to tell him what's bothering me so much. It's that I really don't want to have to ask him for this. But if I want to help Ralph in a real way, it's my only option.

"Yes," I say. I'm sure I don't mean it, but I'll have to do it eventually, and putting it off helps no one. "Just let me get changed quickly, and we can head over."

I open my locker and pull out my deodorant and a hairbrush. It's not much, but there's also not much that can be done to tame my curls and make me look like less of a tomato after such a hard workout. I head for the bathroom, fully aware of just how ridiculous it is for me to ask Caleb for his help, but determined that I have to get over myself and just do it. The worst thing that could happen is that he could say no, right?

CHAPTER 4
CALEB

N*o*, I think.

How could she possibly expect me to do this? She knows how awkward I get around fans, how my thoughts start to race, and how I can't focus on the words I'm saying, just the ringing in my ears.

"Cassie, I…" I start.

But then I see how shocked she is by my using her real name. I don't want her to think I'm upset with her for asking. I'm not upset. I'm embarrassed, I guess.

"I'm sorry, I shouldn't have asked," she says quickly.

Great, now the earth is tilting more, not less. I need to fix this.

"No, no. It's not that. It's just…" I pause. "You know how I get."

It's just Cassie, I remind myself. *She won't judge you.* I think back to the last time I went out to a bar with some teammates. A few guys recognized us and struck up a perfectly nice conversation. But I was so scared of saying or doing the wrong thing that I wound up calling Cassie from the bathroom, begging her to pretend to need my help with something so I could go home early. She didn't even ask what was wrong. She just agreed and called me a few minutes later, put on an Oscar-worthy performance, and we never spoke of it again.

"I know it's hard for you," she says. "I wouldn't be asking if it wasn't important, I promise."

I know that's true. She really wouldn't ever do anything to intentionally put me in a nervous position.

"Tell me why it's important," I prod. "Tell me why I have to do a meet-up with a kid from your school who likes hockey."

She takes a long sip of her Diet Coke and looks at me warily. "He got in a fight today," she says.

"Okay?"

"And his dad died last year."

Well, crap. Now I'm probably going to want to do this.

"And he got into the fight because another kid was mocking him for having a dead dad."

Goodness, kids suck. I don't know how Cassie puts up with seventh graders all day. Probably because she's secretly a saint.

"Okay, okay. Fine. But I'm not just awkwardly meeting him somewhere. I'll get some ice time at the practice rink, and he can train with me for an hour. If he's as good of a hockey player as you say he is, he should love that."

"You'd do that?"

I'd do whatever I have to do to help you, I think. I may have put up a fight for about a minute, but deep down, I knew this was always what was going to happen. Because the world felt tilted, and the look of relief on her face made everything right again. She doesn't ask for help easily, so I know this really matters to her. I can put up with some kid for an hour if it means she keeps looking at me like I saved the world.

"Of course," I say as if I'm not a little terrified of spending an hour alone with someone I don't know, let alone a child.

As if she can read my mind, Cassie says, "I'll come with you and hang out in the stands so you're not alone."

"Great, because I don't know how to handle a twelve-year-old at all," I say with a nervous laugh.

"I know." She laughs even though she knows that's not the full reason I'm nervous about this.

Our usual server, Angela, appears with my second beer and Cassie's second Diet Coke. We thank her and settle into a comfortable silence, eating mozzarella sticks and sipping on our drinks, totally content with letting the grungy music, sticky floors, and greasy food take us into their grasp like a warm hug. There's nothing better than this, I've decided. Just me, Cassie, and our stringy melted cheese against the world.

CHAPTER 5
CASSIE
ONE WEEK LATER

arrive at the practice rink to find Caleb doing some sort of intense drill and Ralph nowhere to be found. Caleb looks up at me and waves, a nervous smile on his face. I know how hard he finds meeting fans—small talk and new people are tough for him. But Ralph's mom was beyond thrilled when I offered up this practice session, so hopefully, it's worth it.

Caleb is wearing one of my favorite things a man can wear. There's something incredibly sexy about a guy in a hoodie and hockey skates that I can't seem to look beyond, even though it's Caleb. I've always loved hockey players since I grew up going to "I" games with my dad. Also, I'm not too big to admit that my best friend is hot as fuck. Not that I'd ever do anything to mess with what we have going here. But still, a girl can appreciate what she sees.

After a few minutes, a woman in her early thirties walks

in. She must be Ralph's mom, except that Ralph isn't with her.

"Hi, Ms. Flowers," she says. "Ralph doesn't seem to want to come in. I'm so sorry to have wasted your and Mr. Mack's time."

No way am I letting Ralph chicken out of this, especially not since I know how nervous Caleb has probably been about this since we talked.

"Why don't I come talk to him?" I ask, mentally crossing my fingers that she lets me.

"If you want to try, sure. But he's being really stubborn. I just don't understand. A year ago, he would have been jumping at the chance to meet his favorite player."

"It's okay, I'll give it a go, and if he can't do it, we seriously don't mind. Caleb needed to work on his drills today anyway," I say.

It's such a lie. Caleb has the day off, and I'm pretty sure he's doing the drills to keep his mind busy, so he's less nervous. I've never seen someone make something so hard look so easy. But I can tell Ralph's mom is doing the best she can, and if we can't get him to come in, I don't want her to feel bad.

We walk outside and find Ralph leaning against the hood of the car.

"Hey, Ralph," I say. "What's up?"

"Oh, uh, hi, Ms. Flowers," he mumbles.

I was honestly expecting him to be rude or standoffish, but he's clearly just nervous.

"Caleb is inside. He's working on some drills. Do you want to join him?" I lift my voice in question, trying to sound innocent.

"Nah, I'm good," he says, looking down at his shoes, clearly trying to avoid me.

"Are you nervous?" I ask point blank because I'm not one to avoid the obvious.

"What? No. That's not it. I just…" he trails off.

Caleb's going to kill me for this, but I know exactly what Ralph needs to hear.

"Want to know a secret?" I ask in a fake whisper.

"Uh, sure?" He looks confused, but I know I can win him over with this.

"I once gave Caleb a black eye," I say with a grin.

"You did?" Now he looks shocked and maybe a little awestruck.

"Yup, we both take boxing classes and the first time we sparred, I kicked his ass."

"Okay, that's pretty cool, Ms. Flowers. You beat up a famous person!"

Suddenly I have his interest, and being the teacher that I am, I'm not about to let a learning opportunity pass me by.

"Yes, but I did it within the rules of a game. Just like hockey has rules for fights and penalties, boxing meant that I gave Caleb a black eye, yes, but the rules kept me from beating him senseless, even if he had been mean to me."

"He was mean to you?"

I may as well have just told him his favorite celebrity is an asshole, which I guess I almost did.

"No," I clarify. "Caleb is the nicest guy alive, but even if he had been mean, that doesn't mean I get to beat the crap out of him. Because there are rules in place to keep everyone reasonably safe. You picking up what I'm putting down?"

"Yes, Ms. Flowers." He's back to mumbling, but at least I've made my point.

"Good. Now, can we please go show Caleb how good you are at hockey?" I ask. "I've been talking you up all week, and you're making me look bad."

I know I'm guilting this kid, but I really did put in a big favor with Caleb, and I need Ralph to understand that his actions affect others. Caleb even had to pull strings to get some ice time at the rink since the Blizzards don't have full ownership of it.

"Yeah, okay. We can go in now," Ralph says as he turns only a little begrudgingly to get his gear out of the trunk of his mom's hatchback.

Ralph's mom mouths a silent "thank you" to me when he's not looking, and I reply with an understanding smile. I really hope this can help him.

Okay, I'll admit that when I told Caleb that Ralph is good at hockey, I wasn't actually sure. I'd heard it around school a bit, but since the kid plays on a club team, I've never actually seen him play. I just wanted Caleb to be into doing a session with him. But *ohmygod* this kid is good.

Apparently, Ralph's dad was also his coach, which made losing him that much harder. I'm no scout, but it looks to me like he has a potential future in the sport if he keeps up with it. I can tell Caleb thinks the same thing because they've been on the ice for almost two hours when we only planned on one. But Caleb kept throwing harder and harder drills at Ralph, and he kept mastering them, so Caleb threw another and another. I think, at this point, he's trying to think of something to purposefully trip up Ralph, but we can't hear what they're saying very well from the stands.

Ralph's mom, Hazel, and I spent the first hour or so in silence, but when Caleb did a particularly impressive skating drill that made him look like a ballerina, she commented on his skills, and suddenly we were talking about the Blizzards players from when we were kids. It turned out we attended a bunch of the same games. Now we're on a roll and can't seem to shut up.

"There's no way we also like the same books," I say, following a truly weird number of things we've discovered we have in common.

I secretly love romance novels, which confuses everyone but Caleb for some reason. Hazel reaches into her bag and pulls out her e-reader. She switches it on and hands it over to me.

"Have a look," she says.

I swipe across the titles and see some of my recent favorites and some that are on my list for future reading.

"You have got to be kidding me," I say. "No one in my life likes the same books I do!"

Not that I have all that many people I'm close to, but still.

"Which is too bad," she says. "I've always wanted to be in a book club."

I hand her e-reader back as I say, "Honestly, me too. I'd love to talk about books with other people."

"Who says we need more people to have one?" she asks.

"What do you mean?"

I think I know what she's saying, and the alarm bells are already going off in my head. She's the parent of a student. A student I'm trying to help. This could get messy.

"We should start a two-person book club!" she says with an alarming amount of excitement.

I give myself a moment to think about it. On one hand, I've never befriended a parent from my school before. On the other hand, Ralph isn't actually in my class, and there aren't any rules against it. If I'm being honest, I probably haven't because I'm not great at the whole friends thing, not because of people being parents.

Finally, I manage to open my mouth and say, "That actually sounds so nice," with only a bit of hesitation.

"*Ohmygod* this is so amazing!" she exclaims. "I need excuses to give myself a night with humans who aren't such a handful all the time."

Her eyes drift down to Ralph. I can understand where she's coming from. She's a widow with a kid who's clearly going through some stuff. She deserves a night off, and I can be the one to give it to her.

Once we've exchanged numbers and set a tentative date for our first book club meeting, Caleb and Ralph exit the ice, both looking completely exhausted. After they've wiped the sweat from their faces and taken their skates off, they make their way up to Hazel and me in the stands.

"We have a proposal for you," says Ralph, clearly giddy about whatever this proposal is while still only sort of trying to act too cool for school.

"Technically, we have two proposals for you," Caleb says, much more cautiously.

"Okay, what are these proposals you speak of?" asks Hazel.

She has a glimmer in her eye that was noticeably missing when she first came into the rink.

"I'd like to do some more one-on-one sessions with Ralph," says Caleb. "He shows real potential, and I think I can help him since he doesn't have a defense-specific coach yet."

I try to hide my shock. Caleb hates meeting new people. He struggles to interact with fans. He must really think Ralph is as special as I do, or he wouldn't be doing this.

"I think I'd be okay with that, as long as it doesn't interfere with your school." Hazel motions to Ralph. "Or your pre-season training." She turns with a motherly tone to Caleb, "I want a Stanley Cup for the Blizzards. It's been too long."

Ralph's dad may have been his coach, but Hazel is a hockey fan, and I appreciate her commitment to the cause.

Caleb clearly agrees because he laughs and nods before saying, "I promise."

"I promise, Mom!" Ralph says with a jump.

"Okay, then that's fine with me," Hazel says, her smile widening.

The guys exchange a fist bump, and my heart swells.

Seeing Caleb so comfortable and himself with someone new to him is doing weird things to my heartbeat, I think. It's just that I'm proud of him, of course.

"Wait, what was the second proposal?" asks Hazel, clearly unaware of the effect seeing my best friend interact with a child is having on me.

"Ice cream!" shouts Ralph with a jump.

Wait, Caleb wants to spend even more time with this kid in one day?

"Okay, fine, yes," Hazel agrees. "We can get ice cream. Are you guys going to join us?"

"It was Caleb's idea!" Ralph says.

Okay, now I'm really confused. Caleb, king of avoiding strangers, is suddenly spending two hours training a random kid and taking him out to ice cream? What is going on?

"We'd love to," says Caleb. "Right, Petunia?"

Not one to turn down ice cream, well, ever, I nod, all the while trying to ignore the look on Hazel's face after Caleb called me yet another flower name. I don't want her making assumptions, but it's probably too late.

Caleb's and my (and everyone else in Denver, come to think of it) favorite place for ice cream is a giant milk jug on a hill. There's almost always some kind of line, but it's worth the wait. We're standing in a line that wraps halfway around the block with Ralph and Hazel, and I think Ralph is getting antsy.

"What if they don't have it, Mom?" he half-asks, half-whines at Hazel.

She lets out an audible sigh, and I can't help but giggle a bit. "Then you'll have to get something else, sweetie."

"Why don't you and me go check the menu for today?" says Caleb.

"Okay!" cheers Ralph.

He's been so happy and enthusiastic since his lesson with Caleb. I'm so grateful Caleb agreed to do this. My heart is seriously swollen or something. I just hope it helps Ralph with the school issues, like I think it will. Hazel gives Caleb a grateful look as he and Ralph step out of the line.

"You guys make an adorable couple," she says once they're both out of earshot.

Suddenly, I'm frozen. I can't think. Are my ears ringing? I think my vision is blurry. I've barely been on a second date with anyone, let alone Caleb. The idea of that is freaking me out right now because I can't seem to find the words I need to explain to Hazel that she's misunderstood.

"Oh," I start and then pause for way too long. "We're, uh, well…"

Another pause.

Get it together, Cass!

"We're not together," I finally finish. "We're just friends."

Why am I reacting like this? It's not like this is the first time someone's assumed we're together. It happens all the time. But it's usually at, like, the line in Chipotle when they ask if we're paying together or something. Not someone who's seen us interact for this long.

"Oh," she says. "Well, that's a shame. He's very easy on the eyes."

As if I'm not totally aware of how hot he is. I spend more time with him than anyone, aside from his teammates and coaches.

"Not that I'm interested, of course," she clarifies.

"I mean, you can be," I say.

Caleb can date whomever he wants, and if he wants Hazel, it's not like I'd stop it. They'd be cute together, actually. So why does it feel like the biggest lie ever as it exits my mouth?

"I'm not at that place yet. It's only been a little over a year," she says with a smile, but I can sense the sadness underneath. "Plus, I'm way too old for him." She laughs.

"And I'm not totally convinced there's nothing between you two."

I open my mouth to protest, but Caleb and Ralph come around the corner. Ralph takes off in a sprint when he sees his mom.

"They have it, Mom! They have it!" he says before basically skidding to a stop when he reaches our spot in line.

"Thank the fucking lord," she says under her breath.

I actually snort a little and have to cover my mouth to keep from laughing. I love this woman.

Once we've made our way through the line, we find a table and enjoy our ice cream (I got the same flavor as Ralph —orange creamsicle—to see what all the fuss was about. I admit it's pretty good) while Caleb talks to Ralph about school and hockey. I've seriously never seen Caleb this chatty. I'm almost more excited about how much Ralph is pulling Caleb out of his shell than I am about Ralph being excited about hockey again. I give myself a mental pat on the back for coming up with this plan and take another lick of my cone. It really is delicious.

CHAPTER 6
CALEB
THE NEXT DAY

We're officially knee-deep in pre-season training, and the coach just put us through an absolute ringer of a practice. I approach my stall in the dressing room and tug my practice jersey off. I'm dripping with sweat. Thank god I don't have to do any media today. I'm definitely not up for people right now, let alone cameras.

"Hey Caleb!" shouts Thomas King, our star forward, from across the room.

"Yeah?" I say as I turn.

He's suddenly right next to me, his blond hair tussled from his helmet. He's an inch or two shorter than me, so he's looking up at me with a face of anticipation that I'm definitely not a fan of.

"Who's this hot chick you were with yesterday?" he says, indicating a picture on his phone I can't see.

I have no idea what he's talking about. I haven't been on a date in over a year. Is he talking about Cassie? Does King think Cassie is hot? Something about that idea makes me want to throw up a little.

"What are you talking about?" I ask, trying not to sound too annoyed.

He hands me his phone. It's a photo on a local gossip Instagram account we all hate. Or at least I thought we all hated it.

"Why do you follow this?" I ask.

"Because I like to know what people are saying about me. Now, who's the chick?"

I have to close my eyes to keep from rolling them. King is a nice enough guy, but he has a reputation when it comes to dating. I'm not sure how much of it is true, and I try to mind my own business, but he's not doing himself any favors right now.

"Dude, you've met Cassie like ten times," I say.

"Not Cassie. Of course I know Cassie. The other one." He points to Hazel.

How on earth am I supposed to explain this?

"Her name is Hazel. She's the mom of one of Cassie's students."

"Why were you at Little Man Ice Cream with the mom of one of Hazel's students? Also, is she still with the kid's dad?" he says with a literal wink.

This time, I can't help but roll my eyes.

"Her son, Ralph, plays hockey. He's been struggling with school and got in a fight."

"Okay? And?"

King still has that look of expectation, like I'm not giving him enough of what he wants.

I let out a sigh and try to regain my composure. I'm really not good at things like this. "And Cassie asked me to hang out with him a bit to see if I could help, so I gave him a hockey lesson, and we got ice cream."

"Why is he struggling in school?" Mitch Greggs, my usual

defensive partner, joins the conversation.

Great. He's scratching his brown beard as he towers over us both, examining the photo.

"His father died last year. He got in a fight with a kid who was making fun of him for having a dead dad," I say.

I'm not sure if I'm supposed to share all of this, but I can feel my hands shaking, and I need to get out of this conversation.

"Jesus," says King.

"That's fucking bullshit," Greggs adds.

"Yeah, so I was just doing Cassie a favor. That's all," I say. There. End of conversation.

Or so I thought.

"You should tell the PR team, they love this shit," says King.

That's the last thing I want to do. I wouldn't want to drag Ralph and Hazel into some publicity stunt, especially not after everything they've been through. "Nah, I'm good. It's bad enough we got stalked by that account."

I secretly hate when the good things we do are used to make the team look good. Sure, we have a platform and can use it to highlight important issues, but that's not why they do it. Like King said, the PR team loves this stuff. Because I'm a team player, I do what's expected of me every season, but I like to keep my work in the community a bit quieter.

When I can get the gossip accounts and social media team to leave me alone, that is.

"I hate that account," says Greggs. "They got me in trouble with Coach like three times last year."

"That's why you don't go clubbing the night before a big game, Greggs," says King. Finally, something sensible comes out of that guy. "Well, I'm in," he continues.

"You're in… what?" I ask.

"This kid. How can we help?" King says.

I've never heard of King doing something like this. Greggs

loves community service work. It's sort of his thing. But King being involved is new. What is happening right now?

"Oh, well, he plays defense, so…" I say, hoping King will drop it.

"I'm sure there are forwards on his team, and Greggs plays defense," King says, his expression filled with a weird amount of hope.

I'm obviously aware that Greggs plays defense, considering we're regularly paired together. I'm also aware that Ralph would probably love to meet more players. So, I stuff down all my fear and nod.

"I'll get some of his team tickets to our home opener. If you guys happen to run into them as they're leaving, I'd have no issues with that."

"Yes!" says Greggs, way more enthusiastically than I anticipated.

What on earth am I doing?

CHAPTER 7
CASSIE
A FEW DAYS LATER

throw a massive hook into the heavy bag before switching to working on some kicks. I don't usually kickbox, but during our last freestyle round of the session, I let myself indulge a bit, as usual. My arms are on fire, and I love the way the bag swings as my leg connects with it. Anthony rings the bell, signaling the end of the round, and I'm simultaneously relieved (because, Exhibit A: my arms are on fire, etc.) and let down (Exhibit B: this is my happy place, and the bell means it's almost over.)

We switch to sitting on the floor to do a short ab workout and stretch while Anthony goes over the usual updates. There'll be a monthly challenge to come to class two times a week (I already come four times minimum, so he stopped signing me up for the challenges because it was making other people sad), and a group of us will be running in a 5k for cancer research (I signed up right away since Caleb had to do it for the team anyway and wanted a buddy), and… wait… *what?*

"… this is the first time I'm inviting any of you to do this, so I hope you'll seriously consider it. An amateur match is no small feat, but if you're able to find a partner to spar with and sign up for some one-on-one sessions with me, we can get you ready. Let me know if you're interested."

An amateur match? That's a thing we can do?

I move into a downward dog stretch while Anthony goes over the other updates for the club, but my mind is stuck on the match. I immediately know I want this. I've been training so hard on the bag and in my personal sessions with Anthony, but to actually fight? That would let me get stronger. And stronger means safer. Safer means I don't have to rely on anyone but myself to be okay.

I look over at Caleb to ask if he wants to get a drink after class as he's stretching. He's in a groin stretch with his legs bent behind him as he moves his hips up and down. If it were any other guy from the team, I would assume they were purposefully trying to be sexual. But because it's Caleb, I know he really is just stretching out like all hockey players do. Does that make it less sexual, though? Absolutely not. He might as well have a woman directly under him.

And that's when I realize I'm not the only person looking at him. Every woman in the class seems to be interested in the way his (admittedly, very well-sculpted) ass is moving in the air. By the looks in a couple of their eyes, they're imagining being the floor beneath him. I clear my throat to get his attention. Knowing him, he'd be mortified to know these people were thinking about him that way. But then he looks over at me as he thrusts again. My mouth goes dry, and something weird happens between my legs.

What is going on?

Is that… lust? Am I lusting after my best friend?

No.

Nope.

No.

Not gonna happen.

I stand up and rip my eyes off of Caleb despite very much not wanting to. I need to talk to Anthony about the amateur match, and this… thing Caleb is doing, whatever it is, is a massive distraction.

"Anthony!" I call out.

"Great workout today, Cassie," he says, offering his fist for a bump.

"Thanks. I was wondering… how imperative is it to have a sparring partner if I want to do the amateur match?"

"It's extremely imperative. We can do one-on-one sessions, but you'd need someone to practice with as much as you possibly can. Do you think you want to compete?"

Yes. But I have no one to spar with. I'm sure Caleb is too busy, and, well, I don't have anyone else.

"Let's ask him," Anthony says right as Caleb walks over to us.

I try to shake my head subtly. I don't want to ask Caleb. He's already doing me a favor with Ralph, and that's one favor too many for my taste. Granted, I probably don't have any other options, but I should at least try to figure something out. Maybe I can pay someone?

"Hey," Caleb says as he fist-bumps Anthony. "Want to grab a drink?"

"Sure," I say with a bit of hesitation. I don't want to leave Anthony alone with Caleb to talk about being my partner, but they're both staring at me, so I turn away and say, "I'll go get changed."

In the bathroom, I change into jeans and a t-shirt after putting on as much deodorant as I possibly can and loosely braiding my hair. I think through my options for sparring partners. I can pay someone, but I don't exactly have a bunch of extra money lying around. I could put an ad out, but I might as well beg to find the creepiest possible person. I can't ask Caleb. I just can't. But what else am I supposed to do? I really want this, and I know he'll help me if he's able to. I take a deep breath as I look at myself in the mirror. I can do this. I just have to be willing to accept help. That can't be that hard, can it?

I walk out of the bathroom to find Caleb cornered by three women. He looks like he wants to crawl out of his skin.

"Caleb!" I shout from across the gym in an effort to save him as fast as humanly possible. "Ready to go?"

"Oh, uh, yes." He turns to the women. "Would you excuse me?"

They (very begrudgingly) clear a path for him, and he meets me at the front door. He places his hand on the small of my back, just like he has so many times before. But after that whole thrusting incident, my heartbeat quickens against my will. What? Is? Happening to me?

Once we're settled into our usual booth, Angela delivers our mozzarella sticks and asks, "The usual for drinks as well?"

"Yes, please," says Caleb with a kind nod.

"Actually, I'll have a bourbon on the rocks, please," I reply.

Caleb's mouth falls open, and I'm pretty sure Angela is also really confused.

"Oh, uh, okay," she replies before walking away.

"Are you okay?" Caleb asks. He has the most concerned look on his face, and I can't help but be a bit touched.

"I'm great. Why?" I ask, trying to be nonchalant.

"You don't drink," he says with the same weary look.

"I don't drink with strangers," I correct. "Are you a stranger?"

"Obviously not. But why has it taken you this long to be comfortable drinking with me?"

He looks a bit hurt, but I don't know how to explain this.

"It's not you. I just really like Diet Coke."

I shift awkwardly in my seat, hoping Caleb doesn't push the conversation further. It's a true statement. I'm not usually a big drinker, even when I trust people. What I don't say is that I'm going to need the liquid courage for what's about to come next.

Angela places a glass of bourbon and Caleb's IPA on our table. She doesn't bother to ask if we want anything else. She just walks away.

I take a long, long drink of my bourbon before dramatically setting the glass down and looking Caleb in the eyes.

"So," I say. "I need another favor."

"Peonyyyyyy," he groans, but there's a glimmer in his eyes that tells me he's not being serious.

Despite the glimmer, I almost just forget about it. I don't want to rely on Caleb any more than I already have. But I want this. I really want this. I can't explain why, but somehow, I think Caleb will understand. Even if he's jokingly shooting daggers across the table through his eyes at me right now. I take a deep breath, another sip of bourbon, and push forward.

"I want to do the amateur fight Anthony was talking about at the end of class." It comes out so fast it's basically all one word. But Caleb seems to have understood what I said, though I don't think he knows what it means for him.

"That's awesome, Carnation! You're going to kick ass."

I wait for reality to dawn on him, but it doesn't. He just sits there with an adorable grin on his face and sips his IPA.

Finally, he breaks his silence. "You need a sparring partner, don't you?"

So, he *does* know that's what I want. And he doesn't seem totally repulsed by the idea.

"And I'm your only friend," he says playfully. I don't try

to deny it because, well, he is. I just sit there silently, hoping he puts me out of my misery soon. "Daffodil?"

I roll my eyes at the name before replying, "Yes?"

"Why are you so nervous about asking me to be your sparring partner?"

I think through all of the reasons why he shouldn't do this. His season starts soon… He can't risk getting injured… He doesn't owe me anything…

"Well, I just figured you wouldn't have the time. You're so busy with pre-season training. And also, there was that one time I gave you a black eye."

We don't talk about the incident that brought us together as friends often. I always assumed Caleb was a bit bitter about it.

But then he sets his beer down dramatically and says, "Best black eye I've ever had. Ten out of ten rating. Would do it again if it meant meeting you."

I don't know why I'm surprised. Caleb has always been a wildly forgiving person, on and off the ice. Someone could brutally slam him into the boards, and he'll shake their hand and do the weird man hug, slap the back thing that looks even more weird in hockey gear, and tell them how great of a player they are ten minutes later. I honestly think it's one of his faults, but now that I'm on the receiving end, I'm not going to lie, I'm pretty pleased.

"Okay… so you'll help me?" I ask, wanting to die of embarrassment.

"Of course, I'll help you. Once the season starts, I won't be able to risk getting another black eye, but for the next month, I'm all yours."

"I'll take it. Thank you, Caleb." My heart has this big, heavy feeling like it's expanding in my chest as I watch him finish off his IPA. And just when I think I've gotten away with this way too easily, Caleb flags down Angela and points at the empty basket of mozzarella sticks. Now, I obviously would love more fried cheese in my life always, but if Caleb thinks we need a second round, that means he's not finished talking. For two fairly non-talkative people, we've already done a lot of that today, so I'm not sure I like where this is going. He's holding my gaze but not saying a word. It's a bit unsettling, staring into his green eyes. I've obviously noticed them before, but the thing about Caleb is when he looks at you, somehow, the world around you just stops, and nothing else seems to matter. I guess it's just one of those things about him.

Angela returns with our mozzarella sticks, and Caleb slowly takes one from the basket, never breaking eye contact. "When are you going to tell me why it took you over a year to be comfortable drinking with me?"

Fuck.

Me.

Why is this the thing he wants to talk about?

"I'm not saying it needs to be today," he continues. "Or ever, if that's what you really need. But I'd just like to know if and when I'm ever going to really know all of you, Marigold."

You do know all of me! I want to scream. *I just hate talking about this!*

Instead, I take a sip of my drink and rip my eyes away from his gaze, looking anywhere but at the annoyingly handsome friend across from me. The thing is, he really does know all of me. He knows my faults, that I'm scared to let people in. But he doesn't know why I am this way. Maybe he deserves to.

"I promise you, you do know me," I begin, still avoiding looking at him. "I just really hate talking about this."

"Okay," he says. "We don't have to, but just know that you're completely safe with me."

I know he means it, and I know it's true. So, I press on through all of the fear.

"In my sophomore year of college, I went to a frat party."

I assume he's about to say something about how that doesn't seem like my scene, but he just sits there, looking at me with a soft gaze.

"It started out really fun, if I'm being totally honest. But then everything went blurry and hazy. And then it went totally black. I'd only had two drinks. I woke up in an alley between the frat house and my dorm to a group of strangers screaming."

I can't bring myself to look at him, so I grab a mozzarella stick and pause the story as I hold on to the warmth of the stick in my hand to keep me in the present moment. It's a trick my therapist from back then taught me: take stock of your five senses. Right now, the taste of the mozzarella as I bite is the only thing keeping me from slipping into the past. I hold on to the hot cheese on my tongue like an anchor and breathe in the smell of the bar. I look at the neon sign on the wall and notice the changing colors of the digital jukebox. I let the music from the class next door fill my ears, the pumping of the bass keeping me where I belong and not back in that alley.

Caleb doesn't push me to continue. Instead, he takes the hand that isn't currently gripping onto melted cheese for dear life. Somehow, it gives me the strength to keep going.

"Some guy had drugged my drink, and when I couldn't walk all the way back to my dorm, he apparently thought the alley was a fine place to…" I pause. "But anyway, a group of girls was walking by, heard him, and figured out what was going on. They stopped him and called the cops before things got too far."

Caleb squeezes my hand, and I look back at him. I expect to see his kind expression from before, but instead, I'm met with anger. He looks like he's ready to commit a murder.

"I'm sorry I didn't tell you sooner," I say quickly, hoping I can make him less upset with me. "It's just really hard to talk about and…"

"Cassie," he cuts me off. I'm jarred by my real name on his lips. "Do you think I'm upset with you?"

"Well, you do look pretty upset right now."

He lets out a sigh before squeezing my hand.

"I'm upset because that happened to you, Rose." A wave of relief falls over me upon hearing another flower name. "If I ever see that guy, I swear to god I'll tear him limb from limb and make him wish he was dead. But you've done nothing wrong. I'm sorry I made you talk about this."

I take in his words. The thing is, I wish I'd told him sooner. Telling him now has made me realize that it's become kind of isolating to keep it all to myself. I really haven't had anyone to talk with about this in years.

"I'm glad we talked," I say. "In college, everyone knew, and it became something I was really ashamed of. Especially because the charges didn't stick, and he wound up back in my classes weeks after it happened."

I see anger flash through Caleb's eyes again as he grabs a mozzarella stick and shoves it into his mouth with force. He holds my gaze as he munches, the anger turning to kindness again, and it gives me more strength to continue.

"My friends didn't believe that I'd been drugged, even though they knew I wasn't a big drinker. They all took his side because the university did, and eventually, I didn't have anyone on campus other than my counselor. My mom insisted I see one, but my dad was less understanding. He said I shouldn't have put myself in that position, that it was my fault it happened."

Caleb squishes the mozzarella stick between his fingers but doesn't say anything. I see the realization flash across his face. He knows how big of a Blizzards fan my dad is, but I've never taken him up on free tickets for my dad. I just go to the games by myself, careful to avoid talking about them when I call my mom so she doesn't pressure me to include my dad.

"So that's why I don't drink with strangers," I say. "It's also why I started boxing."

My counselor had suggested I do something physical to get back in touch with my body. I tried yoga, but ultimately, the idea of learning to defend myself seemed to make me feel like I was taking control of my life. Like if I don't drink with strangers and I know how to keep myself safe, I'll be okay.

"Thank you for telling me," Caleb says.

He doesn't let go of my hand. He just holds my gaze with his big, kind green eyes and rubs my hand lightly with his thumb. It's the most reassuring moment of my life. No questioning if I could have done anything differently. No anger with me for putting myself in such a bad position. Just kindness and understanding.

We sit in our booth for the next few minutes in silence. As I eat a mozzarella stick with Caleb's hand holding onto mine, I know there's nowhere else I'd rather be. No one else I'd rather be with in this moment. It was terrifying to share this piece of myself with him, but knowing that he knows actually makes me feel stronger. Maybe if I can face this fear of talking about it, I can face other fears too.

CHAPTER 8
CALEB
THREE WEEKS LATER

never thought I'd be willingly putting myself into the position to be punched in the face by Cassie Flowers again. Life comes at you fast, I guess. Just like her fists, which happen to be flying angrily in my direction at a truly aggressive speed. But unfortunately—or maybe fortunately, since it's challenging her—I've gotten better.

I dodge her killer left hook for a third time as Anthony hits the bell to signal the end of our session. It's the last time we'll do this before my season starts, and while Cassie's gotten a few good hits on me in our previous sessions, I've largely been able to hold my own. Which is good not only for my ego but also for Cassie. I think it's helping her to have someone closer to her level. She's going to need it if she wants to compete in this match, especially when we usually just train on bags in class.

"That's enough for now," says Anthony while we both gulp down water. "Caleb, you've really improved."

"Yeah," says Cassie with a glare. "It's annoying the shit out of me."

"You're welcome for willingly letting you hit me on a biweekly basis," I say. "Also, we both know you needed someone to hold their own against you if you want to compete in this thing."

Cassie laughs. It's the laugh she has that fills the whole room—it's joy and fun with just a slight edge of sarcasm and wit. It's so perfectly her that my heart does this weird flippy thing in my chest. It's been doing that a lot ever since our heart-to-heart at Anthony's. Something shifted that day for me, and I can't shake this nagging feeling that I can't quite put my finger on. It's like now that I know this big thing about her, we're both opening up more. Whether it be about something dumb or something big, I feel tempted to share my whole self with her. I ignore the feeling for what feels like the fiftieth time and turn my attention back to the frustrating, beautiful woman in front of me.

"You're going to be great, Orchid," I say, reaching out to rub her back.

That's the other thing that's shifted lately. I keep reaching out to touch her as though I want to be as reassuring as possible or something.

"Maybe I'll be great," she says, avoiding eye contact while she shoves her shoes into her duffle bag.

I lightly grab her arm to get her to look at me. When she does, the edges of my vision blur. It's just me and her, and nothing else in this room, in the world, matters.

Because Cassie looks scared.

I straighten. "You'll be ready. You'll keep training with Anthony, and when the fight comes, I know you're going to kick ass."

She nods. I'm not sure she's fully convinced, but the fear has left her eyes, so my anxiety level lowers. But I can't bring myself to let go of her arm. And it's taking everything in my control not to slide my hand down and lace my fingers through hers. Why does this keep happening lately?

I finally force myself to remove my hand from my best friend's arm and mentally roll my eyes at myself. What is going on with me?

"Want to go to Anthony's?" she asks.

"Of course," I say. "As if there was a world in which we don't do that."

Angela has already placed our mozzarella sticks on the table along with the two, yes, two, IPAs we ordered.

Cassie shines a soft smile at me as she takes a sip of her beer. It's different from the bright, bold smile she shows the rest of the world, and I like to think she saves this one just for quiet moments between the two of us.

I think I've been pretty successful at hiding my reaction to her drinking around me. It's a weird mix of annoyance that it took so long for her to feel comfortable with me and relief that she finally got there. I only wish I could have done something differently to help her get there sooner.

"Are you ready for your opening game?" she asks.

I try to hide my nerves with a quick nod. It doesn't work. And I know Cassie can tell because I'm tempted to sit on my hands to keep them from visibly starting to shake.

"Caleb, you won the Norris Trophy in your second season in the NHL. You're going to be great."

Ah, yes, the Norris. The trophy for best defenseman in the NHL that I happened to win last year despite the team not making it to the Stanley Cup. I feel eternally guilty about that fact, and the guilt is renewed whenever someone brings it up. I should have been able to get the team there, but I had a nagging leg injury and couldn't play to my best level in the second round of the playoffs.

"Caleb."

"Hmm?" I hum as if I don't know exactly where this conversation is going—as if I don't know Cassie better than I know myself.

"Why do you get super weird when someone brings up the Norris?"

"I don't get super weird," I lie.

"Caleb."

God, I love it when she says my name. It gives me the fuel I need to be honest with her.

"Okay. Fine. I just hate that in the same year I got one of my dreams, I couldn't get my team to the Cup."

And there's that just-for-me smile again. My heart does the flippy thing while I take a sip of my beer in an attempt to recover.

"You realize you said 'team' just then, right?"

Now I'm confused. Or maybe I'm just distracted by the freckle on her neck. I've known it was there forever, so why am I fixating on it right now?

"Yes?" I say, trying to focus on the conversation and not on how much I seem to want to put my lips on that freckle.

"You're one part of a larger *team*. You're one of the best defensemen the world has ever seen, sure. But you're not solely responsible for getting your team to the Stanley Cup. It has to be a group effort."

I know she's right. And I also know that hearing Cassie say I'm one of the best is going to be the single biggest bump to my ego I've ever had. Cassie knows hockey; she did it long before we met because her dad is a huge Blizzards fan. I know winning the Norris should be enough to make me feel like I'm good, but of course, it would be Cassie who actually breaks through.

I can't resist the urge any longer. I reach across the table, take her hand, and give it a quick squeeze. I'll let go right away, I tell myself.

"Thank you," I say.

I don't let go.
But neither does she.
Interesting.

CHAPTER 9
CASSIE
TWO DAYS LATER

"Alright," I holler in my teacher's voice. "Does everyone have their ticket ready to go?"

Ten eager faces of aspiring twelve-year-old hockey players nod up at me from outside of the Blizzards' arena.

"Okay, get in a single file line behind me and try to be as quiet as humanly possible until we're inside."

Of course, they aren't quiet. It's the Blizzards' home opener, and these kids are rabid hockey fans, but you can't blame a girl for trying.

"Thank you for doing this," Hazel whispers as we walk through the doors.

"Oh please, it's way better than sitting with the WAGs. I'm happy to do it." WAG is what the Wives and Girlfriends call themselves. They have matching jackets during the play-offs and everything. It's not really my scene. I'm not built for that life, and I know it. It would mean giving up my independence, and I'm incapable of that. "Since I'm neither a wife nor a girlfriend, I don't really fit in with them."

"Not a girlfriend to anyone?" she asks.

She has that look of hope on her face, like she's ready to live vicariously through me. And I don't blame her. That's the least she deserves after losing her husband. But I have nothing to offer her.

"Not attached to anyone," I say.

Instead of looking bummed, she looks relieved.

"Interesting," she says.

I'm about to ask her why that's interesting, but we've reached the front of the line, and it's now my job to get these kids through the chaos of security at the arena.

Other than one of Ralph's teammates forgetting his phone in his pocket and going through the metal detector four times, things go well. The kids immediately run toward the team store. Well, all but two. Ralph stays by his mom's side until she hands him some cash and tells him to go buy something.

Henry, a sweet kid, hangs out with me. He's quiet at first until I bring up Caleb. Then he's all about talking hockey stats for his favorite players. I can't help but notice he's the only kid without any Blizzards gear on. Then I remember Ralph saying we had to invite him because he's never been to a game. Ralph seemed to think it cost too much for his family. It breaks my heart that I can come to any Blizzards game I want, but this kid loves hockey and has never even been to one. I really want to make this one special for him. He deserves to have the best night of his life. I pull out my phone and shoot off a quick text to Caleb. What's one more favor on the massive list of things he's helped me with lately?

Cassie: Can you hook a kid up with some merch after the game? The one Ralph said couldn't afford to come to a game doesn't have anything. I can meet you in the hall so you don't have to come in and meet everyone.

Once almost all of the kids have acquired various Blizzards' gear, we head to the Club Level. Caleb got the kids a suite because, of course, he did. He asked me to keep a surprise.

"Ms. Flowers, can we get some snacks?" one of the kids asks.

"You won't need them where we're going," I say with a hint of mystery.

"Where are we going?" another says with a leap into the air.

"You'll see," I say with a glint of mystery. I can't wait to see their reactions. Especially Ralph and Henry's.

I'm so glad I agreed to keep the suite a secret. There are pompoms on all the seats, unlimited soda, and enough food to feed a small army. Caleb really outdid himself. The kids are going wild, and I love it.

"This is so cool, Ralph!" says one kid as he snatches a pompom from a seat and waves it in the air.

"Yeah, thanks for inviting us!" Henry says with so much gratitude in his voice that I, the most jaded woman ever, could honestly cry.

"I can't believe you know Caleb Mack!" another kid says while filling up his soda cup.

The compliments continue to pour in, and the look of pride on Ralph's face is rivaled only by the look of relief on Hazel's. They're both so far from the looks of fear I've seen them both have in recent weeks. And it's all because of Caleb. My heart swells thinking about the impact he's had on their lives.

Just when I think I can't be more proud of Caleb, he plays like an absolute beast during the game. While the kids are completely enthralled by the game, I'm just completely enthralled by him. How good his skating has gotten, how strong his shot is, and the way his smile spreads across his face from the bench when one of his teammates makes a good play. He winds up scoring *three* damn good goals, and the Blizzards win five-two against The Wild. He scored a freaking hat trick, and he's not even a forward. I'm so overjoyed—I can't even believe it.

The kids start to pack up their stuff right as my phone buzzes. It's Caleb replying to my text from before the game.

Caleb: Of course. I'll come up as soon as I'm done with press. I'll even come in.

He says *of course,* as if I didn't ask him something we both know is going to be hard for him. But he's been getting out of his shell more lately. Maybe Ralph is good for him, too.

Me: You're the best.

Caleb: I know.

He adds a winking emoji for effect.

We hang out in the suite a bit longer, the kids completely hyped up on sugar at this point, until there's a knock at the door.

"Who's that?" shouts one of the kids.

"I don't know. Why don't you open the door?"

The kids all rush over to the door as Caleb's face slowly appears.

"Hey, guys! I heard there are some hockey fans in here."

All the kids say different versions of *"ohmygod-you're-caleb-mack"* at the same time while they rush him. I find myself taking a sharp inhale. What was I thinking asking him to do this? He's got to be melting down inside. But a warm smile shines across his face. It's his real smile too. Not the one he uses with the press or at galas. He's genuinely happy to be here.

He pulls out a sharpie and signs anything the kids ask him to. When he gets to Henry, he reaches into his duffle bag.

"Can't let you go home without some gear, man," he says as he rummages through the bag.

Eventually, he pulls out a jersey. I know instantly that it's his game jersey. Players don't actually own their jerseys. What strings did he have to pull to get this? It's even from his first-ever hat trick in the NHL. And he's giving it to a random kid he's never met. If the suite wasn't enough to make me melt, this definitely is. I'm a goddamn puddle, and I don't know how to feel about it.

"Sorry, it's a bit sweaty. Do you want me to sign it?" he asks.

Henry is in complete awe as he nods silently.

Caleb signs the jersey and hands it over to Henry, who quietly thanks him before rushing over to his friends to show it off.

"Tell me again why you aren't dating him," Hazel whispers in my ear.

"It's complicated," I reply.

"Doesn't seem that complicated to me," she says before quickly following it up with, "Sorry, not my place."

I just smile at her and don't say a word. Because what am I supposed to say? You're right. It's not that complicated? That I've never even entertained the idea of letting someone get that close to me? That I'm already terrified of how I feel with him as a friend, and I don't think I could handle anything more?

So I stay quiet and watch as the kids pepper Caleb with questions until Hazel announces it's getting late and they need to leave. Hazel insists she can handle getting the kids to their parents, so after dragging the kids out of the suite, it's just me and Caleb standing together by the door after waving them off.

I turn to him and say, "Thank you, Caleb."

"Of course," he says like it wasn't a big deal. But I know it was, and it means the world to me. "Anything for Ralph," he continues.

Anything for Ralph.

Not anything for me.

Why does that bother me so much?

"Some of the guys want to go out to celebrate. Do you want to come?" he asks.

I absolutely do not want to go out. I have to be at school by seven tomorrow. So why do I find myself saying, "Yes, that sounds great."

Because I like Caleb's teammates, and I want to hang out with them? Is that what I'm going to tell myself? Because the truth: that I don't want this night to end, that I want even more time with Caleb, is too much to bear.

CHAPTER 10
CALEB

'm a bit shocked Cassie agreed to go out with us. She's always encouraging me to go out with the guys, but she rarely tags along. Yet here I find myself, sitting in a quiet booth of a speakeasy in downtown Denver with Cassie pressed against my side. I'm pretty sure it's just because the booth is small, and there are a lot of us, but I like it, regardless.

I reach forward to grab my beer—and to slyly see if she's also pressed up against Greggs. I don't know what I thought looking would do, but when I sneak a glance, I see there are several inches of space between them, and my heart beats a bit faster. I lean back and put my arm across the back of the seat. Not across Cassie's shoulders. That would be completely insane, and I'm only teetering on the edge of insanity right now.

The past few weeks with Cassie have been interesting. I find myself saying that word—interesting—to myself a lot. I notice how my body reacts when I see her. That any room I walk into I instinctively look for her first. I don't know what any of it means, but I do know that it's… interesting.

"Did Ralph's team enjoy the game, Cassie?" King asks.

I tune back into the conversation at the mention of Cassie's name.

"They loved it!" she says. "It helps that you guys put on a pretty good show for them. Nice work."

"That was all Mack," says Greggs.

Oh goodie, attention. I take a swig of my beer and nod, hoping that everyone moves on. Thankfully, hockey players are a fairly self-centered bunch, and these guys know I hate attention more than I hate the St. Louis goalie, so they turn their attention back to Cassie. I'm not sure I like that either, though.

"Well, three-fifths of it was Mack," Cassie says. King looks dazed and confused, so Cassie continues, "Because he scored three of the five goals?" Then she leans into me, resting her head on my shoulder.

I freeze.

My brain short-circuits.

What. Is. Happening.

But it's over as fast as it began. She shifts back to where she was sitting before, still pressed into me but not full-on, snuggling me like a koala bear. I find myself wishing she'd come back, which I wasn't really expecting. The group keeps talking while I panic internally. Why can't I get it together?

"Ralph's mom told me one of the kids in the group has to quit the team, though. He can't afford all the gear and fees," Cassie says.

Suddenly, I'm paying attention again because I know she's talking about Henry, the sweet kid who needed Blizzards gear.

I know hockey is expensive. My parents worked so hard for me to be able to play at a competitive level. Something about Henry not being able to afford it breaks me. It reminds me of my friend Peter. When we were kids, we played the D-line together at the same level. He was a really great player, but he had to quit in high school because his dad got laid off. All of that talent and hard work was thrown away just because hockey is an expensive sport. When I started playing Juniors, Peter and I fell out of touch, but I've always hated that I'm in the NHL and he isn't. If Henry's even close to Ralph's level, he's got real talent. I can't let that be thrown away. Not for a second time.

"We need to do something," I find myself saying with an aggressive amount of urgency as I slam my beer on the table.

"Woah, uh, okay," says King. "What do you have in mind?"

Well, now, that's an excellent question. Half of my team is staring at me in shock, probably because this is the loudest I've ever spoken in my life, and I don't know what to say next. But then I feel Cassie's hand squeeze my thigh in support.

"Hockey isn't accessible here," she chimes in. "Kids don't have teams at their schools, so they have to pay for their own gear, and there are huge fees to play in private clubs."

"That sucks," says Greggs. "I wish we could help this kid." But he takes a swig of his drink and doesn't offer a solution.

"Maybe we can," I somehow get myself to say. "But it's not just about him. If it was, I'd just pay for it myself. There are a lot of other kids this is happening to, though."

What I'm not saying is that the idea of repeating the Peter situation when I have the power to fix it this time isn't an option.

"Look, man, if you're serious, you know I love doing work with my animal shelter non-profit," says Greggs.

Yes, our six-foot-five defenseman is obsessed with tiny

little puppies and kittens. It's quite a sight when he brings fosters around, let me tell you.

"I'm sure we can figure out how to make this happen," says King.

I'm suddenly deeply regretting every life decision I've made up to this point because I don't know what they mean, but I have a feeling I'm not going to like it.

"Make what happen, exactly?" I ask.

"Your new non-profit! Caleb's Kids! Or something. I don't know. We'll workshop the name," Greggs says with far too much enthusiasm.

Nope. Absolutely not. Not happening.

I can't be the face of something like that… can I? I mean, I do the basic community service work required of a professional athlete, but I've never really gone above and beyond like Greggs has. Mostly because it involves a lot of time with people and a lot of attention. Plus, the few times I have gone above and beyond, the PR team has taken over, which I hate. It's not so much that I mind getting good press for the team. It's just the added attention… it's all too much.

So, I can't do this, right? There's no way I can handle it. I'll find another way to help Henry.

Then suddenly, Cassie's lips are right by my ear, and my brain is short-circuiting again. Since when has she had this effect on me?

Shivers run down my spine as her lips all but brush against my skin. "I'll help," she whispers. Honestly, she could ask me to do anything right now, and I would say yes.

So, I guess that's how I wound up researching how to set up a nonprofit at two o'clock in the morning after scoring my first hat trick in the NHL.

CHAPTER 11
CASSIE
A FEW DAYS LATER

I pull up outside of the address Hazel texted me. It's a cute white house with blue shutters and planter boxes a few neighborhoods away from mine. It's the kind of house I hope to be able to have someday, though I'll probably never be able to afford it in the Denver real estate market on my teacher's salary. At least not alone.

I get out of my car and walk up the wildflower-lined sidewalk to the door that matches the blue shutters. There's a little knocker on the door in the shape of a rose; I use it to let Hazel know I'm here.

"One second!" a voice yells from inside. A few moments later, the door flies open to reveal the always-gorgeous Hazel. "Hi! Sorry, I was cleaning up a bit. Ralph has a tendency to leave the results of a tornado in his wake every time he leaves the house."

I'm not sure what to say, so I extend the bottle of wine I

brought with me and say, "I think I remember you saying you desperately need a glass of wine."

"Oh, bless you. I definitely do. Come in, come in!" she says as she gestures and leads me into the living room.

There's a plate filled with cheese, other themed snacks, and two empty wine glasses already set up. I'm glad Hazel wanted to host our first two-person book club because there's no way I could have pulled this off. I take a seat while Hazel opens the wine in the kitchen and try not to snoop.

But I can't help it. There aren't too many family photos up. Mostly, there's framed art from when Ralph was younger and photos of him playing hockey alongside his awards and trophies. My gaze lands on one family photo of Ralph, Hazel, and a handsome man I assume is Ralph's father. They're all standing on the beach, holding onto each other while they laugh. My heart aches for Hazel, knowing that if this photo is any indication, she lost a great love. And I can tell Ralph lost a great father based on how he is in school.

Hazel emerges from the kitchen triumphantly with the open bottle of wine in one hand and the cork in the other. "Here we go!" she says.

She pours us both *very* full glasses and plops down across from me on the sectional.

I tentatively take a sip of wine. Technically, I don't know Hazel very well, but logically, I know she's not a threat. I ignore that nagging voice in the back of my head saying, *you shouldn't have put yourself in that situation*, and let myself take in the flavor.

It's delicious, so I take another sip before asking, "So, what did you think of the book?"

"I'll answer that question if you answer one first." Hazel has a conniving look on her face as she shoves a bite of cheese into her mouth.

"Okay," I say with hesitation. I think I know where this is going, and I don't like it.

"Why aren't you dating Caleb?" she asks flatly.

Well, I guess we're just diving right in then. It's not like she's the first person to have asked the question, but I like Hazel a lot more than I like those other people. For the first time ever, I don't know how to answer the question.

"Well... I... Uh..." I stumble.

"Sorry, you don't have to tell me," she says. "You two just seem so coupley together already, and you're clearly close. Why not take that next step?"

Once again, I don't know how to answer. Normally, I'd say something along the lines of, *he's like a brother to me*, or, *I don't see him like that*. But the truth is that I'm not capable of being in a relationship with anyone, including and especially Caleb.

Caleb deserves the entire universe, not to mention all the other universes in the multiverse. I'm not even that good of a friend. I've asked him for a lot of favors lately, and I feel really guilty about it. There's no world in which I can be the person he, or anyone else, deserves, so I've never even explored the idea. It'll just be me in my shitty little apartment until the bitter end.

But explaining all of that to Hazel seems like a bit much, so I just mumble, "It's complicated," and take a sip of my wine.

"Right. Sorry. Not my business," she says.

Now I'm worried I've upset her when, in reality, it's me and my incapacity for emotion that's the problem. "No, no," I say. "You're totally fine. I'm just not great with... feelings."

"I can understand that," says Hazel. "We all have our stuff. I guess I just think you're both really great, and I want great people to be happy. What you're doing for Ralph is really amazing. I can't thank you enough."

"That's all Caleb," I say. "I'm just glad he and Ralph hit it off."

"Me too," she says. It seems like she has more to say, but she nibbles a cracker instead, leaving me to fill the silence.

"I guess I've never explored the idea with anyone, not just Caleb," I say before I can stop myself.

"Really? I mean, if you want to be single, I definitely won't judge you for that."

"I'm not sure it's a want," I say.

It falls out of my mouth, and I immediately want to shove it back in. What is it about Hazel that makes me feel so dang comfortable? Here I am, just airing my deepest inner thoughts during our first time hanging out. What is wrong with me?

"I see," she says in a way that tells me she very much does not see.

"It's more of a need," I admit. "I'm not built to be a partner. Not to anyone."

"Well, I'm not sure that's true, sweetie," she says. "If you truly want to be single, there's no harm in that at all. But if you're holding yourself back from something special because you're afraid, that's another thing entirely."

I'm not afraid… am I? I like to think I'm generally a pretty fearless person. I'm training for this fight; I take on twenty-seventh graders every day. I'm hardly a coward… right?

Hazel takes a sip of her wine before continuing, "I'm not going to push you, of course. Like I said, you guys could be really great together, and I'd hate for you to miss out on that because of a story you're telling yourself that's not even true."

But it is true. I'm not able to be the partner he needs. He's the best person in the world, and I'll never be able to be anything close to a match for that. Hazel clearly doesn't understand how incapable of love I am—or how wonderful Caleb is—if she thinks we'd be good together.

I nod along like I agree with her and take a bite of cheese, praying that she changes the subject.

"Well, now that we got that over with, what did you think of the book?" Hazel asks.

I reach into my bag to pull out my copy of the book, eager to talk about anything other than my handsome best friend. "I'm so glad you asked."

CHAPTER 12
CALEB

've put Ralph through two hours of intense drills. After seeing him work one-on-one again, I'm even more convinced this kid has a future in hockey. His defensive skills are top-notch, but what's really going to set him apart as a defenseman is his puck-handling and offensive ability. I can't wait to see him play an actual game against other kids. I can only imagine he'll completely dominate them.

"Alright, I think that's enough for tonight," I say after Ralph manages to get past me and score in a really embarrassing (for me) fashion.

"What, do you have a hot date or something?" he says in that annoying tone that only a twelve-year-old can, and I laugh.

"No. But I did promise your mom I'd have you home in an hour, and last I heard, you wanted ice cream."

"Oh, well, in that case, let's go!" he declares, completely

forgetting about grilling me about my (nonexistent) dating life.

There's an ice cream shop a short walk from the practice arena. Ralph and I talk about his other favorite players in the league on the way there, but he insists I really am his favorite, which is both sweet and also a terrifying reminder that a lot of people look up to me, and I can't mess up.

"So, speaking of dating," Ralph says dramatically between licks of his ice cream.

"Got a crush on someone?" I ask in a pathetic attempt not to talk about myself.

"No," he says way too quickly, which tells me he totally does. But I'm not going to pry. "I'm talking about Ms. Flowers."

I really shouldn't talk about this with a twelve-year-old.

"What about her?" I say as if I don't know what he means.

"Are you guys, like, dating or whatever?"

I laugh because I'm uncomfortable, and I don't know what else to do. The idea of dating anyone at this stage of my career has always been off the table. The NHL takes and takes from us until there's nothing left to give to the other parts of our lives. Some of the other guys try to make it work, but I've always been singularly focused on hockey, and I don't know how else to be. But the idea of dating Cassie is a non-starter. She deserves so much more than I can give her, especially during the hockey season. I'm not the partner she needs, and I know it.

"We are not 'dating or whatever,'" I say. "We're just friends."

"Why?" he whines.

"Why… don't you mind your own business?" I say as I mess with the hair on his head to annoy him.

"Because my own business sucks," he says under his breath.

Oh. Right. That.

Crap.

"I'm sorry, man."

"Thanks," he replies before taking a long pause and shifting uncomfortably in his seat. "Mom keeps saying it's going to get better and that the therapy will help, but I wonder if she's wrong. It's not getting easier."

I'm in uncharted territory here, and I have no clue what to say. So, I rest my hand on his shoulder and try to show him that I'm here for him, even if I can't find the right words.

"Dad loved hockey," he continues. It's the first time I've really heard Ralph talk about his dad, so I wait for him to continue. "He taught me everything I know before he died."

"Your dad must have been a great player."

"He was going to play in college and maybe even go pro," Ralph says. "But then my mom got pregnant with me, so he had to go straight to working out of high school."

I nod along, hoping that he'll keep talking about his dad. Hoping that I can be a safe space for this kid.

"He played in the Fire vs. Police game every year, and Fire always won because of him. At least that's what Mom says."

Wait a minute. I always go to those games. I think I know this kid's dad. And I think I'm about to have my world rocked.

"Ralph, was your dad's name Eric?"

"Yeah, why?"

Holy crap. This kid's dad was Eric Cast. He was one of the top forward college recruits when he was eighteen. Everyone assumed he'd be a top draft pick whenever the time came. He wound up becoming a firefighter instead. Whenever he played in the Fire vs. Police charity game, he was such a dominant force that the police always wound up literally falling all over the place trying to catch him.

Suddenly, Ralph's skill on the ice makes so much more sense.

And suddenly, I feel my duty to mentor this kid triple.

"Your dad was an incredible player, Ralph. I've watched him."

"Really? How?" he asks.

"I always sneak into the charity games. I wear a disguise and everything." I can't help but laugh at myself a little for admitting that last part.

"No way!"

"Yep. And your dad was incredible. Just like you are," I say as I wrap an arm around his shoulders and give him a little squeeze.

Ralph blushes while he licks the last of his ice cream out of the cone.

"I do have one question, though," I say. "Why do you play defense? Your dad was a forward."

"Oh, that. Well, I've always been a bigger kid. I played both offense and defense until we had to pick last year, and Mom thought that defense might help me get my… anger… out in a more productive way."

It reminds me of Cassie a little bit. How she started boxing because she wanted to learn self-defense, but now she kind of uses it as an outlet for her anger. I've always wondered what it's like to be mad at everything instead of afraid of it. Something tells me it's not much better.

"Is it working?" I ask.

"I think it might be," he says. "I haven't gotten in a fight since the first week of school."

"Good. If you stay focused on your grades and hockey, you'll be good to go."

"Grades?"

"Hey, Man. I was an honor student in college. Being a smart player isn't just about being able to smash other dudes into the boards. And also, I'm best friends with a teacher from your school."

"This word you're saying. This 'friends' word. I don't think you know what it means."

I give him a playful shove. "Shut up."

"Wow, I really hit a nerve."

Yes, you did, I think. Because even if I could never actually act on it, it's not like I haven't thought about it.

"Let's get you home," I say instead.

Once I'm home from dropping off Ralph, I feel the immediate need to tell someone about his dad being Eric Cast.

"Hey, you," Cansie answers immediately.

"Hey, what are you up to? I have something crazy to tell you."

"I'm taking a bath," she says.

And my brain freezes. She's in the bath… like, right now? Just talking to me while she's naked?

"Caleb?"

"Right. Yes. I have something to tell you…"

Don't think about it. Don't think about it. Don't think about it.

"Okay? And?" she asks.

"Ralph's dad is Eric Cast," I say it like the huge bombshell it is.

"I'm aware… Caleb, is this why you called me? To tell me that you know Ralph's dad's name? Because I was really enjoying the bubbles in this tub."

Ugh. Now, I'm definitely thinking about it. *Focus, Man.*

"He was supposed to go pro, but Hazel got pregnant when they were young, and he had to go to work right away. That's how he became a firefighter," I explain.

"Oh, I didn't know that. I guess that explains why Ralph is so good at hockey?"

"Definitely. Anyway, how was your book club?"

"Oh, it was, uh, good!" she says way too cheerfully to be convincing.

"Are you okay, Violet?"

"I'm fine." After pausing for a minute, she continues, "I

was just wondering, do you know what kind of a house you want eventually?"

"I have a house."

"You have a condo. There's a difference."

I've thought about it a lot because I can't stay in my modern bachelor pad forever. It's not really my vibe, and there's only one bedroom. Which works for me for now, but once it's time to retire and hopefully start a family, there won't be enough space.

"Yeah, I've thought about it," I say.

I don't elaborate because it feels silly to say that I want a little white cottage with a cozy vibe and just enough space for my non-existent family. That's not really the usual hockey-player move post-retirement.

"What kind of vibe do you want? Do you want to live in Cherry Hills?"

Cherry Hills is the most affluent part of the city. It's where most of the athletes and coaches who stick around Colorado wind up living. I honestly have zero interest. Where I want to live is also really expensive. Everything is in Denver, but not to the same degree.

"No, I think maybe Washington Park. I like older houses with history. I don't need a new mansion to be happy."

I just need the people I care about. *People like Cassie.* I shove the thought down before it can take hold in my brain. I guess Ralph's questioning got to me a bit.

"I love Wash Park," she says quietly. So quietly, I almost can't hear her.

I almost tell her that we can be neighbors, but something stops me. It's this little inkling in the back of my mind telling me that she'll be there in the house with me. But logistically, that doesn't seem possible, so I brush off the subject altogether.

"Are you ready to help me with this nonprofit?" I ask,

desperate to change the subject before I say something weird I can't take back.

"I'm so ready! I'm really proud of you for doing this, Caleb."

I love the way she says my name—like it's a secret. And then I remember that she's saying it while she's in the bathtub. Covered in bubbles, apparently, and suddenly I can't breathe.

"Are you there?" she asks.

Actually, in my head, I'm in that bathtub with you, I think, much to my own horror.

"Uh, yeah. I'm here, Lily." Even I could tell my voice was deeper and hoarser than usual when I said it, which I guess means it's her turn to be quiet.

"My water is getting cold. I'm going to let you go," she says.

I'll warm you up, I offer in my head. Thank god it's only in my head.

"Have a good night, Dahlia," I say.

"You too, Caleb."

CHAPTER 13
CASSIE
THE NEXT DAY

Caleb looks exhausted.

Not just exhausted—he looks terrified, maybe?

We're sitting at our favorite coffee shop near my place. It's a bit far from Caleb's downtown condo, but he says they have the best espresso in town. Part of me wonders if he just likes my neighborhood more than the busyness of downtown. My cozy, historic area certainly suits him better than the sleek, modern condo he got after his first year with the team.

Right now, I'm worried that espresso is the last thing he needs because he's completely freaking out. His hands are visibly shaking, and his eyes look like they're going to pop out of his slumped head.

"Caleb," I say a bit too sternly.

But somehow, he seems more relaxed when he looks up from his tablet, and his eyes lock with mine. He's been pouring over nonprofit information since Greggs and King convinced him to start one, and I think all the unknowns are getting to him.

"Yeah?" he asks.

"You know you don't have to do this, right?" I reach across the table and take his hand. I don't care if it seems couple-y or whatever. He needs to take a breath, and I know I can get him to.

"Yes. I do have to do this. It's not just about Henry, Sunflower."

My heart hitches in my chest when he says a nickname name like that, as though he's desperate. Like I'm needed. I'm not used to being so tied to a person, and it's all becoming a bit terrifying, if I'm being honest. We've been friends for over a year, but things have become more intense lately. It's Caleb who needs me, though, so I press through the fear.

"Why don't you just ask Greggs?" I ask.

"I don't think that's a good idea," he says.

He's avoiding eye contact now, which I know means he's just nervous to ask, though I'm not sure why.

"He seemed really excited about this idea," I say. "Just text him."

Caleb doesn't say anything. He just stares at his phone sitting on the table.

"If you don't, I will," I say.

His eyes fly up at me.

"You have Greggs' number?" he asks.

Is that a tinge of jealousy peeking through? Why would Caleb be jealous of my talking to Greggs?

"Of course I do. I'm your emergency contact. I need to be able to get in touch with someone from the team. Greggs seemed like the least annoying option," I explain.

A visible look of relief washes over him.

"I'll text him," he says with so much reluctance that I'm honestly shocked when he picks up his phone and starts typing.

A moment later, a reply dings through.

Caleb heaves a sigh of relief. "He's going to connect me with someone who can help. Apparently, he got a consultant to help set everything up to help with the fundraising and grants and stuff."

"That's great!"

But he just sits there silently, looking pensive.

"You don't need a whole team if you don't want one, Caleb," I say because I think he's worried about managing people. He hates even having a manager and publicist constantly bugging him to do more stuff he's not comfortable with. "You can make this whatever you want it to be. It doesn't have to be as big as Greggs' thing."

"I know," he says. "I want it to be even bigger. I'm just trying to figure out how."

Well, okay then.

CHAPTER 14
CALEB
A FEW DAYS LATER

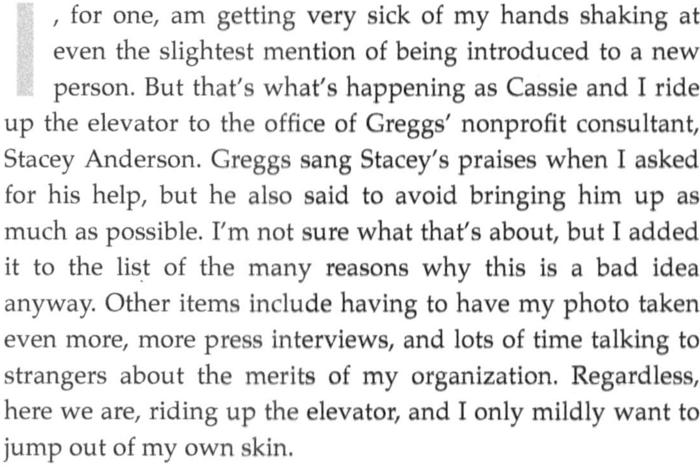

I, for one, am getting very sick of my hands shaking at even the slightest mention of being introduced to a new person. But that's what's happening as Cassie and I ride up the elevator to the office of Greggs' nonprofit consultant, Stacey Anderson. Greggs sang Stacey's praises when I asked for his help, but he also said to avoid bringing him up as much as possible. I'm not sure what that's about, but I added it to the list of the many reasons why this is a bad idea anyway. Other items include having to have my photo taken even more, more press interviews, and lots of time talking to strangers about the merits of my organization. Regardless, here we are, riding up the elevator, and I only mildly want to jump out of my own skin.

Cassie must be able to tell that I'm nervous because just before the elevator dings and the door opens, she gives my hand a little squeeze. It's reassuring and kind, and it's definitely giving me the wrong idea. Ever since we talked while she was in the bathtub the other night, I've become hyper-aware when we touch. It feels like there's a zing of electricity that flows through my body whenever we do. Even the slightest brush of her hand against mine as we walk down the street has me all hot and bothered, and it's really inconvenient. Not only am I not interested in dating anyone right now, but Cassie is my best friend. Feeling this way about her is off the table.

We exit the elevator, and I try to get my brain back on the task at hand. Meet with Stacey, get her to help with the nonprofit, and stop lusting after my best friend. Easy as pie.

We reach the door to Stacey's office suite, and my hand is stuck hovering over the handle. Cassie nudges me with her elbow. It's enough to get me to push the handle down and open the door.

"Hello," a friendly voice says as the door opens to reveal a tall, dark-haired woman in stilettos and perfect-looking makeup.

"Hi," I say with a hesitant and mildly awkward wave. The woman reaches out her hand, and I shake it, nervous that she'll be able to tell I've been shaking. "I'm Caleb."

"Stacey," she says. "And you are?" She turns to Cassie and reaches out her hand again.

"I'm Cassie, a friend of Caleb's. I'm just here to help out however I can."

"Perfect! Why don't you both take a seat, and we'll get started."

She gestures to a pair of chairs across from her desk as she strides to the other side of it and takes a seat. It's a small office, but the view is amazing. Something tells me that's exactly why Stacey chose it. Between the view and her professional clothes, you can tell she takes how she presents herself to clients seriously. I like her for this project already.

"So," Cassie says. "How does this work?"

I appreciate her taking the lead in the conversation, and I smile at her as a way of silently saying *thank you.*

"Why don't you tell me a bit about the idea you have, Caleb? I'd love to hear what inspired you to want to do this," Stacey says.

"Well, I... uh..." I pause to regroup. *Get it together, Caleb!* Cassie places her hand lightly on my thigh, and it immediately grounds me enough that I'm able to press forward. "I've known for a long time that hockey is an expensive sport to play. There are steep fees, the gear costs a small fortune just to start, and once you're old enough, the travel can be costly. Growing up, my best friend actually had to quit when one of his parents got laid off. So, when one of Cassie's students brought up that a friend of his might also have to quit, I decided I wanted to do something. I couldn't help my friend then, but I can help countless kids now."

"It's really great that you want to use your celebrity for good," Stacey says. "How do you feel about capitalizing on your star-player-status to help get the word out about this?"

I think about it for a moment. On the one hand, the thought kind of makes me want to hide in a corner for the rest of eternity. On the other hand, I want this organization to be a success. If my name can help more people know about the work we're planning to do, that feels worth it.

"I'm good with it," I say with a confident nod.

I'm honestly proud of myself for the confidence I feel, and I think Cassie is proud of me as well because she gives my knee a little squeeze, and I can see her grinning out of the corner of my eye.

"Wonderful! I think we should do a kickoff gala. Really hit the ground running and set things off with a bang. We'll get items signed by the team just like we do for Mitchell's gala every year, and we'll auction them off. I already have some great ideas of donors to invite who will love this cause."

"That sounds great," I say, trying not to think about having to ask my teammates for their help with this.

I know they'll do it without question, but that doesn't mean that I don't have to ask them.

"Then let's plan to meet next week to discuss details once I'm able to lock in a date and location. In the meantime, I'll get the paperwork started so we're legally set up correctly for this. What are you thinking you want the name to be?"

Crap. A name. I know I need one, but I honestly haven't gotten to that. I was so overwhelmed by the nonprofit paperwork that I completely forgot about it. And now Stacey is looking at me expectantly.

"What about Smashing Barriers?" volunteers Cassie, as if on cue. Always there to cover for me.

"Oh, I love that," says Stacey.

"It's perfect," I say.

I reach out to give Cassie's hand a quick squeeze. It's a small gesture that we've always done, but usually, it's just the two of us, and as soon as I do it, I'm hyperaware of the woman across the desk from us. And yet, when Cassie squeezes back, I don't let go.

CHAPTER 15
CASSIE
ONE WEEK LATER

"**P**eonies aren't even in season!" King yells as he jumps to his feet, wildly flailing his arms in frustration.

"We can have them flown in!" Greggs replies. "They'll look way better than the basic shit you're proposing!"

Greggs and King have been going back and forth for twenty minutes about the centerpieces for the gala while Caleb's eyes have completely glazed over.

Since our meeting last week, Stacey hit the ground running and got everything set up so that Caleb could start fundraising for his nonprofit. She's smart and talented, and I'm quickly becoming obsessed with her. She's laughing to herself as these two massive hockey players fight over centerpieces and silent auction items. I'm not actually sure how Greggs and King got invited to this meeting. Something tells me they may have invited themselves, actually. But I'm glad they're here. Despite their outbursts over which flowers are native to the state of Colorado, I think they're helping keep Caleb calmer.

"Is Greggs always this… into the details?" I whisper to Stacey.

"Believe it or not, this is him being tame. Last year's foster event was almost a 'complete disaster' because the font on the invitations wasn't 'dog-ish' enough. Whatever that means." She rolls her eyes.

I can't help but laugh, knowing that the guy who regularly beats the absolute shit out of professional hockey players on the ice cares so much about flowers and fonts.

"I kind of want to kill him sometimes," she continues. "But he does so much good for the organization, I guess I just put up with it."

Based on how many times I've caught Greggs sneaking a look at Stacey today, something tells me he isn't just giving her extra attention because he cares about dogs. I think maybe he's getting in his own way and actually likes her. A lot. I decide to play wing-woman to thank Greggs for helping Caleb. Well, and because the pining is honestly too much to witness and not want to help. The poor guy is clearly completely gone for this woman.

"He's a really great guy," I say. "I'm so glad he's helping Caleb figure all of this out."

"Yeah, it's very nice of him. So, you and Caleb…"

Oh.

Oh no.

Is she interested in Caleb?

And why does that make me feel… jealous?

This is not going according to plan at all.

"We're, uh, just friends," I somehow manage to say. I've said it a million times before, so why does it feel like a lie this time?

"I'm just asking because he keeps looking over at you. I wasn't sure if there was some there… there."

Well, that's… interesting. I guess we've made eye contact a few times, but he just looks away quickly and returns back to trying not to kill his teammates. It's no different than when he finds my face in the stands and gives me a quick wave and a wink during warmups. Or when we lock eyes during a funny moment in boxing class. Or when our hands brush as we walk down the street eating ice cream or sipping coffee. It's just how we are… right?

CHAPTER 16
CALEB

"So, when are you going to ask Cassie out?" Greggs says in a far-too-loud whisper.

I'm suddenly snapped back to the hell that is my current reality from the nice little place I'd created in my brain to ignore my teammates' weird obsession with *my* nonprofit's gala.

"Who's asking Cassie out?" It comes out much more desperate than I intended.

"Um… you?" says King. "Who else?"

Oh, thank god.

Wait.

What?

"I'm not asking Cassie out," I say. "She's my best friend."

I sneak a glance across the room to where Cassie and Stacey are sitting. Cassie is staring right at me. I quickly look away, praying she didn't hear us talking about her.

"Then why does she keep looking over here?" asks Greggs.

"Maybe because you can't stop staring at Stacey like the thirsty freak you are," offers King.

"Shhhhhh!" Greggs says dramatically, holding a finger over his lips and glaring at King.

"Wait, are you actually into Stacey?" I ask, apparently too loudly because Greggs is shushing me now too.

"Of course I am," he whispers. "But I think she hates me."

"Why would she hate you?" I ask. Shockingly, I'm actually starting to like Greggs.

"You guys know I can be a bit… intense…"

"You? Intense? Never…" says King with more sarcasm than I thought was possible.

"Shut up," Greggs says. "Well, anyway, I think I've gone a bit overboard with some of the nonprofit stuff, and I think I pissed her off."

I sneak a glance over at Stacey, but my eyes fall on Cassie instead. Considering she's usually in workout gear when we hang out, it's been almost jarring to see her in a sundress today. Jarring and breathtaking. That, combined with the way her natural curls frame her face, might be enough to kill me, honestly. This growing attraction I have for her and the jealousy that comes with it is becoming a problem. If Greggs or King wants to ask her out, they should. Cassie has made it abundantly clear we're just friends, and it's always been enough for me. Well, until right now, apparently. Because right now, I want to pluck her off the couch and drag her across town to my condo. Which is not something I'm used to.

"This isn't about me, though," says Greggs. "It's about Caleb needing to grow some balls."

"I have… plenty of… balls, thank you," is the best response I seem to be able to come up with because my eyes are still glued on Cassie.

Greggs and King both (understandably) laugh before King says, "Dude, you so obviously want her."

"We're just friends," I reply defensively.

"You can tell yourself that all you want, but you clearly want more," King says.

Do I?

I honestly don't know.

Because despite my growing physical attraction to her, the idea of dating Cassie—of dating anyone, really—scares the living daylight out of me. Sure, Cassie is completely gorgeous, fun as heck, and the best person I know, but it's not about her. How am I supposed to just... open myself up to losing my best friend like that? On top of all the stress my hockey career would put on our relationship?

No.

I can't.

I can't lose her.

But I also can't admit why to these guys.

"We'll see..." I fake-concede, knowing full well I have zero intention of risking my friendship with Cassie for some weird, pent-up lust I can't seem to shake.

"Nice!" they both say and fist-bump.

Well, at least that will get them off my back. For now, anyway. But I have to figure out how to get over this thing I have for Cassie. It's inconvenient at best and dangerous at worst. I could really end up hurting her if I don't get it under control. I try to turn my attention back to the centerpieces and table settings at hand, vowing to shove my attraction for Cassie deep, deep down. Right where it belongs.

CHAPTER 17

CASSIE

A FEW DAYS LATER

Caleb hates my Blizzards' jersey. Sure, he loves that I love his team. But he doesn't love that I refuse to wear his jersey. But I've had this Patrick Roy jersey since I was a teenager, and I'm not giving it up. Especially when all the other women in the family section have stuff bedazzled with their respective player's names. I'd look way too much like Caleb's girlfriend if I did that. And despite being a teacher, I hate bedazzled shit. I'll take my Patrick Roy jersey any day.

I'm also totally convinced that wearing this jersey has been Caleb's lucky charm. For the past six games I've been to, he's been nothing short of incredible. I'd wear a burlap sack if it meant he kept that up. Especially knowing how much he wants to win the All-Star game. Normally, the All-Star game is just an exhibition game where the players come to show off and blow off some steam. But because Caleb is Caleb, he wants his team—The West—to win. Badly.

The game is tied 2-2, and Caleb has, once again, been unstoppable. He got an assist on the first goal and scored the second himself. But the Eastern Conference is giving it everything they've got, and if we don't score again in the next three minutes, this game will go into overtime.

Now we're down to two minutes remaining, and Caleb is racing down the edge of the ice when an Eastern Conference forward smacks into him. The refs have been so far up that player's ass that they refuse to call a penalty, so Caleb (for the second time in his entire career) takes a swing for himself. It's a good thing we've been working on his right hook because the hit is actually pretty solid. The downside is that he winds up in the penalty box.

And without Caleb on the ice, the defense isn't nearly as strong.

The West loses.

Caleb is going to be so bummed.

I'm sitting in the Vegas Strip hotel lobby waiting for the team to return when a guy in a Vegas jersey saunters over to me. Whether he intends to mock my team or hit on me is unclear, but I shoot him the same do-not-even-think-about-it look I would either way and take a sip of my beer. He saunters toward the hotel elevator, leaving me to my IPA.

A few minutes later, Caleb walks in. His hair is wet and spikey from his shower after the game, and he has a big bruise on his cheek. But he smiles when he sees me and envelopes me in a big bear hug.

"Does this mean you'll wear my jersey now?" he asks as he gives me an extra squeeze.

"I'll wear your jersey when you win the Stanley Cup," I say, giving him a little poke in the ribs for good measure.

"Ouch, way to hit a guy when he's down." He laughs and wraps his arm around my shoulders.

"Oh shush, it'll happen. You played great today."

"I shouldn't have let my emotions get the better of me. Even if the refs were being ridiculous," he says.

Greggs wanders over to us and places his hand on Caleb's arm. "No way, man. You have to stand up to yourself. Penalties are a part of the game. You know that. This isn't your fault."

"But that doesn't mean it doesn't suck," says Caleb.

"It totally does," I chime in. "So, why don't you all go get changed, and I'll take you out? We are in Vegas, after all."

"You're the best, Cass," says Greggs, who completely towers over me as he gives my head a playful rub before turning to King. "We're going out to celebrate. These are Cass' orders, so no one is getting out of it! Let's meet back down here in twenty minutes."

Despite some grumbling on Caleb's part, King and Caleb file into the elevators and make their way to their respective rooms. Caleb flew me out for the All-Star Weekend because I had a three-day weekend off from school, and he was convinced that I, not my Roy jersey, was his lucky charm. I guess he was wrong. But I'm glad I'm here because otherwise, he'd just be moping around his hotel room by himself, even if the rest of the players went out.

I open my suitcase and pull out the only Vegas-worthy dress I own. It's black with a plunging neckline, and it's far too short for any other location. It barely covers my ass. But for here, it's perfect. I set it aside and pull on my robe to get ready in the bathroom. After messing with my hair a bit to make the usually unruly mop of curls do something resembling an actual hairstyle, I add some eyeshadow to my minimalist makeup from the game. Once I'm almost ready to get dressed, there's a knock at my door.

I walk across the room and look through the peephole to

see Caleb wearing a sports coat and button-up. I open the door to reveal him wearing jeans that hug his legs in a way that would make anyone who's attracted to men swoon. I'm not too big to admit that my best friend is one hell of an attractive guy. I'm not fucking blind.

"Hey you," he says as he walks past me and into my room without permission, which would bother me if it was literally anyone else.

"I just need to put my dress on. One second," I say, pulling my robe closed across my chest. I'm comfortable with Caleb, but not *that* comfortable.

Caleb perches on the end of my bed while I head to the bathroom to change. I adjust my boobs to make them look extra perky in the dress (yes, I'm a teacher, but a girl's gotta live) and give my hair one last fluff. I step into my heels and slide the bathroom door open. Caleb's on his phone, probably looking at all the bad takes about his game on Twitter.

"Are you on Twitter? We've talked about this, Caleb," I say.

He looks up at me, and his mouth falls open. I'll admit I'm a bit pleased with the response to my outfit.

"Jesus, Buttercup. You look incredible. I'm going to have to work overtime to keep guys away from you tonight."

"Buttercup?"

"It's a flower."

"You know I can take care of myself," I grumble as I grab my purse.

He laughs. "I know that better than most people."

"You ready to celebrate a great trip?" I say while we exit my room into the hallway before double-checking that the door lock is latched.

"Celebrating doesn't feel quite right yet, but I'm ready to go out with my best friend," he says with his kind, genuine smile as he extends his elbow.

•   •   •

The club is clearly louder than Caleb would like, but the other guys are living their best lives. I've tried to get Caleb to go dance twice, but he refuses. So, I order us drinks—an IPA for us both—and watch as the bartender pours them and places them on the bar. I grab them quickly, and we settle on the couch in the VIP section King managed to secure for us. Most of the players Caleb is slightly closer with are in committed relationships, so they always try to live vicariously through him by trying to get him to hit on women when the team is out. But Caleb always refuses and chooses to hang out with me, at least when I'm around. Who knows what he's doing when I'm not.

Admittedly, I like that he's next to me tonight. He's clearly taking the loss hard, and I want to be the one who's here for him, not some random woman at a club in Vegas he'll likely never see again. I shudder at the thought and take a sip of my beer.

We both finish our beers in comfortable silence, but I can tell the alcohol has done nothing to help his mood. He's moping.

"Alright," I say as I stand up. "I'm dancing."

"I'm not letting you go out there by yourself. There's a ninety-eight percent chance you get accosted by a finance bro in a vest if you're alone."

"I can handle myself, Mack," I say, knowing full well that using his last name will piss him off and make him want to join me even more.

He stands. My plan is working.

"I'm coming with you," he says.

"Okay." I take his hand. "But I'm requesting that techno song you say you hate but secretly love."

"Fine, but if I start dancing, it's only because the beat is too catchy for its own good."

I drag him to the dance floor, which is something I've done before the few times we've been out together. But this time, he laces his fingers through mine, which I know for a fact he's never done before. Because that's a thing that couples do. A warm feeling starts in my gut as he gives my hand a squeeze.

What the hell?!

I shut down the ooey-gooey-ness growing inside me by repeating *he's your best friend* over and over again in my head until we reach the dance floor.

Caleb is undeniably hot as fuck tonight, and he's obviously wonderful. But the idea of dating has never really been on the table for us, and it never will be, even if I might think about it sometimes. Caleb has always been singularly focused on his career, and, to this day, I'm about as emotionally available as a sack of rocks. But most importantly, now that I've actually let someone into my life a little bit, I absolutely, without a doubt, cannot stand to lose him.

We find a spot on the dance floor, and I must have done something horrific in my past life because the music immediately slows. Caleb locks eyes with me and takes a step forward. I let out a cackle of a laugh because that's what I do when I'm uncomfortable. His gorgeous smile spreads across his face, and I feel like I'm tipsy even though I've barely had a drink.

"You can't even slow dance with me when I just lost, Lavender?" he cajoles. His palm is resting on my shoulder now. And for some reason, my breath is caught in my throat a little.

"Of course I can," I say defensively because it's true. This can be a completely platonic slow dance. That's a thing, right?

I step forward and wrap my arms around his neck. He pulls me even closer until our bodies are pressed together. We start to sway to the music, and I rest my—admittedly tiny— head on his broad chest. I can hear his heart thumping, and I'm glad to know I'm not the only one whose heart is beating a million miles a minute right now.

The song starts to come to an end, and Caleb's lips come within centimeters of my ear. He says something right as the beat of the song he claims to hate starts. I don't know what he said, but it sounded like it might have been *you really do look incredible tonight.*

I don't get a chance to ask because the song's beat continues to grow louder and louder, and Caleb is full-on bouncing around with his arms swinging like a monkey. Warmth fills me seeing him having a good time, even if he does dance like a baboon. I start to bounce, too, and before I know it, my arms are swinging in sync with him. I'm sure we look ridiculous, but neither of us can bring ourselves to care because we're having fun. And that's why I love our friendship so much. Caleb brings me outside of my asshole self and makes me have *fun.* Which is definitely not something I was used to when we first met. I'm not sure Caleb was either. But we bring it out in each other, as evidenced by the fact that I almost smack into a guy wearing a Vegas jersey.

"Hey, watch it!" the clearly belligerent man yells.

"Sorry! I'm getting a bit carried away, I guess," I holler back.

He mumbles something that sounds an awful lot like *cunt* under his breath before turning to walk away, and before I know it, Caleb is launching himself toward the guy. I reach out to pull him back, but he escapes my grasp, yanking his arm through my fingers and flinging his fists toward the guy, who doesn't even realize he's being hunted down by a professional hockey player.

"Caleb!" I yell as I reach out for him again.

It's not that I don't want this guy to get punched in the face. Hell, I'd like to do it myself. But Caleb *cannot* get caught in a fight at a nightclub. The headlines would be a disaster.

Greggs and King must have been watching us because suddenly they're flanking either side of me, stepping toward Caleb to lock his arms at his side. Once they have him restrained, I place my hand on his shoulder. He's shaking, which I'm used to. But this time, I can tell it's not from fear; it's from anger.

"Caleb," I say again.

"He called Cassie the c-word," Caleb says to Greggs, clearly trying to get a rise out of him too.

"He *what*?" Greggs yells.

"Guys!" I holler in my teacher's voice. "That's enough! I don't need to bail any of you out of jail tonight."

"That won't be necessary," a deep voice says from behind me. "But you do need to leave. Now." I turn to see a big bouncer with his arms crossed staring us down.

"But…" Greggs starts.

I hold up my hand to shush him and nod to the bouncer. "Not a problem at all. We'll see ourselves out. Right, boys?"

"Right," says King, who's been remarkably silent this entire time.

He grabs Caleb's bicep and pulls him toward the door, with Greggs and I falling in line behind them.

CHAPTER 18
CALEB
THE NEXT MORNING

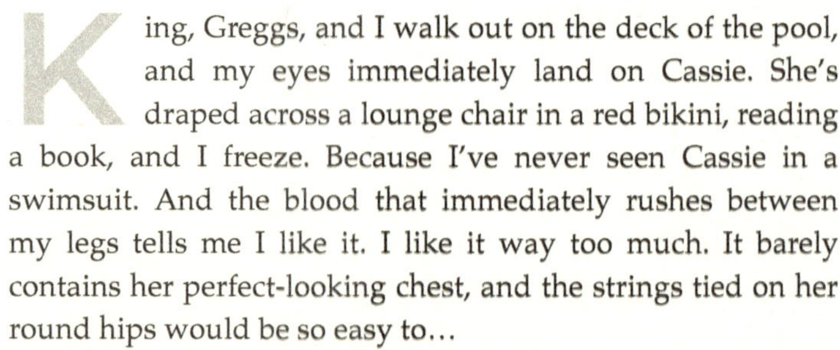

King, Greggs, and I walk out on the deck of the pool, and my eyes immediately land on Cassie. She's draped across a lounge chair in a red bikini, reading a book, and I freeze. Because I've never seen Cassie in a swimsuit. And the blood that immediately rushes between my legs tells me I like it. I like it way too much. It barely contains her perfect-looking chest, and the strings tied on her round hips would be so easy to…

"Holy shit," says King when his eyes fall on her. "Is that Cassie?"

"Finish that thought, and I'll rip your face off," I say before I can stop myself.

"Alright, dude. Take a breath. She just looks… different."

As if she senses us all staring like a bunch of creeps, Cassie looks up from her book and waves us over.

"Different is one way to put it," says Greggs as we cross toward her.

"Greggs, I realize I would instantly lose, but I will fight you regardless if you don't shut up," I say under my breath, afraid that Cassie will hear me.

"Hey, guys!" she says with a huge grin that melts my insides even further because she's even sexier when she's happy, and I truly do not know what to do with myself.

"Hey Cass, thanks for a fun time last night," says Greggs with a wink.

I full-on choke on the sip of water I just took because he couldn't mean what I think he means... right? Because I dropped Cassie off at her room and Greggs was nowhere to be seen. He hadn't... They hadn't... right? Right?!

"No problem. Sorry, that douche got us kicked out, though," she says.

Oh, thank God.

Except I'm still choking.

King slaps his hand on my back way too hard and says, "You good?"

"Wrong pipe," I manage to squeak out like a prepubescent twelve-year-old.

Cassie pats the space next to her on her chair for me to sit. As soon as I do, she rubs my back, and if I wasn't already dangerously close to pitching a tent out here, I certainly am now. Finally, I get myself together enough to stop coughing but not enough to get the very hot images of the things I evidently want to do with Cassie out of my head.

So, I grab the newest fantasy book in my favorite series out of my bag and settle in on a separate chair from Cassie in hopes that maybe the distance will help me calm the heck down.

Flying Cassie out for the All-Star Weekend was a massive mistake. Not because I didn't want her here; I wanted that desperately. But because once you see your best friend looking like the hottest thing you've ever seen, it's really hard to obey your very strict I-will-not-jackoff-to-my-best-friend rule.

It's not like I haven't thought about Cassie like this before. But now that I've seen it? It feels like it's game over. Honestly, what am I supposed to do with this?

She's your best friend, I tell myself yet again as I lay in bed. I said I wanted to take a nap before escaping the pool situation, which was true at the time. But the problem is, I've made the mistake of opening Cassie's Instagram page. Even just looking at her silly grin in the photo I took of her on a hike we both went on but hated the entire time last summer is making me think unsavory thoughts. Well, that and the selfie she posted on her close friend's story in that damned bikini.

I'm always so focused on my hockey career that I don't really let myself get distracted with dating or even just hooking up at all during the season. So, let's just say it's been a while. Like, since before I met Cassie. So, more than a while I guess. And the need for release has suddenly completely overcome my entire existence.

Shower. That'll help.

I climb out of bed and walk into the bathroom. As I'm turning on the cold water, my phone buzzes. It's a Snapchat from Cassie. I brace myself as I open it. It's a selfie of her, Greggs, and King. But I only see her because, if I'm being one hundred percent honest, I've only ever really seen her.

I grumble to myself about Greggs and King getting to hang out with Cassie as I let the cool water pour down over me. To distract myself, I try to name the capitals of all fifty states, which is really hard for a Canadian. It's enough to get me to calm down, though. Well, at least it is for now. But I don't know how much more of this I can take.

CHAPTER 19

CASSIE

'm sitting at our gate waiting for the guys to get through security. None of them have TSA Pre-check because they're used to flying private with the team, so it's taking them forever to get through security. Just as I'm reaching into my bag to pull out a book, I see them barreling toward me in the distance. It's impossible not to notice three hockey players confidently making their way through virtually any crowd, but when my eyes land on Caleb, I find myself thinking that maybe it's more than that. There's something magnetic about him, and the way he smiles at me when he sees me staring is enough to floor me.

Okay. Yes. My best friend is hot. I accepted this a long time ago. So why do my insides go all gooey when he approaches me with a water bottle outstretched in his hand and says, "You never drink enough water."

He's not wrong. I don't. But has he really noticed my water intake?

I grin up at him and take the bottle from his massive hand, our fingers brushing together enough that my stomach does a flip somewhere deep inside me. *What. Is. Happening. To. Me?*

Caleb settles into the seat next to me, with Greggs and King across from us.

"You didn't get me a water bottle," says Greggs with a grin.

"Huh?" asks Caleb.

"You got Cassie a water bottle," Greggs continues.

"So?" Caleb says defensively.

"Nothing," Greggs says with a knowing look. "Just saying."

"Well, stop saying." Caleb's grumpy now, and it's honestly a little cute how pouty he's being. Even if I have no idea what's happening.

It's not until I look at my boarding pass that I realize Caleb upgraded me to first class. When I try to interrogate him about it, he immediately denies it, but there's no other explanation for the fact that I'm now seated in the second row, sipping a mimosa, with Caleb in the window seat next to me, and no one to my right because, unlike my original assigned seat, this is an aisle, not a middle in row thirty-four.

I'm not complaining, but it is a bit of a waste. I'm going to immediately fall asleep as soon as planes take off, regardless of my seat assignment. And the champagne in the mimosa is just going to make that even more likely. I might even fall asleep before the safety instructions are over…

I fell asleep on Caleb.

No.

I snuggled Caleb.

Snuggled!

What on earth is wrong with me?

And why didn't he shove me off?

When I woke up in his arms, his hand was gently rubbing my back.

Rubbing my back!

What the hell?

Okay. How do I move? I have to move.

He's still rubbing my back. It's so calming and… and what if I don't want to move? What if there's a part of me that's hoping that little jolt I just felt isn't the plane starting to descend? What… does this mean?

I'm honestly too sleepy for all the questions, so I guess that's a plausible explanation for why I'm nuzzling into Caleb further, closing my eyes, and going back to sleep.

CHAPTER 20
CALEB
ONE WEEK LATER

t's been a week since the All-Star Break, which means that it's time for the inaugural gala of my *Smashing Barriers* (Greggs lost the naming argument, thank god) nonprofit. After all the hard work of getting this thing pulled together, I'm nothing short of completely terrified as my Uber approaches Cassie's apartment. I'm in an uncomfortable suit and willingly walking into a room full of people who are there because they want to talk to me. Why did I think this was a good idea?

I text Cassie to let her know we're waiting outside and get out of the car to greet her. My palms are all sweaty, and I'm pretty sure I'm shaking a little. The sounds on her street seem louder than normal for some reason.

But then everything goes still and quiet.

Because Cassie just walked outside.

And *oh my God*. She's breathtaking.

I don't mean that in a she's pretty way. I mean, she legitimately knocks the wind out of me as she walks toward me. A sundress was one thing, a bikini another. But this? This is something else entirely. I'm completely undone as she approaches me and gives a little twirl. Cassie's not really the twirling type normally, but I greatly appreciate the opportunity to take all of her in.

It's not like it's even a revealing dress or anything, but something about her radiates joy and sunshine in a way I can't fully understand. The front of the dress is a high-necked halter, for crying out loud. The back, on the other hand, scoops deep and low, and honestly, I don't know how I'm supposed to resist touching her all night. Especially now that she's standing inches in front of me. This is definitely not helping my attempts to ignore my attraction to her. I can't ignore it anymore, I realize. Because she's too incredible, and I'm too useless to do anything but stare at her and want her.

"You look incredible," I say. Well, we both say it at the same time, actually.

"I wear suits all the time," I say. "You, on the other hand…"

I don't finish the thought because she steps closer, and I can swear she's looking at my lips. Then suddenly, her lips are right by the sensitive spot under my ear, and I think my brain is going to short circuit.

"You like it?" she whispers as if there's any other reaction I could possibly have to seeing her like this. As if she hasn't completely forced my world to shift tonight.

"It's perfect," I say. I don't have other words to offer her because perfect is the only one that seems to fit.

"Should we get going?" she asks, taking a step back from me. I have to resist the urge to pull her back, pull her close against me, and never let go. "I hear the flowers at this thing are supposed to be 'completely on point,'" she says, doing her best Greggs impression.

I let out a laugh and begrudgingly turn toward the car.

Despite wanting to keep Cassie just for myself right now, I need her help if I'm going to get through tonight.

I hold the car door open for her and help her settle in. When she takes my hand, I swear a pulse of electricity courses through my entire body while she seems totally unaffected as she places her purse on her lap and closes the door.

I should have known that Greggs and King wouldn't stop being involved with this when the planning was done. But I'm actually shockingly grateful. They're both working the room with the same commitment they would if this was their own event, which means I have less ground to cover on my own. I think I even overheard Greggs talking up the silent auction to someone I know is a huge donor to these sorts of things. Between them and Cassie, we might actually reach our fundraising goal for tonight.

Cassie hasn't left my side the entire night. She effortlessly moves us from group to group, making sure that I talk to all the people I absolutely have to but steering those conversations toward things I'm comfortable with. This basically means I've just talked about hockey all night, but that's really why these people are here. They might like a good cause, but what really drives people to events like this is the other people there. In this case, some of the best players in the NHL.

Cassie's in the middle of a conversation with one of the top donors in the state when Greggs approaches us.

"Hey, man," he says. "Are you ready for the silent auction?"

"What do you mean?" I ask.

"It's almost time to read off the winners. You gotta get up there and do your thing!" he says like it's the most obvious thing ever.

Oh god.

Why did no one warn me about this?

"Do my… thing?" I squeak out.

"You just read off who won each item. It's super easy."

Easy for a guy like Greggs, maybe.

I need to get out of here.

"Um, will you, uh, excuse me for a minute?" I say to no one in particular as I make a mad dash for the bathroom.

By the time I make it to the bathroom, my hands are sweaty, and I'm full-on shaking. I close a bathroom stall and try to hold my head in my hands, trying to get a grip, but there's no use. It's coming, and I can't stop it. My breathing becomes labored, and my vision blurs around the edges, almost turning red.

Get it together, I try to tell myself.

But it's no use because there are all those people, and they all expect so much from me, and I just cannot take it. Cannot handle the pressure for one more second. The shaking worsens, and I can feel tears stinging my eyes.

"Caleb?"

Ugh.

It's Greggs.

"Hey man, you in here?"

And King.

"Do you want us to get Cassie?" Greggs says.

The last thing I want is for her to see me like this, even if she'd know exactly what to do to help. Because I'm letting her down. I'm letting everyone down.

"No," I croak out.

"Open the door, Caleb," Greggs says softly.

I didn't even know he could produce such a kind and understanding tone, but I know it's him because when I don't open the door, he just forces it open with his body. Greggs and King both suddenly fill the doorway. But when I look at their faces, they aren't as angry as I expected. They both look totally fine, even though I'm letting them down after all they've done to help make this night a success.

"Alright, buddy, breathe in," King says before pausing.

I'm breathing in and out too fast. I can't seem to catch my breath at this point.

"Try again. Breathe in," King says. "Slowly."

I breathe in.

"And, slowly, breathe out," he says, dramatically demonstrating how to do the most basic human functions that I seem to be incapable of right now.

I let out a breath slowly.

Is Greggs rubbing my back right now? I think he might be, which is a bit strange, but I'm having a full-on panic attack, so that's the least of my worries.

"In." Pause. "Out," King continues.

He repeats himself until my breathing is back to normal, and I fully open my eyes. After a few moments of silence, Greggs stands up. It's only then that I realize we've all been sitting on the floor of the bathroom together. If hockey Twitter knew about this, they'd have a field day.

"Here's the plan," says King. "Greggs and I will come up with you to do the silent auction announcements. If it gets to be too much, just tap out, and we'll take over."

"And I'm going to give you the number of my therapist. I think you should consider giving her a call," Greggs chimes in.

"Your… therapist?" I ask.

"I have bipolar disorder," he says like it's not a massive bombshell. "I see a therapist and psychiatrist regularly."

"I had no idea," I say.

"That's because I see a therapist and psychiatrist regularly, dude." He laughs. "And I try to keep it private, stigma and all that, but I trust you."

"And you can trust us," says King. "Anxiety must suck, but we'll help you get through tonight."

"Anxiety?" I ask.

Is that what this is?

"My dude, you just had a panic attack," says King. "You hate crowds. You avoid attention like it's the plague. I think it's safe to say you have social anxiety."

"But we'll leave it up to the professionals to decide for sure," adds Greggs. "Because you're going to think about calling her… right?"

"I'll think about it," I say, unsure that I actually will.

"I'll take it. Are you ready?" Greggs asks.

"Let's do this," I say with a nod.

I emerge from the bathroom to find Cassie standing outside the door. I lose my breath all over again, but this time, it's because of her.

"Everything okay?" she asks.

I look to Greggs and King, and they both nod their encouragement.

"I freaked out about the crowd," I say. "But I'm okay now."

Suddenly, she's pulling me into a hug. It's kind and sweet and very much not like her to just randomly hug me like this in public, where people will make assumptions.

But she doesn't let go.

Instead, she somehow pulls me closer and brings her lips up to my ear. "You've got this, and I'm here for you."

It's exactly what I need to hear.

It always is.

Because Cassie is exactly what I need.

She always has been.

And suddenly, I realize we've always been headed in this direction. We've always been on the path of me standing here, vulnerable in her arms. Because it's inevitable. We're inevitable.

And it's then, as we're wrapped in each other's arms, swaying in the hallway, that I realize it.

I'm in love with Cassie.

CHAPTER 21
CASSIE

Watching Caleb, with Greggs and King beside him, I'm so overwhelmed with pride for him. I know this isn't easy for him, and I know how much he wants tonight to be a success. As he presents each silent auction winner, he becomes more and more comfortable. Near the end, he even cracks a joke.

When he emerged from the bathroom, I was so worried about him. All I've ever wanted in our friendship is for him to be okay, and tonight, he wasn't. And I couldn't be there for him until it was over. That thought kind of broke me a bit, so when he finally came out and told me what happened, I did the only thing I could. I hugged him in the way he deserved and let him know that I was there for him. Always.

What I didn't expect was what that show of affection would do to me. Because now, as he's reading off these auction winners, I want to run up on stage, wrap my arms around his waist, and never let go. It's a weird urge for someone who doesn't even really like hugging her own mother, but it doesn't go away. I want his arms around me. I want my head on his chest like it was on the plane. I want to be as close to him as humanly possible.

When the presentation is finished and all the winners have received instructions from Stacey to pick up their auction items, I expect Caleb to make himself scarce quickly.

Instead, he stays on stage, opens his mouth, and says, "I just have a quick thing to say if you all don't mind giving me another moment of your time."

He fishes in his pocket for a second before pulling out a stack of note cards. His hesitant expression turns into a broad smile when his eyes lock with mine.

"This night would not have been possible without a great many people. Please give a round of applause to the event staff," he says, and the crowd applauds politely.

"I also want to thank my teammates, all of whom are here tonight. You all never stop showing up for me, and I hope you know how much it means to me. This cause, these kids, love hockey just as much as we all do, and the fact that we raised what we need to support their love of this sport means more to me than winning any trophy. But, of course, I do hope we get to hoist The Cup this year."

The crowd erupts in support, and a few of the guys whoop and holler.

"Most importantly." His eyes are back on me again. "I want to thank my best friend. Cassie, you are my rock. We've been through so much together, and I mean it honestly when I say that getting punched in the face by you was the best thing to ever happen to me. Thank you for your help tonight. Thank you for everything."

And with that, I have melted into the floor from the ooey-gooey-ness that is my soul. There is no structural integrity left in my body, I'm sure of it. All that's left of me is mush. Mush with a heart that's been closed off for so long. But somehow, Caleb, with all of his shyness, kindness, and laughter, has managed to crack it open. And I'm not sure what that means or what to do about it. But I do know that when Caleb walks off stage, I'm going to take his hand and not let go until I have to. I tell myself I'm doing it to try to help keep him calm and try not to think about the fact that it'll give me a bit of what I want without crossing a line.

"I'm not letting you sleep on the couch, Aster."

"And I'm not letting you not sleep in your own bed the night before a big game."

"I sleep in hotels all the time before games."

"Five-star hotels with *beds*, Caleb."

We're standing in Caleb's living room, both refusing to go to his bedroom. The gala went late, and Caleb insisted that I could sleep in his apartment instead of making the long trip back to my neighborhood. I didn't for a second think that that meant kicking him out of his bed.

"Can we be adults about this, please?" he asks with a sigh.

"I *am* being an adult. An adult that sleeps on the couch," I say as I cross my arms like a child.

He looks at me like I'm ignoring some super obvious solution and says, "I mean, I have a king bed. Let's just share it."

What?

Has this man lost his mind?

Clearly, he has no idea what his little speech back at the gala did to me, or he would not be suggesting two best *friends* share a bed. So why am I nodding my head? Like, up and down? As one does when they're agreeing to something?

"Okay," the words fly out of my mouth, and my immediate instinct is to slam a hand over my lips and never remove it so as to not allow myself to speak ever again. Because, again, *What!*

"Great!" Caleb says cheerfully as he stands up from the couch.

When we got back, we both changed into a set of his oversized Blizzards warmups. What is it about men and gray sweatpants? I realize just how bad of an idea this is right around the moment I notice. I appreciate how good his ass looks in those sweats as he makes his way down the hall. If he knew what I was thinking, he surely wouldn't agree to share his bed right now. Right?

But I betrayed myself with all my nodding and okay-ing, and now here I am, walking down the hall, following Caleb into his bedroom. What I don't realize until I'm sitting on the edge of his bed is that I've never been in here before. We've always hung out in the main living space because, you know, *friends*. It feels oddly intimate but not monumental. This is always what was going to end up happening. Which leaves me feeling confused and cozy at the same time.

"Begonia," he says in an annoyed tone.

I whip my head toward him to discover he's shirtless. Well, not permanently. He's just changing his shirt. But that honestly feels even more intimate than it did a second ago, and I'm officially so confused.

"Yes?" I reply.

"You can get under the covers. I promise my sheets don't bite."

Right. Okay.

I can do this.

Adults. We're being adults.

And, of course, he's right. His sheets do not, in fact, bite because they're actually incredibly soft, and this pillow is the perfect amount of squishy and firm. I don't think I've ever felt more comfortable than I do as Caleb switches off the light and slides into bed next to me.

After a few moments of silence, each of us lying on our backs facing the ceiling, I say, "Do you want to talk about it?"

"Talk about what?"

"What happened at the gala? In the bathroom."

"Oh. Right. That," he says.

I sit in silence for a second before I realize I'm maybe crossing a line for him. "We don't have to if you don't want to," I say.

"No, no. It's not that," he says. "I'm just trying to figure out exactly what it was and what that means. Greggs and King think I have social anxiety. I've always just assumed that I'm shy. It's just a lot to wrap my mind around, I guess."

I think through the interactions Caleb and I had early on. I like to think we've always been comfortable with each other, but I realize he was even nervous with me. He asked a lot of questions but let me do most of the talking for a long time. He hates talking to the press, even when it's for a puff piece that'll make him look good. He always mumbles and gets shaky when he meets new people. The few times I've hugged him when he's nervous, and his heart is always clamoring in his chest. Maybe Greggs and King are right.

"I think they might be right," I say.

"Me too," he says quietly.

Suddenly, the space between us is too wide, and I can't stop myself. I reach out and take his hand in mine, lacing our fingers together. "And that's okay," I say. "It doesn't change anything. This is a good thing, Caleb."

"It is?"

"It just means you might be able to get some help, so it's not so overwhelming and scary."

He gives my hand a squeeze, and I expect him to let go, but he doesn't. Instead, he pulls my hand to his chest, and I can feel his heart beating.

"I meant what I said tonight," he says. "I couldn't have done this without you."

Then he does the most shocking thing in the world and raises my hand to his lips. He kisses the back of my hand, and my brain scratches like a broken record. What is going on here? And why do I like it? It's over just as quickly as it started, though, and he releases my hand.

"Goodnight, Daisy," he says.

I laugh. "You've used that one before."

"I didn't have a chance to look up new flower names this morning," he says with a yawn.

I'm about to make a joke, but then he lets out a little snore, and I realize he's already asleep. So, instead, I fall asleep with the image of Caleb googling flowers at the start of each day, a grin on my face.

Why is it that the moment I fall asleep, Caleb turns into a fucking magnet? I swear. He's the flame. I'm the moth. My subconscious cannot help itself. And neither can my half-conscious body because, at about three in the morning, I partially wake to find that my head resting on his chest and our legs are intertwined. There's a small part of me that freaks out when I notice his shirt is mostly no longer on his body, and I can see his (incredibly impressive) abs and pecs in all their glory. It's the same part of me that never lets anyone get close. The part of me that was hurt all those years ago and doesn't trust a soul.

Except I do trust a soul. I trust Caleb. So I guess that's why the part of me that wants to nuzzle into him further and go back to sleep wins the brief argument.

I smell coffee.

Coffee and bacon.

AKA the most perfect combination in the history of the world.

I blink my eyes open, expecting Caleb to still be mostly under my body, but he's not there. Then I remember that bacon doesn't cook itself (much to my sadness, you know, every morning of my life). So I pad my way down the hall like I live in the place.

The problem is that I wanted Caleb to be in bed with me, I realize. But when I round the corner into his kitchen, his back is to me, and he's shirtless. A record scratches in my brain again while the less-than-appropriate part of my brain examines his back muscles like I haven't seen this man shirtless before. Of course I have, but it hits differently because I was just sprawled all over him in bed for eight hours.

"How did you sleep?" he asks as he turns around.

Then I think there might be a record scratching in his brain because he's definitely staring at me. Was the cuddling too much? I mean, I personally don't even know what it means, so I'm sure he's just weirded out. Which, of course, he is. Why wouldn't he be? His best friend nuzzled into his chest in the wee hours of the morning. That's weird. What I did was weird. So why did I do it?

"Black-Eyed Susan?" he asks.

Oh. Right. How did I sleep? It's too revealing to say, *oh, you know, amazingly well, because your chest is a perfect pillow*, so I settle for "Good."

"Coffee?" he says, holding out a mug. "I have cream and sugar for myself, but I know you take it black."

We get coffee together all the time, so Caleb knowing my order isn't surprising, but I'm still touched as he passes me the coffee and motions for me to sit at the bar with a serious look on his face. Uh oh. Is he upset about the cuddling?

"I need a favor from you," he says.

"Whatever you need," I reply, praying that he doesn't bring up last night.

First, I'd die from embarrassment, but I also don't know if I don't want a repeat. My brain is so very confused about the whole thing.

"I need you to take me to therapy," he says.

Wait, what?

My confusion must be on my face because he continues, "Not like, go in with me. But just drive with me, and then maybe we can get coffee together afterward so that it's bookended by less scary things. I called Greggs' therapist this morning, and she was able to squeeze me in tomorrow."

"Okay," I say. I obviously support him going to therapy. I'm mostly surprised that he's willing to go and that he got in so quickly. "Wait, you said Greggs connected you?"

"Yeah, apparently, the dude has bipolar disorder. But he keeps it private, so you can't tell anyone."

"Of course," I say, reaching for Caleb's hand and giving it a squeeze. "You need to know how proud I was of you last night."

How proud I have always been of you, I think, but don't say.

"Thanks. As I said, I couldn't have done it without you."

He squeezes my hand back, and our eyes lock. I swear I could kiss him right now, which would be truly insane. So, it's a good thing that right as his eyes fall to my lips, the kitchen timer beeps.

CHAPTER 22
CALEB
THE NEXT DAY

There's a little honk that manages to escape Cassie's beat-up Honda as she pulls up outside of my condo building to take me to therapy. We could have taken my (much nicer) car, but she insisted that she wanted to drive so I could focus on not, you know, panicking and whatnot.

When I get into the car, I almost blurt out that I love her right then and there because she's as stunning as ever, and although it might be wrapped in vibranium, she actually has a heart made of gold. And I'm one of the lucky few who gets to see it. It's terrifying to realize you're in love with your best friend, though, and I'm still not sure what it all means yet, so I keep my mouth shut.

My favorite song is on the radio when I take my seat. She reaches across the console and squeezes my hand. It's just for a quick second, and it's a perfectly normal gesture for us to do, but after I had to stop myself from kissing her yesterday morning, her touch feels different. Electric, almost.

Cassie pulls onto the highway, and another one of my favorite songs comes on the radio. This one's more upbeat than the last, and I notice Cassie is bobbing her head along to the beat. Before I know it, I'm singing—first under my breath and then fully yelling by the time the bridge comes along.

Song after song, they're all my favorites. As Cassie pulls up in front of the therapy office, an old house in a historic neighborhood of Denver, I realize the radio has not been playing. It's a playlist. I lunge for Cassie's phone, and she can't react fast enough to stop me.

I read the playlist title as a question. "Caleb's Favs?"

She lets out something between a sigh and a… growl? "I just thought it might help you relax before therapy."

"You made me a mixtape," I say, feeling incredibly touched.

"It's a playlist, that's different," she says, clearly feeling weird about it for some reason.

"Fine. You made me a *millennial* mixtape."

"Shut up," she says playfully. "Go to therapy; you're going to be late."

"Fine. Coffee when I'm done?".

"Yep, I'll be here."

It's a simple enough thing to say, but she says it with gravitas. Maybe she doesn't just mean she'll pick me up after my session. That maybe she'll *always* be here.

I get out of the car and walk toward the old house. When I approach the door to the office, my heartbeat quickens. I realize it's the first time since I got into Cassie's car that I've even thought about my anxiety, therapy, or anything that Cassie knew I'd be nervous about. She showed up for me today in a big way, and as I ease the door to the office open, I feel the strength I need to take this head-on and be truly honest with this therapist, which is something I wasn't anticipating earlier this morning.

Once I've hit the button to let Dr. Chells know I'm there

and sit on the couch, my body starts to betray me a bit. My hands are shaky, and my heartbeat begins to pick up. I'm a few minutes early, so I pull out my phone and my headphones and navigate my way to the playlist Cassie made me. I click on the song we left off at in the car, and I envision myself back in the car with Cassie, wherever she's driving right now, her head bopping along to the music. That image, combined with the beat of the music, is enough to keep me calm until my therapist appears in the doorway.

"Are you ready?" she asks as I stand up from the waiting room…couch?

Nope, I think.

"Yep!" I say far too cheerfully.

Once I've settled on yet another couch in her office, Dr. Chells sits across from me. "So," she says. "What brings you in today, Caleb?"

"Well," I start before pausing. I take a deep breath in and try to clear my head because right now, it's all mumbo jumbo, and I need to focus. "I had a panic attack a few days ago. It's happened before, but this time, my friends were there, and one of them suggested that I might have social anxiety."

"I see. Do you think you have social anxiety?"

"I think I might. I don't like big crowds or strangers. When I have to talk to people I don't know or talk to the press, my hands shake, and my heartbeat quickens. Even if it's just one-on-one."

"What happens in your head when this happens?"

I think about it for a second. I'm usually so overwhelmed by my body's physical response that I don't even notice. "It feels like my brain turns to mush, to be honest. I can't put a thought together, but also, somehow, I'm thinking at a mile a minute. Does that make sense?"

"It definitely does make sense. You mentioned a panic attack. When you've been anxious but been able to stop yourself from having one, what's worked for you?"

"My best friend," I say. "She knows exactly what I need to get calm, and we've never even really talked about it. It's like the day we met. She just intuitively knew me and what makes me tick."

"She sounds pretty special."

She is clearly about to say something else but I interrupt. "She is," I say. "She's the best person in the world."

Dr. Chells lets out a little laugh before saying, "We'll unpack that statement at some point. But first, I want to talk about the stress you're under and how it might be impacting your anxiety."

We take the next forty minutes to talk about hockey, the pressure I put on myself, my fear of letting people down, and how all of that might be increasing my anxiety. We also talk about Cassie and how she helps me when I'm anxious, though I leave out my feelings for her. I'm not ready to share that with anyone yet, even my therapist. We agree to meet as much as I'm able to with the intense schedule I have, and she gives me some journal prompts to work on when I'm at away games. I'm not sure what Cassie did while I was in therapy. I'm so in my own head as I crawl into her car that I don't think to ask.

I'm deep in thought as Cassie and I drive to the nearby coffee shop we've been wanting to try out. I'm focused on the last part of my session with Dr. Chells—the part where we talked about Cassie. For some reason, things have always been easy with us. To this day, I don't know why a shy guy like me and a closed-off girl like her are able to make it work, but we are. And it's working right now, with my favorite music playing in Cassie's crappy old car. She doesn't ask how therapy was or make a big deal about it. She knows I wouldn't want that. Instead, we just listen to music with the windows down and drive to coffee, which is something we've done a million times. So why do things keep feeling different?

Because you're in love with her, I remind myself. I've had a few days to fully accept this fact now, but what I haven't accepted is what on earth I'm going to do about it.

Once we arrive at the coffee shop, we each place our orders and find a table near the back where, presumably, no one will bother us. I don't get recognized as often during the regular season as I do during the playoffs, but today is not a day that I'm willing to risk it. I feel raw and vulnerable, and I'm just frankly not in the mood.

Cassie hops up to grab our coffees when her name is called, and I find myself admiring her grace and beauty as she walks away. I'm unsure of a lot right now, namely how I'm going to work through this anxiety, but I know with absolute certainty that she is perfection. She's confusing and closed off to most people, but I see her so clearly, and I love what I see. I also love how she sprawled all over me the other night. And I have a hazy memory of her snuggling further into me at some point. I certainly wouldn't mind a repeat of that. Or something more…

She turns around and I feel the heat flow to my cheeks. She definitely knows I was staring at her, but she couldn't know what I was thinking, right? Then she smiles at me, almost knowingly, as she walks back to our table, and I wonder if she actually knows. After all, I was dangerously close to kissing her the other morning. Maybe she knows, and she's trying to figure out what to do to make me stop.

She hands me my latte, sits down with her plain black coffee, and gives me a soft look. "We don't have to talk about it, but we can if you want to."

Oh God, maybe she does know. What am I supposed to do here?

I must look like I just saw the ghost of my very much alive grandfather because she quickly says, "About therapy. We don't have to talk about therapy, but we can."

Oh.

"Oh."

She stares, a slight smile starting to spread across her face.

"It was good," I continue, trying to make up for my awkwardness. "I liked her a lot, and I think it will be helpful to keep seeing her."

"That's great!" She reaches for my hand, and I can't help but squeeze hers back. "I'm really glad Greggs suggested it."

I am too. It was scary and weird, but the more space I have from the session, the lighter I feel.

"Shit," Cassie says in a harsh whisper, snapping me back into the present moment. She's staring over my shoulder at the door.

"What?" I say, starting to turn.

"Don't!" she yell-whispers. "A guy just walked in wearing your jersey."

Ugh. Maybe he won't recognize me. I pull out a Colorado baseball cap from my backpack for good measure. I'm actually a Toronto fan, being from Canada and everything, but the Colorado hat helps me blend in better.

"It's fine," I find myself saying.

"It's... fine?" Cassie asks.

"Yeah, I mean, I'd rather not deal with it, but if I have to, I'll be okay."

It's the first time I've said something like that and meant it. I really will be okay. If I can get up off the floor of the bathroom and give a speech, I can handle talking to a random fan for a few minutes.

Still, Cassie doesn't seem convinced and reaches for my hand across the table. I offer her mine back, mostly because I want the excuse to touch her, even for a short second. I'll take any opportunity I can get to be closer to her at this point, I think.

It's not a short second, though. We sit there, holding hands across the table and sipping on our coffees until the guy in my jersey is long gone. Until the coffee shop closes. We chat, and we laugh, but we never let go.

CHAPTER 23
CASSIE

A COUPLE OF WEEKS LATER

"'m going to kiss you now, Cassie," Caleb says as he hovers over me, one arm braced on each side of my head.

Then, just as he said he would, he kisses me. His teeth dig into my lower lip as his hips grind into mine. Immediately, I want more. I want his skin on mine. I want his clothes on the floor. I want him.

I want Caleb.

It's not the thought I assumed I'd be having as my alarm blares through my bedroom. Usually, I let out a groan and hit snooze. But right now, I'm very much awake. Based on the sweat currently covering my body, I don't just want Caleb. I want him, *a lot*. He's been in Seattle for the first round of the playoffs since yesterday afternoon. He's been away for games hundreds of times before during our friendship, and I've never felt like this about him not being here.

And I've certainly never dreamt about him grinding his

hips into mine while we make out. That was entirely new and entirely terrifying. I acknowledged a long time ago that Caleb is attractive, but I didn't acknowledge that I'm attracted *to* him until very recently. Now that it's setting in, I have the immediate instinct to run and hide. Where would I run? I have no idea. But the idea of having feelings beyond friendship for Caleb is so terrifying I can barely see straight.

My second alarm buzzes with the reminder that I have boxing training with Anthony in forty-five minutes. The gym is across town, so I have to get moving, which is probably good because if I think about Caleb naked anymore, we're going to have a problem.

I miss Caleb even more once I'm in the middle of training with Anthony. I know it's a good thing that he offered to step in to help train me once Caleb's season started because he's a professional fighter, which means I'll be in the best shape possible when it comes time for my amateur fight. But in the meantime, it means that I have to work that much harder not to get hit in the face.

I dodge another insane hook and land a jab of my own, which he seems surprised by. Surprised enough that he steps back and says, "I think we're good for today."

"I can keep going," I say, bouncing from foot to foot, arms in my ready position.

He laughs. "I know you can, but I'm an old man."

He's older than me, but I'd hardly consider him an old man. Still, I give in, and we settle on the bench to the side of the training area. I take off my gloves and start undoing my hand wraps. Being covered with sweat and filled with accomplishment is one of my favorite feelings. I feel safe here. This place allowed me to learn to defend myself. It taught me discipline. It gave me Caleb. Almost everything I love is because of this gym.

"Am I going to be ready?" I ask.

I've been working really hard, training almost every day. But there's part of me that wonders if I can really do this.

"You were already a great boxer, Cassie. Of course, you're going to be ready."

"Thanks, Anthony."

I don't really believe that I'll be ready. I have a lot of work to do, and the fight just keeps getting closer and closer. The thought of not at least putting up a good showing kills me. I have to be competitive.

"When does Caleb get back from Seattle?" he asks nonchalantly as if I haven't been subconsciously counting down the minutes.

"Tomorrow morning. They have a game tonight. If they win, they have one more game before they go on to the next round of the playoffs."

I start to pack up so I can get home and shower before the game starts.

"Sometimes I still can't believe Caleb Mack is a regular at my place," he says. "You'd never know he was a famous guy when you meet him."

I think about Caleb's panic attacks and anxiety. He's so afraid to let people see the real him, even though the real him is the most wonderful person in the world. I know he has to do the work himself to get to a place where he feels more confident, and the anxiety lessens, but I do wish there was something I could do to help.

"Yeah, he's pretty special," I say.

I get home with just enough time to throw some leftovers in the microwave, shower, and settle in for the game. There's no amount of alcohol that could take the anxious edge I have off, even though we technically don't have to win this game since we won the first three, but if we do, we're that much closer to The Stanley Cup. That, and I really just hate seeing Caleb's face when they lose. It's like he takes it as his own personal failure, and it breaks my heart a little more every time it happens.

After the first period, we're down by one, and I'm shocked when I see Caleb appear on screen to take an interview. He usually avoids having to do these as much as possible. But he takes the questions like a total champ and seems completely fine as he walks away from the reporter when they're done badgering him about the team's failure to make opportunities in the Kraken's zone. Even though we're down, I find myself bursting with pride that Caleb was able to do that so well.

The Blizzards win their game. It was touch and go in the second half of the second period, but they pulled out all the stops in the third. Caleb played well, per usual, and King was on fire. I watched Caleb do yet another interview after the game, and he was just as great as the one he did after the first period. He talks in clear sentences, he makes eye contact with the reporter, and he even makes a little joke and laughs.

It's been about thirty minutes, and I've just been scrolling through Twitter, watching fans talk about how great the Blizzards are playing this post-season, when I realize it's eleven-thirty at night, which is way past my normal teacher bedtime. I'm about to finish off my glass of wine and crawl into bed when my phone buzzes.

"Hello?" I answer.

"Cloverrrrrrrr!" It sounds like Caleb, but wherever he is, it is loud, and he sounds… drunk.

"Caleb? Where are you?"

"I dunnoooo… Some bar? Greggs and King made me come out with them, but I don't want to be out with them. I want to be home with yoooou," he sings.

Caleb must be really drunk if he thinks I'm in his condo right now.

"I wish you were here too." I laugh. "But I'm not at your home. I'm in my apartment."

"Noooooo," he says like I'm an idiot. "I don't mean my condo. I mean our house. The one in Wash Park."

Oh.

Oh.

He said *our* house. Like he wants to live with me. Well, okay then.

"Oh, right, of course," I say, trying to sound normal and not completely shocked by this entire interaction.

"Caleb!" I hear a voice yell in the background. "Who are you talking to, dude?"

It's Greggs. I'm simultaneously relieved and terrified that Caleb is with Greggs right now.

"It's Cassie," Caleb hisses. I can tell he's talking to Greggs because he used my real name. "You can't talk to her. She's mine."

Mine.

I don't know why, but that phrase shakes me to my core.

"I know, I know," says Greggs. "Just tell your girl I say hi."

Greggs... knows?

His... girl?

"She's not my girl," Caleb yells. And then I hear him try to whisper, "Not yet."

How on earth am I supposed to react to that? This is the first time Caleb's ever admitted to anything like this, and it's making my brain freeze.

"Hey, Caleb? I think I should go," I say because he's clearly not in a place to be able to have this conversation.

Even if my subconscious from this morning wants it, he's drunk. I don't want to let Drunk Caleb force Sober Caleb into something he doesn't actually want just because he's a little physically attracted to me or something.

"Wait!" he yells. "Are we ever going to talk about it?"

"Talk about what?" I ask as if I don't know.

"The other night," he says. "The ssssssssnuggling."

"We can talk about it when you're sober. When you get home," I say. Hopefully, he doesn't remember this conversation, and I can just pretend like it didn't happen.

"I'm holding you to that," he says.

"Goodnight, Caleb."

"G'night, Iris."

CHAPTER 24

CALEB

haven't seen Cassie since I got back from Seattle. We only had one day between games, and she had parent-teacher conferences that night. The good news is that Ralph is doing great in school. Cassie confirmed with Hazel that things seem to be in a better place for him now and texted me to let me know, which is great, really. But it also means that Cassie and I haven't really talked since I was a drunken mess on the phone. It's all a bit hazy, but I know for a fact that I said something about the cuddling. Part of me doesn't regret it. Even if I'm still not sure I can handle the commitment of a relationship and hockey at the same time, I want to know where we stand. The other part of me, however, is completely mortified.

I just arrived at the Blizzards' arena in my standard gray suit, where the social media team snapped some pictures of me walking in, per usual, before I changed into my warm-up gear. Now, I'm sitting in the dressing room, just waiting for the rest of the team to arrive. Tonight is hopefully our last game of this series. If we win, it'll not only be a sweep, but we'll go to The Stanley Cup.

I pull out my phone to text Cassie to make sure she has her ticket for tonight. As awkward as it might be after my drunken buffoonery, I need her here. When I look up at her section in the stands, it grounds me. She's always there, in her giant old Roy jersey, yelling at the top of her lungs like your drunken uncle at a football game, and I love it. I love how into the game she gets and how defensive of me she gets. I've always known that Cassie is someone you want on your side, but in those moments where she's truly tuned into the game, or into a sparring session for that matter, there's no one else I'd rather have fighting for me.

Caleb: You all set for the game tonight?

Cassie: Yep! I'll see you after, right?

I take a deep breath and try to get up the guts for the latest of many times today to bring it up. But I'm a coward, so I settle for:

Caleb: Of course! I'll meet you at the entrance to the bar.

She replies with a heart emoji, and I know it doesn't mean what I think I want it to mean but I'll take it. For now. Because my team has started to make their way into the dressing room, I need to focus on this game.

The buzzer blazes, announcing that it's time for us to take the ice for warmups. I'm right behind King and right in front of Greggs as we file in one after another.

Greggs leans over to me while I start to get my legs moving and says, "I see that Cassie is here."

I hadn't even looked for her yet, and part of me is annoyed that Greggs saw her first, but then I search her section for her face, and just as I expected, I'm suddenly grounded when I lay eyes on her. And just as I expected, she's in her Roy jersey. Her soft curls fall around her face and she gives me a shy wave. I wave back and get back to my drills and stretching because as much as I'd like to stare at Cassie all day, I need to focus on this game, and focusing on her is a surefire way to be distracted.

The first period goes off without a hitch. I play a standard amount of time, which is good because that means that our depth is holding up their end of the deal. At the end of the period, we have one goal, made by King, assisted by yours truly, and Seattle is at zero. We file into the dressing room to get notes from our coaches and captain, Grant Lance. I'm not super close with Lance, but I really respect him as a player and a leader.

Despite that respect, I sneak a quick look at my phone.

Cassie: Nice assist. Now, get me a goal.

Well, okay then.

I shoot back a laughing emoji and do my best to focus on what Lance has to say. Granted, I've played a pretty solid game, so there's not a lot of feedback for me specifically.

Once our twenty minutes are up, we file back onto the ice to do it all over again, but this time, I'm determined to get a goal for Cassie.

I don't just get one goal. I get two. We're up four to one (Lance got a goal, too) as we file into the dressing room once again. I sneak a quick look at my phone before tuning into Coach's feedback.

Cassie: That's more like it.

I'm feeling invincible after such a great period, so I get ready to fire off the first thing that comes into my mind despite the alarm bells in the back of my head screaming at me to stop. My finger hovers over the send button, but I hesitate. Is this a good idea? It's potentially the most outgoing thing I've ever done, and it's a huge risk. But before I can delete it, Coach is clearing his throat, clearly annoyed with me.

Caleb: I didn't forget about the cuddling conversation. We're talking about it. Tonight.

Crap.

I sent it.

And now Coach is annoyed with me too, so I can't wait to see if Cassie replies.

"Sorry," I mumble under my breath, coming back to my usual quiet ways as I shove my phone into my bag.

"I'll forgive you because of how you're playing tonight, but you know the rules, Mack."

Evidently, I don't know the rules of hockey, however, because I'm very clearly tripped by a Seattle player in the third, and the refs do exactly nothing about it. I even motion to them that they missed the call, something I never do, because I'm so frustrated. Then, I find myself looking at Cassie's section again, eager to see her reaction. I can't help but chuckle to myself when I see her leading her section in the classic hockey chant of "Refs, you suck! Refs, you suck! Refs, you suck!"

That's my girl.

Despite my being tripped and eventually taking a penalty for retaliating against that guy, my team kills Seattle's usually solid power play, and we wind up holding our four-to-one lead. In the dressing room, I quickly change out of my gear and take a quick interview that shockingly doesn't make me too nervous. Greggs and King have already left for the bar, and I know Cassie is waiting for me. What I don't know is how she's going to react to my forwardness earlier. Even I don't know what came over me when I typed that, so I'm sure she's at least a bit shocked.

Do I know I'm in love with Cassie? Yes. But do I know what I want to do about it? Not at all. Which makes this whole thing that much more terrifying and confusing. But the adrenaline of the game got into me, my finger slipped, and now, I have to face the consequences.

I've been standing outside of the bar trying to convince myself to go in for what feels like at least five minutes when my phone buzzes.

Cassie: We can't talk about it if you don't get over here.

Well, okay then.

You can do this, Caleb. Just tell her you have feelings for her. What's the worst that could happen? Other than losing the only person who's ever really seen you…

Dang it.

I shake my whole body and put one foot in front of the other to eventually get myself through the doorway of the bar. I dodge and weave my way through the crowd to the private room in the back, hoping no one recognizes me. I also hope that the music in the private room is a bit quieter.

But the moment I walk through the door, I see Cassie and the noise all falls away. She's on the dance floor with Greggs and King already, but as always, we seem to be able to sense each other because she looks over and immediately runs toward me.

Before I know it, her arms are around my neck, and our bodies are pressed together. It starts as our usual greeting of a hug, but I don't let go, and neither does Cassie.

"You were incredible tonight," she says, her eyes falling to my lips before our foreheads fall together as the breath escapes me.

There's a tension between us that's stronger than it ever has been before, so I let my hands wander to her waist and pull her against me. Her reaction to my text earlier was surprising, and it's enough to get me to say what I feel. It's terrifying and bold, but I can't wait anymore.

"I'd really like to kiss you right now," I say, though, just to be sure I'm not misreading this entire situation. And because it's true. Nothing's ever been more true. "Is that okay?"

"Y-yes," she says, breathless.

I take her chin in my hand and lift her head. I wish I could take a photo of her face right now, eyes wide but wanting, lips full and ready. But when her teeth sink into her bottom lip, I'm a goner. I lower my head quickly and press my lips into hers.

Immediately, electricity zings through my whole body. I try to keep myself under control, but I'm kissing Cassie.

I'm kissing Cassie a lot.

Maybe too much?

Her tongue slips into my mouth right then, so I guess it's not too much. I feel myself stiffen against her, but she doesn't move away. Instead, she grinds her hips into me ever so slightly, only making me even more hard. She lets out a soft moan against my mouth as her hands dig into my hair.

Kissing Cassie is absolute bliss, and I've decided I don't intend on ever stopping. That is until one of my teammates (I think it was Greggs, that a-hole) whoops and hollers. Suddenly, I'm very much aware that we're in a room full of my teammates, but the idea of not… exploring this thing with Cassie further might break me, so I pull away from her momentarily and whisper, "Can we get out of here?"

CHAPTER 25
CASSIE

I don't know what I expected kissing Caleb would be like, but it paled in comparison to the real thing. I think I assumed he'd be timid and shy about it or something. But I could not have been more wrong.

A few moments after we left the after-party, we arrived at Caleb's condo building. I've never been more grateful that he lives in a high-rise downtown because it means I'll be kissing him again soon. I don't really know what's come over me, but the moment our lips crashed together, I wanted more. And more and more and more. I couldn't get enough. His hands pulled me closer and explored my body... And his *tongue*. I wouldn't mind seeing what else he can do with that thing, *good lord*.

We walk into the elevator, and the doors shut. Caleb looks at me, and suddenly, my back is pressed into the wall, Caleb's body towering over me, one hand leaning on the wall, the other ever so slightly lifting my Roy jersey up so his hand can rest on my hip.

"I swear I would rip this old man's jersey off of you right now if there wasn't a chance Mrs. Phyllis from floor seven might get on this elevator."

"The jersey really bothers you that much?"

"Any clothing on your body would bother me at the moment." He grinds his hard cock into my waist to prove it. "But another man's jersey? Yeah, it's been driving me insane."

Suddenly, the doors open to the eighteenth floor, and I'm being quite literally whisked out of the elevator as Caleb scoops me into his arms and basically runs down the hall. I thank my lucky stars that this man, the man I'm pretty sure I'm about to bone, is a professional athlete, as a laugh escapes me. Caleb has been so bold tonight. I'd be shocked if I didn't know him so well. But I do know him, and I know that when he decides he wants something, he'll do everything he can to get it. I guess I happen to be the thing he wants.

Caleb's condo door swings open, and my feet find the floor. My back is immediately pressed into the closed door as Caleb's lips immediately find mine.

"You have no idea how much I want this," he says.

"I think I do." I reach between us and take him—well, as much as I can hold—in my hand, forcing him to inhale, his head falling back. I love seeing him like this, both confident and undone at the same time. "Your dick doesn't have a great poker face."

Caleb pulls my arms above my head and braces his hands over my wrists. His mouth falls to my ear. "Should we see about you? Are you wet for me, Cassie?"

My mouth goes dry at the sound of my real name. Ever since he found out my last name is Flowers, he's stopped calling me Cassie. I'm not sure that's why it's so shocking, but I also really like the way my name sounds on his lips.

His mouth falls down my neck before he stops to nip at

my collarbone. How he knows exactly what I want before I even do, I don't know, but this man is going to singlehandedly break me, even if it's just for tonight.

"I'm taking off your jersey now, Cassie."

God, I really do love how he says my name. And I love how his fingers brush against my stomach as he lifts my jersey off my head. I say a *thank you* prayer to the lingerie gods that I chose to wear something other than my usual tan bra tonight. Caleb seems to have the same thought because when he sees my unlined black lace bra, he takes a sharp inhale. My jersey falls to the floor and his hands start to explore, a bewildered look on his face.

First, they run up my stomach and around my back before they settle on caressing my chest. My nipples immediately react, and his fingers pinch them lightly as he peppers light kisses along my collarbone, down my chest, down my stomach…

"I'm going to take off your jeans now, Cassie," he says, looking up at me for my approval.

All I can manage is a quick nod because Caleb's gorgeous face looking up at me, head between my legs, is too much to bear.

He undoes the buttons on my jeans and slides them down my legs. His hand slides inside my lace thong (thanks again, lingerie gods) and pulls them down.

"I knew you'd be wet for me. Good girl, Cassie," he says with a smirk, his crooked smile shining up at me from below.

Lord have mercy.

"I'm going to lick your pussy now, Cassie," he says, once again looking up at me for approval. I nod and let my head fall back.

Then his tongue is on me, and my mind goes completely blank. It's just Caleb and me, his tongue causing a visceral reaction across my body. "Ca-Caleb," I moan. He moans, too, when I dig my fingers into his hair, and the sensation of it is enough to push me right to the edge.

"I'm going to put my fingers inside of you, Cassie," he says. I don't object, and two of his fingers slip inside me a moment later. "Is that good?"

I look down at him, and he's all smirk again as his hand moves slowly in and out of me. I nod quickly, unable to find actual words, as his mouth finds my clit again, and he circles it lightly with his tongue. I knew he could do incredible stuff with that thing.

"I want you to play with your tits, Cassie."

I would do pretty much whatever he wanted at this moment, so I lift my hands from his hair and unclasp my bra, slide it off my shoulders, and let it fall to the ground. Caleb inhales and takes what I look like topless in. I lift my hands to my chest and tease my nipples lightly. The sensation, combined with Caleb's fingers inside me, nearly pushes me to the edge again. Then his tongue is back on me, and suddenly I'm gone, organism chasing over me, my body shaking against the door.

I take a few deep breaths before looking down to see Caleb grinning up at me.

"Let's go to bed," he says, standing up.

"How are you suddenly so forward, Caleb Mack?"

He takes my hand and guides me down the hallway toward his bedroom.

"No, not like that. I don't want you to freak out tomorrow. We're going to sleep," he says.

"But, I didn't... You didn't..." I stutter.

Caleb turns to me seconds before walking into his bedroom. "Forget Me Not," he says flatly. "I couldn't care less about that right now. I just watched the girl of my dreams come from a few swipes of my tongue. I'm on cloud nine right now."

The girl of his... dreams? I don't think I can mentally

unpack that statement right now, so I follow him into the bedroom.

"I still might freak out," I say, trying to be honest.

He chuckles. This man is chuckling right now!

"I know. But I'd like to do what I can to lessen the freak-out." He holds out a massive Blizzards t-shirt and continues, "But if you want to make this easier for me, you could cover your incredible tits up."

I take the t-shirt and shrug it over my shoulders. I'm drowning in it, but at least I'm not naked anymore. However, I'm surprisingly not completely weirded out by being naked around Caleb.

"It is okay if I sleep in my boxers? I actually don't usually wear stuff. I'm like a furnace at night," he says, hands at the ready to take his button-up off.

I think back to the night we wound up cuddling, and he was, in fact, a furnace. "That's fine. It's not like I haven't seen you without a shirt on," I say, thinking it's true and I'll be fine.

Then he takes his shirt off and slides his undershirt over his head. And now I'm rethinking my answer. Is it possible that he's even hotter than he usually is right now? Or is it the pheromones? I don't know, but it's only made worse when he unzips his jeans and pulls them down his legs. How have I never noticed his thighs before? I mean, I guess I knew they were big, given that he's a hockey player, but good lord. He smiles at me as if he has no idea what images are running through my head right now.

He also clearly has no idea that I'm already freaking out. My best friend just ate me out. I grabbed at my tits in his presence. How are we ever going to come back from this?

"Ready for bed?" he asks, plopping down on the bed and patting the space next to him. I crawl next to him and lay down, facing up at the ceiling. "Gardenia." I turn to face him. "Come here."

I snuggle into his chest despite the fear that's suddenly rolling through my brain. Suddenly, I'm not freaking out anymore. He's warm and cozy, and his kindness seems to radiate from his (very sexy) body.

"Mmm," I find myself humming, nuzzling into his chest further.

"Hey," he says as he plays with my hair. I shift my head to be able to see him. He looks nervous. "Are you freaking out yet?"

"We have plenty of time for that tomorrow," I say with a grin, knowing full well that it's coming.

He takes my chin in his hand and lifts my head up until our lips are almost touching. "I'm going to kiss you goodnight," he says. "But just know, I plan on kissing you in the morning, too."

I feel a grin spread across my face despite myself. "Okay."

He brings his lips to mine, and I feel the most comfortable I've ever felt in my entire life. The kiss is slow and sweet, like we're both savoring it. When our lips finally part, I'm still not scared. I feel safe and seen, like I'm truly at home for the first time. I nuzzle back into Caleb's chest as he reaches for the light on the nightstand with his long arm.

"Goodnight, Hibiscus," he says.

"Goodnight, Caleb."

I wake up, once again, to the smell of bacon and coffee.

I could get used to this.

The thought is enough to wake me fully, just enough to sit up in bed and realize Caleb's not next to me. There's a sudden ache in my chest at the absence of him, even though logically, I know he's just down the hallway in the kitchen.

During the night, I eventually stopped snuggling him and moved to my own side of the bed, but his presence was still so calming. Just knowing he was there next to me seemed to be enough to keep me from panicking.

Seeing him as quickly as possible is probably the best way to stop the ache in my chest, so I pad my way down the hall and walk into his expansive, modern kitchen. I don't even think to look at myself in the mirror first, which might have been a mistake. I'm sure I look awful.

Caleb turns toward me, and a smile quickly spreads across his whole face. "There she is," he says, walking toward me.

He envelopes me in a hug, just like he has so many times before, but this time, I let my head fall against his chest and allow myself to just be held by him for a moment. "How did you sleep?"

"Perfectly," I say. "But I'm still waiting for that good morning kiss you promised."

He brings his lips down to mine, and I lift my head to meet him. Our lips press together, and it's warm and calm and good. So good I feel myself smiling against his lips.

"Glad to see you haven't started your inevitable freak out yet," he says, stepping away and walking toward the coffee maker. "But I know it's coming, and I want to talk about it. Sit."

He motions toward a stool near the island before turning to rummage through his cabinets.

A moment later, I'm sitting on the stool, and Caleb's placing a cup of coffee in front of me.

"I know you better than anyone, Hyacinth," he says. "So, I know you're going to panic. But I need you to know that I'm not going anywhere. No matter what you choose after that freakout, I'll still be here. Whether it's as a friend or something more, I've got you. I always will."

"So you want something more?"

"I think I do," he says. After taking a sip of his own coffee, he continues, "And I hope you're willing to at least try it out with me. We can test the waters, see if this is something we want to do for real."

"I don't hate the idea of testing the waters," I say. It's like he knows exactly what I need to feel comfortable with this.

"How about this: we go on a few dates. Real dates. If, after we give it a real try, we decide we don't want to move forward, we go back to being friends."

"Do you really think we can do that? After what happened last night?" I ask.

"Well, I'm not losing you, so we don't really have a choice, do we?"

"Test dates…" I ponder out loud. "What do you have in mind?"

"I'll plan a couple of dates, and you plan a couple of dates. We'll trade off. It might take a while with the playoff schedule, but maybe after three dates, we can decide if we want to be just friends. And I'll go back to that, no questions asked, if it's what you want."

I'm still not sure this is a good idea, but Caleb seems to have thought it through, and I know I can trust him. Even if the idea scares the living daylight out of me, I can try for him.

"Okay." I nod. "But I don't have sex until the third date. And I'm not staying over until after the test dates are over. And I don't drink on dates."

"Noted." He laughs. "Now, can we eat? I'm starving."

CHAPTER 26
CALEB
THE NEXT DAY

I walk into the practice rink's dressing room with my head down. I might be thrilled that I finally got to kiss Cassie (among other things), but it happening in front of my whole team wasn't really part of my plan. Knowing them, it's going to be a whole thing now, and I really just want to be free to explore this thing without so many eyes peering at us.

I'm right, of course, because as soon as Greggs sees me, he rushes over with King not far behind. At least they aren't making too big of a scene. Yet.

"So?" asks Greggs.

"So…" I reply, attempting to play it cool.

"You don't have to go into detail, but at least tell us you guys are together now," says King with a hopeful look. Don't these guys have lives of their own to worry about?

"We are… not," I say.

"*What?*" Greggs all but yells.

"Not yet," I continue in a yelling whisper. "We're testing the waters, seeing if it works."

"Oh, it's gonna work," says King.

"Yeah," says Greggs. "You just have to woo her."

"I'm not sure Cassie is the wooing type," I say.

"Everyone's the wooing type. Hell, I'm the wooing type," says King. Greggs nods along. "So, what's the plan?"

Apparently, they do not, in fact, have lives of their own to worry about, so I go through our agreement of three dates and going back to being friends if we decide it's what's best.

Greggs is incredulous. King is shocked.

"You won't be able to go back to being friends with her, dude," King says.

I nod along, pretending to agree because I just want this conversation to stop. I might be scared about taking all of this on during the playoffs. Lance has been having a heck of a time with his wife being pregnant right now, and he's a veteran with all of this. How do I know Cassie and I will be any different? Still, I have to try. I know Greggs and King are saying this because they want to help, but the alternative to testing the waters is potentially losing Cassie forever, which isn't much of an alternative at all. In fact, I won't stand for it, which gives me only one option.

"Guys, I think I have to woo her," I say.

"No shit," says Greggs, face flat.

"That's what we've been saying," says King at virtually the same time.

This next part is going to be painful beyond belief, but these guys are the people I'm closest to next to Cassie, and I can't exactly ask her. "How do I... um... how do I... do that?"

"What does she like?" asks King.

"I am not telling *you* that," I say.

Why would he even ask me that? I'm not about to tell my teammates what we did or that some weird sort of confidence came over me when we did it, and I'm still sort of shocked by the whole thing. I'm not telling them anything.

"I don't mean it like *that*. I just mean, what does she do for fun?"

Oh, right. Well, that's actually a good point. I haven't been on many dates, but for the most part, I've been miserable on them. I can't have Cassie feeling that way, or I'll lose her.

"She likes boxing a lot. That's what she spends most of her time doing outside of teaching stuff," I say.

"That's badass," says Greggs.

"I have the perfect date idea!" King yells, and heads start to turn toward the corner we've basically huddled in.

"Dude, I'd rather not have the whole team in my business with this."

"Right. Sorry. But you should take her axe throwing."

It's… perfect, actually. It's a standard date activity with a perfect Cassie twist. "How did you come up with that so quickly?"

"Dude's been on a million first dates," says Greggs. "But not very many second ones."

"Shut up," says King. "At least I don't look like the heart-eye emoji every time a certain nonprofit consultant I employ walks in the room."

Greggs elbows King in the ribs right as the coach enters the room.

"Greggs, if you're going to elbow someone, can it at least be a player from an opposing team?" says Coach.

"Yes, sir."

"Great," Coach says. "Now get on the ice. We have work to do."

CHAPTER 27
CASSIE
A COUPLE OF DAYS LATER

have no clue what to wear on this date.

Not just because it's a first date with my best friend, that would make it hard enough. But then he texted that I needed to wear pants and closed-toed shoes, and now I'm all in my head about it. What on earth could we be doing that involves the need for closed-toed shoes?

After about twenty minutes of pondering, I gave in and texted Stacey. It was a moment of weakness, but she has an incredible sense of style, and she said I could text her if I ever needed anything. I guess a fellow woman's advice on what to wear is a need before a first date… right?

About twenty minutes after I text her, the intercom is buzzing. Moments later, before I can even buzz her up, there's a knock on my door. I answer it to find the impeccably dressed Stacey holding a number of cute sneakers and a bag of… wine?

"Do you have a bottle opener?" she asks, pulling a bottle of red from the bag.

"I do, but I don't drink on dates."

"Do I look like a six-foot tall, sexy-as-hell hockey player to you?" she asks.

"Um… no?"

"You're freaking out, and you need to loosen up. Have a small glass with me now so you aren't totally frozen on this date."

Well, with logic like that…

I point to the drawer with the bottle opener and start looking through her shoes. Despite being tall, Stacey usually wears heels when I see her, so I'm a bit surprised by the selection of appropriate shoes.

"I love shoes," she says, clearly reading my mind. "I wear heels for work, but I adore sneakers. I wear them whenever I get the chance. Now, what are you wearing for your outfit? That will help us pick shoes."

"I… don't know. This?" I point to my v-neck tee shirt and loose jeans.

"Ah, I see more of my services are needed here than I thought. None of my clothes would fit you. You'd be swimming in them. So, we'll just have to work with what's in your closet."

She marches past me into my bedroom and immediately starts throwing clothes on the bed.

"I love this one." She holds up my first day of school top. A yellow blouse that reminds me a bit of a number two pencil, though I'd never admit that out loud.

"I usually wear that for work," I say.

"We just need to accessorize it differently," she says. "Belts?"

I point toward my dresser, and she starts rummaging through it.

A few minutes later, I'm fully dressed in an outfit I never

would have thought of putting together. I look cute and pulled together and actually feel confident.

About ten minutes after Stacey leaves, there's another knock on my door. My breath hitches in my chest as I walk toward the sound, knowing that the moment I open that door, everything changes. I take a deep breath, undo the lock, and open the door.

Caleb's standing there in a button-up shirt, jeans, and sneakers. He has a single pink rose in his hand and a sheepish half-smile on his face.

He extends the rose and says, "Hey."

"Hey," I reply, taking the rose and giving it a sniff.

"I know flowers aren't really your thing, but there was a guy selling them on Sixteenth Street, and I couldn't say no to him."

"It's perfect," I say because... it is. "I'll go put it in some water, and then we can head out."

I rummage through my cupboards for a vase and finally settle on a small mason jar. As I turn, I find Caleb leaning against my doorframe, the edge of his shirt riding up just a bit. He looks sexy as hell.

"Ready to go?" he asks after a moment.

Shit.

I'm staring.

"Yep!" I approach him and, because, apparently, I've completely lost my mind, I plant a kiss on his cheek when I reach him.

"Sorry," I say, suddenly very aware of the fact that this is our first date, and I'm so out of my element, and I don't know how to act at all.

"Cassie, I got down on my knees and watched you come from my tongue. I think it's okay for you to kiss me on the cheek if you want to."

There he goes, using my real name again.

This whole Caleb being confident about sex thing is hot as fuck, and it's making me want to nix my three-date rule and take him to my room right now. But we've set clear rules to make this trial run work, so I settle for kissing him lightly on the lips and leading the way out the door. We need to do this thing right if we both want to make it out unscathed.

"Aren't you going to tell me where we're going?" I ask as Caleb starts his SUV.

He looks over at me with a smirk. "Nope, it's a surprise."

I don't even bother checking his GPS. Caleb knows this city like the back of his hand despite being Canadian, so he won't be using it. Instead, I lean back and appreciate the view of Caleb as he navigates through the evening traffic. How many times have I done this? A hidden glance here, a sneaky stare there... hundreds of little looks hidden between the snarky jokes and belly laughs of friendship. Has my stomach always done this fluttery thing when his eyes lock with mine at stop signs? Or is that a byproduct of the whole we've-made-out-now thing?

Eventually, he tears his eyes from mine, and we pull into a parking lot outside of an old warehouse. It's creepy as hell.

"Here we are," he says.

"Do you murder all of your dates? Is that why I never get to meet them?"

He mumbles something under his breath and opens his car door, so I follow him and open my own.

I approach him on the sidewalk, and he reaches out for my hand. We've held hands hundreds of times before in little hidden moments here and there, but this time, it feels intentional. And monumental. I lace my fingers through his and give his hand a squeeze. He squeezes back, and my heart does this weird, flippy thing.

We walk up to the door, and there's no sign, just a photo of an axe.

"Oh my god, you are actually going to murder me," I say.

"No," he says. "But I am going to win."

"Win at what?"

"Let's go inside and find out."

Caleb's winning.

He's winning, and it's driving me crazy.

But I'm also having the best time. It feels like I'm on a first date with my best friend, which I guess is exactly what's happening. But I feel so comfortable and just plain happy, I'm not sure what to do with myself. I was so nervous it'd be weird, but it's not. It feels perfect, actually.

The best part is I can give Caleb shit about his axe-throwing skills one second and plant a kiss on his lips the next.

God, his lips. They're so nice and soft, and... shit, I'm staring at him again.

"You can kiss me again if you want to." He laughs, and my cheeks burn pink.

Then his hands are wrapped around my waist, and I'm being pulled against him. The rest of the world goes blurry, and it's just the two of us. Our noses brush together.

"I'm having a really great time," I say.

"Any signs of a freakout on the horizon?" he asks.

"None yet. But I'm sure there's one in our future."

He presses his lips into mine softly, and all the breath leaves my body.

"Well, I'm ready whenever it does. Because I'm not letting you go, Cassie. One way or another, you're stuck with me."

God, this man.

I let my head fall against his chest and breathe him in. I know what he smells like, but there's something about tonight, something about right now, that I just want to remember. He wraps his arms around me more tightly and squeezes me against him. I basically only come up to his lower chest, but it feels like we fit perfectly despite the height difference, and I love being this close to him. I realize that, in a weird way, I've wanted this for so long. I've always longed to be closer to him. I just didn't know how.

"I'm not letting go either," I say.

He kisses the top of my head, and we separate just a bit, but I can tell that neither of us wants to let go. We both care more about being together than we do about who wins at axe throwing.

By the time we make it back to the street outside of my apartment, I honestly can't remember who won. All I can remember is Caleb's laugh. Caleb's arms around me. Caleb's lips on mine. And I want more.

Caleb puts his SUV into the park and looks over at me slowly. I don't know why it's so hard for me to tell what he's thinking lately; maybe it's the test dating thing, I don't know.

But I'm not exactly expecting him to say, "As much as I'd love to come upstairs and do unspeakable things with you, you have a three-date rule, and I want to respect that."

"If you count all the times we've hung out before, we're actually woefully behind," I say, inching myself closer to him across the center console.

He inches closer too, until our foreheads are touching.

He lifts my chin up and says, "Just a kiss goodnight today, baby."

Then he kisses me softly, slowly, like he has all day and could just spend the rest of his life kissing me in this car. Like I'm the sweetest thing in the world.

"Goodnight," he whispers softly when we pull apart.

And now I'm a total puddle. All it took was one mention of a cutesie name and a sensual kiss, and I'm done for, apparently. The flower nicknames were one thing, but that just felt like a joke between friends. *Baby* is… different. It has a weight to it.

"Goodnight, baby," I say, testing out the nickname. I'm surprised to find that I don't hate the way it feels on my lips when it's directed at Caleb. In fact, I like it. Probably too much.

"I'll see you when I get back from L.A.," he says after he lightly kisses the tip of my nose.

"I can't wait," I say, forcing myself to lean back and start to get out of the car.

And it's true, I can't wait to be near him again. To kiss him again.

"I'll text you," he says with a smile the size of Texas as I stand up.

"Let me know when you get home safely," I say, waving like a giddy moron as I turn to enter my building.

"Always do."

He waits for me to make it inside before pulling away. I close the door to my apartment and lean against it. My heart feels swollen somehow. Like sooner or later, I won't be able to keep it inside my body.

CHAPTER 28
CALEB
THE NEXT DAY

'**ve** spent a fair amount of my adult life on planes. I have a set routine I go through involving an eye mask and headphones for any flight with the team. Part of it is that I need to focus on the goal of the given trip: to win. But if I'm being honest, another part is that I don't like having to talk to the other guys on the plane.

Today, I decided to forgo my headphones and give the whole chatting on the plane thing a try. It's one of many ways I'm trying to get out of my comfort zone since starting to work with Dr. Chells. I take a seat in an empty row and figure that if someone wants to talk to me, they can join me, but I'm not ready to just sit down and start talking with a guy I honestly barely know on a personal level. Of course, moments after I sit down, Greggs appears in the seat next to me.

"No eye mask, Sleeping Beauty?" he asks.

"Not today," I say, hoping he won't make a thing out of this.

A few moments later, Grant Lance, our captain, takes a seat in the row in front of us. He's on a video call with what appears to be a very upset Mrs. Lance.

"Stella, I'm sorry. I know how important this was to you," he says.

"It's not just important to me," she says. "It's important to literally every person who's ever been pregnant."

"I know," he says with a sigh.

"Look," she says. "I know what I signed up for. I know this timing sucks with the playoffs. But you could have at least tried to make it work."

"I did try. It wasn't possible. There will be other ultrasounds, honey."

"Wrong answer," Greggs mumbles under his breath to me. I elbow him in the gut, but admittedly, he's not wrong.

"There will not be other first ultrasounds for our first child, Grant," Stella says flatly.

Grant lets out an audible sigh and rests his head on the seat. "I know, honey. I said I'm sorry."

The plane has gotten so quiet you could hear just about anything, so Stella's sob rings through the entire cabin.

"Like I said, I know what I signed up for," she says. "But that doesn't mean I don't have a right to be upset." Then she's quiet for a few moments, just a few whimpers coming through the phone. Grant doesn't say a word. "I had to listen to the heartbeat by myself, Grant," she says quietly.

"Please put all electronic devices on airplane mode. The door has closed, and we are preparing for takeoff," the pilot says over the intercom.

"Goddammit," Grant says. "Honey, I'm so sorry. I have to go."

"I know you do. Can you promise me something, though?"

"I can try?"

"Make it worth it," she says. "If you don't play your absolute best tomorrow night, I will never forgive you."

"I will," he says. "I promise. I love you."

"I love you too."

And then the line is dead. And the plane is silent. Grant turns around in his seat and examines the team. "Well, you heard my heartbroken wife. Let's make this worth it."

A few guys holler their support, but I just nod and dig around in my bag for my headphones. All I could think about while Grant and Stella were arguing was Cassie. Is that what our future will look like? Just a series of missed ultrasounds and birthday parties? I already don't know if I'll be able to be at her fight in a few weeks. What if I'm out of town when our kid is born? It's happened in the league before. It could easily happen to me.

I know I'm getting ahead of myself. Cassie and I have been on one date, and even if it was the best date of my entire life, we have a long way to go before we have to figure out these issues. Still, it serves as a good reminder of why I haven't dated much before. The thing is, I might just be being selfish, but I like to think Cassie is worth trying for. I just hope I can balance it all because she deserves better than what Stella got today.

CHAPTER 29
CASSIE
THE NEXT DAY

Caleb and the rest of the team are in L.A. to play their first game in the next round of the playoffs. I'm fairly used to watching his away games alone, but Stacey texted me and asked if I wanted to go to a local bar to watch this one. Apparently, she doesn't let her dislike of Greggs get in the way of her Blizzards fan status. I asked if I could invite Hazel to get her a break from mom-ing, and Stacey was thrilled by the idea, which is how the three of us wind up getting hit on by rabid Blizzards fans in a sports bar in between the second and third period.

"I'm good, thanks," I say for the third time to the same guy who really, really wants to buy me a cheap beer.

"She's taken, Dude. Backoff," yells Stacey over the bumping music, watching triumphantly when the guy slumps away.

"Wait, what?" yells Hazel.

"I… uh… I'm not… Taken. I just, uh… kinda?"

How do I explain that I'm test-dating my best friend?

"*Who?*" Hazel basically yells.

"Who do you think?" Stacey says with a smirk.

"*Ohmygod!*" Hazel says like it's all one word at the top of her lungs.

"We're just test dating," I say, trying to get control of the conversation.

"Test dating? That sounds fake."

"I don't know what to call it. We're testing the waters, seeing if it works for us to be together. If it doesn't, we'll go back to being friends."

"Oh, it'll work," Hazel says.

Why is everyone so certain of that but me? It's been going well, of course. Like, in the I-can't-stop-thinking-about-Caleb's-lips-on-mine-all-day kind of way. But I still don't know. There's something so terrifying about this whole thing, and I can't seem to get past it, even if I'm having an incredible time with him.

"Don't freak her out," says Stacey. "Look how terrified she seems right now."

"So what's the deal with you and Greggs?" I ask in the most thinly veiled attempt in the history of humanity to change the subject before taking a gulp of my Diet Coke.

"The deal is that we drive each other insane in the worst way possible, and, other than meeting you fine people, I deeply regret ever agreeing to take him on as a client."

Does she really have no clue he's been sneaking glances at her every time they're in the same room? Not to mention, I find Greggs kind of lovely... what on earth did he do to earn this reputation?

"He's playing like an absolute beast tonight," says Hazel.

"Yeah, if he wasn't such a controlling ass, I'd be his biggest fan," laughs Stacey.

The other player who's playing like a beast is Caleb. He's always been good, but anytime he and Greggs have been on the ice together tonight, they've been unstoppable. It's like they're in complete control of the game. I've never seen the team work like this before. I don't think Lance, the team's captain, has ever played this well. And he is already quite good. It makes me really excited about our Stanley Cup chances. Really excited for Caleb. He even scored the most recent goal.

The intermission is almost over when my phone buzzes.

Caleb: That goal was for you, baby.

A blush immediately rushes to my cheeks, but I still don't find myself as repulsed by the nickname as I would have expected. My phone buzzes again. And again.

Caleb: I'll FaceTime you when I get back to my hotel.

Caleb: If you want to talk, that is.

I can feel myself smiling at his adorable shyness as I type a motivating response.

Cassie: I'll talk if you get another assist in the third.

Caleb: You got it, baby.

Not only do I get my assist, but Caleb manages to dominate the third, and the Blizzards win 5-2. It's a great first showing of this round of the playoffs, and Caleb is indisputably the reason it happened. I'm back in my apartment after dropping off the slightly tipsy Hazel and Stacey at their respective homes when my phone rings. It's Caleb on Face-Time, so I swipe way too eagerly to answer.

"Hey, you!" I say as his rosey-cheeked face fills my screen.

"Hey, baby."

Despite my best efforts to play it cool, I can feel a smile spread wide across my face. "You were incredible tonight."

"I miss you," he says matter-of-factly.

"I miss you, too," I say because it's true. I even got caught zoning out in the faculty meeting this morning thinking about our kiss last night, much to my horror.

"What's our date night plan tomorrow? It's your turn to plan something," he says. We'd agreed that I would plan this date since it's in the middle of the playoff series, and Caleb is super busy.

"I figured we'd do a classic: dinner and a movie," I say.

"Wow, are we in a nineties rom-com?"

It sort of feels like we are, but I'm not going to be the one to admit it.

"I will be wearing a dress I fully intend to drive you insane with all night. Feel free to counter with your outfit choice."

"You drive me insane no matter what you're wearing, baby. But I'll be sure to roll up my shirt sleeves. I know how that drives you crazy."

I? What? How?

"How do you know that!"

"Because every time I do it, you get this weird look on your face. I figured it out a long time ago. Why do you think I always wear long sleeves around you."

"I assumed you got cold easily!"

"Jasmine, I'm from Canada, and I play hockey for a living. As a wise prophet once said, 'the cold never bothered me anyway,'" he half says, half sings.

We continued to talk until I had to go to sleep for school, and Caleb had to rest well because it's the playoffs. As I'm falling asleep, I find my mind wandering back to the fact that Caleb's known that I've been attracted to him for… how long, exactly? God, that's so embarrassing. Except… he liked it. Enough to choose his shirts accordingly. I store that knowledge somewhere in my brain for later and let myself get whisked off to sleep, wishing that Caleb was next to me as I do.

CHAPTER 30
CALEB
THE NEXT DAY

assie warned me about her dress, but I still was not prepared. It shows off every curve of her perfectly, especially her incredible chest. Seriously, how did I manage to get this woman to go on a single date with me, let alone three?

Tonight, she's wearing heels instead of sneakers, which feels a little strange, but I'm not complaining because her legs are absolutely wild. She even does a little twirl in her doorway when I bring her another single flower before we leave for our date.

Once she cuts the stem and placed it in the jar next to the first one, which fully bloomed while I was in L.A., she takes a few strides to close the space between us. I place one hand on her hip and interlace my fingers through the other. I lift her hand to my lips and give it a quick kiss along the knuckles.

"I missed you," she says quietly.

I know she said she missed me yesterday, but to hear her say it in person has me a bit shocked.

I'm not an idiot. I know I've been leading this whole thing so far because we both know that Cassie's convinced she's not built for this. And that's okay. I'm not sure I'm built for it either. But to hear her admit face-to-face that she missed me makes my heart do funny things in my chest regardless.

"I missed you too, baby," I say.

I wrap her up in my arms and give her a squeeze. She feels so right in my arms, even with her being a few inches taller in heels than I'm used to, that I don't want to let go. But we have a date to get to, and I have wooing to do.

"What do you mean you don't know how to skate?" I try not to yell.

Cassie is a ball of laughter across the dinner table from me at a too-fancy-for-our-behavior restaurant.

"How is this even possible?" I continue. "You love hockey!"

"I love *watching you* play hockey. There's a difference."

"Well, I know what we're doing for our fourth date," I say.

"Caleb, that's so cheesy. Then we really will be in a nineties rom-com."

I point to her alfredo pasta covered in cheese. "You love cheese."

"Fair point," she says as she scoops a big bite into her mouth.

This night feels like so many we've had before, but just different enough that I'm nervous. I keep expecting her to freak out, but she seems genuinely fine. If someone's freaking out, it's me. That fight Lance had with Stella on the plane kind of got into my head.

"Freakout, check-in," I say as we're walking to the car before going to the movie.

"I'm not going to go to the bathroom at the movie and never return if that's what you're thinking," she says with a laugh.

"Okay, great, because I heard this is a great movie. I'd hate for you to miss it."

"Oh, I'm staying entirely for my goodnight kiss."

The kiss is long and sweet and perfect, and I don't want it to stop. It's almost enough to make me throw out most of my worries and ask Cassie to be with me before we even finish test dating. We're standing outside of the entrance to Cassie's apartment building, and it's taking every inch of self-control I have not to throw her over my shoulder and march upstairs to her bedroom. But Cassie said she won't sleep with me until the third date, and even though I can tell she's having very similar thoughts (her hand is dangerously low right now), I'm not letting her break her rule. She needs to know how seriously I take this. How seriously I take her.

"Goodnight, baby," I whisper against her lips.

"Goodnight," she says, interlacing her fingers through mine and giving both my hands a squeeze.

"Will you be at the game tomorrow night?"

"Of course, I wouldn't miss it."

"Wear my jersey, baby," I say before giving her lips a quick peck.

"Win a Stanley Cup, baby," she quips back.

I don't know whether to feel frustrated that she won't just wear the dang jersey or overjoyed that she's taken to calling me baby. I settle for overjoyed because her lips are on mine again, and I can't remember ever feeling anything different. I slip my tongue in her mouth, and her whole body softens against mine. I could do this all night, except Cassie has school tomorrow, and I have morning skate early, so I settle for one last peck on her cheek before she turns to go upstairs.

CHAPTER 31
CASSIE

have to drag my own body up the stairs to get myself to leave Caleb. Stupid three-date rule. Why had I even said that? It's not like I'd been on a date in years, anyway. I know I was nervous about things with Caleb moving too fast, but for crying out loud, this is getting ridiculous.

I slide my key into the lock and step inside. I take my heels off and step onto the gross carpet that fills my whole apartment. I'm reaching for the light switch when I realize it.

"Fuck," I groan.

My feet are wet. I wiggle my toes and feel the usually gross carpet that's now even more gross somehow. I force my eyes to adjust to the dark and eventually see that my entire apartment is filled with water. I shove my feet back into my unbearable heels and march outside, dialing my landlord as I go.

"What do you mean you don't know how long it will take?" I screech into my phone as I wait in line to check in at a cheap motel near my apartment. It's not the nicest, but it's safe, and that's all I really care about right now. "It's past midnight, I have work tomorrow, you're refusing to pay for my hotel, and *you won't tell me when it will be fixed?*"

My landlord gives me some legalese answer, so I hang up. Even though the pipe has stopped spewing water into my apartment, the damage is done, and my landlord seems to think he doesn't need to tell me how long it will take to replace all of the carpet and half of my furniture.

Once I've checked into my motel, I find my way to my shitty ass room and drop my duffle on the floor of the open-air hallway. I finally get the key to work in the old reader and manage to shove the heavy door open. I throw the duffle onto the bed and survey the situation I've found myself in.

I really can't afford to stay here for more than a few nights, but I also don't really have a choice. My parents live too far from school, and I wouldn't want to live with my dad anyway. Hazel has Ralph at home. Stacey lives in a one-bedroom with a stylish but very uncomfortable couch. Unless I call Caleb, this is what I'm stuck with. And I am *not* going to call Caleb. I might have a few weeks ago, but now? It feels like too monumental of a thing to ask. Especially when we haven't even had sex yet.

I unzip my bag and pull out a pair of pajamas, a toothbrush, and some face wash. I have to be at work in just a few hours, and then I have Caleb's game tomorrow night. I need all the sleep I can get after the turn this night has taken. I shoot a text to Stacey and Hazel so someone knows where I am, and I'm in bed, completely zonked out, in about five minutes flat.

I get the world's most jarring wake-up call at the exact time I'd asked for, much to my sadness. I barely slept, and now I have to manage a room of unruly pre-teens for several long hours before I see Caleb.

Great.

When it's finally time for the game, I apply far too much concealer to try to cover up the dark circles under my eyes. I know I have to tell Caleb about the flood, but I don't know how yet. He already hates how shitty my apartment is. Just a few months into our friendship, he tried to buy me a condo in his building, which was insane. Then again, right about now, I'm wishing I'd taken him up on it.

When I arrive at the game, I grab a Diet Coke and make my way to my section, weaving through eager Blizzards fans and the occasional L.A. fan. I'm a little surprised when I arrive at my seat to find Stacey in the seat next to it.

"Hey, stranger," she says as she stands to give me a hug.

"Hey! I didn't know you'd be here."

"It was the weirdest thing; the ticket showed up with some flowers today, but the note wasn't signed," she says.

"What did the note say?"

"Something nonsensical about flowers." She shrugs. "Whatever, I'll gladly take the ticket."

Stacey clearly doesn't know that this is the friends and family section for the team. Greggs obviously sent the ticket, but I'm not about to intervene in whatever... that... situation is, so I keep my mouth shut. He would have told her if he wanted her to know.

I turn my attention to the game. If they win tonight, they'll sweep the series and go on to the next round of the playoffs.

Despite King and Lance scoring early in the first period, L.A. is not having it today. They're playing a much more aggressive game, and I swear Caleb almost gets into a fight with their captain near the end of the second. During the intermission between the second and third periods, I pull out my phone. I know I shouldn't, and I'm sure he won't see it until after the game, but just in case he sneaks a peek at his phone, I want Caleb to know that I'm here, supporting him through this tough game. I type out a quick text and slide my phone back into my pocket.

Cassie: I know I shouldn't say this, but you almost beating the shit out of that guy was really hot.

It's either I go for the shock factor, or I'm going to get all mushy about how amazing he is, and I don't want to get ahead of myself.

The third period goes about as well as the second, and the Blizzards lose. It just means that they weren't able to sweep the Kings, and they're still very much in the playoffs, but I know Caleb was secretly hoping they could do it. As he's skating off the ice to do press and get changed, he manages to find me in the stands, and a small smile crosses his face when our eyes meet. I don't know what he's so happy about, but I do know that I'm thrilled that Greggs rented out a quiet cocktail bar to hang out in after the game. I need to see Caleb. Need to wrap my arms around his neck. Need to feel his lips on mine. I may have decided not to tell him about the flood just yet, but I know he'll make me feel better anyway.

CHAPTER 32
CALEB

I walk into the cocktail bar Greggs rented out, and I'm shocked to say I don't hate it. It's dark, quiet, and exactly my speed. It's definitely not a place I would have expected Greggs to choose, but we all contain multitudes, I suppose.

Of course, as soon as my eyes adjust to the darkness, they land on her. They always land on her. She's in that darn Roy jersey that completely swallows her up, but I've never seen anything more beautiful. She's sitting with Stacey in the corner, sipping on her Diet Coke. I know the moment she sees me because she stands and walks over quickly, like maybe she wants to be near me as quickly as possible. I don't hate it.

"I'm sorry about the game," she says as she reaches me.

I immediately reach out and enclose her in my arms. I don't know why, but it feels like we both could use a good hug.

"How was your day?" I ask as she looks up at me expectantly.

"How was my day? It was… fine."

Something is wrong. She hesitated. And now she's burying her head in my chest again.

"What's wrong?" I ask.

"What? Nothing."

Well, that's clearly a lie, but I know better than to push Cassie to share something before she's ready. So, we sit with Stacey, and I pull Cassie onto my lap. We never really had the PDA conversation, so I'm honestly a bit surprised when her lips are instantly on mine.

"I missed you," she whispers, her lips barely leaving my own.

"You just saw me last night, baby. But I missed you too."

Our foreheads fall together, and for a brief moment, it's like we're in this impenetrable bubble where nothing can get to us. That changes in an instant because of a man named Greggs.

"Hey guys!" he all but yells before plopping down mere inches from me.

I try not to let my annoyance show as I say, "Hey, dude."

"Hi, Greggs," Cassie says with a small smile.

I hate that I don't know what's wrong. If I knew, maybe I could fix it. Or at least be there for her.

"Sorry about the apartment, Cassie," Greggs says.

"Oh, I, uh… yeah," Cassie says as she looks down at her Diet Coke.

What is Greggs talking about?

"They're taking way too long to fix it," Stacey says.

"Fix what?" I ask because I can't help myself.

"Nothing!" Cassie says too quickly and too high-pitched to be convincing, blush rushing to her cheeks.

"You didn't tell him?" Stacey asks with a concerned look.

Cassie turns to me but doesn't make eye contact. "My apartment flooded."

"What? When? Why didn't you call me?" The questions roll out of my mouth one after the other.

"A pipe burst. This morning. I... don't know."

"Where did you sleep?" I ask, not sure that I want to know the answer.

"Caleb..." she says, finally bringing her eyes to meet mine.

"Where did you sleep, Cassie?" I use her real name to really hit home about how unhappy I am.

"Well, I have a room at the hotel down the street from my place. I didn't get much sleep because I was on the phone with the landlord for a long time."

"That's a motel, Cassie."

"Caleb," she says, her shame turning to annoyance.

"You're not sleeping in a rat-infested motel," I say, preparing myself for the fight I'm sure is coming. But I'm not taking no for an answer. Not this time.

"You don't know that it's rat-infested."

"Alright, let's go look at it. If there are no signs of rats, I'll consider letting you stay there."

I know Cassie can take care of herself, so I'm mostly joking. But she gets a look on her face that makes me wish I hadn't made the joke.

"*Letting* me?" she says.

"Yes, Cassie. What if something happens to you?" I think she knows I'm joking now because there's a slight sparkle in her eye that makes me think I've almost won.

Almost.

"Nothing is going to happen to me, Caleb."

"Alright, I didn't want to do this. But you're leaving me no choice," I say.

I'm on my feet in two seconds, holding Cassie up off the ground with ease.

"What are you doing?" she yells.

I throw her over my shoulder like a little sack of potatoes and march toward the door. "We're going to get your things from the motel, and then you're moving into my apartment. Duh."

"*Duh*? What's obvious about that?"

She's kicking somewhat wildly in the air in an apparent attempt to break free, but I can barely tell because my grip on her isn't going anywhere.

"Every part of it. I'm not letting my best friend and test girlfriend stay anywhere that's not nice and clean and safe. You're the most important person in my life, and I'm not letting anything happen to you. I know you won't let me spoil you, but at least let me make sure your basic needs are taken care of."

"Well, when you put it like that..." she says slowly. "I guess I can stay with you tonight. If you're sure, it's not too much of an imposition."

"Never say anything that dumb to me ever again."

Now she's laughing, and I know I've won. Not just the argument, but now I'll get to share my bed with Cassie tonight. That's definitely a win in my book.

"We are not having this argument again. You are not sleeping on the couch," I say.

"I just think we need to be careful. Things are... new," she says.

I can't help but roll my eyes. "Cassie, I've known you for years. I've tasted you on my tongue, for crying out loud. I think we can handle sharing a bed again." I take a step toward her, pick up her hands, and give them each a light kiss on the knuckles. "I have zero expectations for anything more than getting a good night's sleep so we can go get your stuff in the morning before I have practice."

"Zero expectations?" she asks.

"You have a three-date rule. I respect that, and if you need to wait longer, I'll respect that too. I'm not in this for sex, Cassie. I want you. All of you."

She looks at me with glossy eyes, and I realize I've never seen Cassie cry. Not once. I'm not sure what I'll do if her tears break free from her eyes.

"Thank you," she says, stepping toward me and burying her head in my chest. "I want all of you, too."

Her voice is muffled, but I know she said it, and it makes my heart soar. Cassie Flowers wants me. How is that even possible?

I lift her chin and give her a long, hot kiss. A little breath escapes her mouth, and I think I just took Cassie's breath away with a kiss. That sort of thing could go to a guy's head.

"Now, can we go to bed, baby?" I say.

"Yes, I'm so tired."

Once we've brushed our teeth, changed out of our respective clothes, and set an alarm for the morning, Cassie and I crawl into bed together. A little part of me feels like this is the first of many times we'll do this routine. I can only hope it lasts after her apartment is fixed because feeling her bring her back against my front and snuggle into me might be the greatest feeling in the world. I fall asleep with Cassie in my arms, on my mind, and owning my whole heart. I just have to figure out how to handle hockey and a relationship with Cassie at the same time. Hopefully, I can do better than Lance. Cassie deserves at least that much.

CHAPTER 33
CASSIE
THE NEXT DAY

'm staring at an empty drawer, unsure of what to do with myself. And with my stuff. Logic would state that I should place all the clothes I'm close to dropping on the floor into the drawer instead. But there's something about this that feels monumental, like I won't be able to take it back.

Of course, I know that I won't be living with Caleb forever. This is temporary. But I can't help but feel like it isn't. Like if I place these clothes in this drawer he so kindly emptied for me, I'll be committing to forever. It's not that I don't think I want that… eventually. It's that I'm honestly still a little unsure.

"Are you really freaking out about a dresser drawer?" Caleb says from behind me.

"What? I, uh… no?"

I look over my shoulder to find him laughing.

He strides across the room and wraps his arms around me

from behind. First, he gives me a squeeze as he says, "Baby, it's a drawer, not a wedding. You need space for your stuff, or we'll be tripping all over it all the time. Please don't overthink this." Then, he takes the clothes out of my hands and carefully places them in the drawer. "See? That wasn't so bad, was it?"

I turn in his arms to face him and wrap my arms around his neck. "I guess not," I say as I place a quick peck on his lips. He pulls me even closer, and I find, once again, the breath escaping my body. How does this man have this embarrassing effect on me? I find myself resting my head on his chest, and at that moment, I don't think there's a better feeling in the world.

Then he lifts my chin and gives me an honest-to-god incredible kiss, the kind of kiss that could compel even me to write poetry. I decide that the best feeling in the world is kissing Caleb Mack.

"I wish you didn't have to go," I say against his mouth.

I didn't realize I said it out loud until he pulled back.

He places a soft kiss on my forehead and says, "I know, baby. Me either, but Stanley Cups don't win themselves."

I know that Caleb needs to be focused on hockey right now. It's the most important part of the most important season of his career so far. I immediately feel embarrassed that I let my little confession slip.

"Hey," he says, lifting my chin until our eyes meet. "I like that you miss me when I'm gone."

"I always have," I find myself admitting.

A big grin spreads across his face, and he envelopes me in a bear hug. "I do have to get going," he says after a few moments.

He gives me a long, hot kiss goodbye, and I swear I don't know what's come over me because I think my knees might give out a bit. "Don't eat all my cheese," he says after our lips have parted.

He leans over to grab his duffle bag and starts for the bedroom door.

"No promises!" I holler as the apartment door closes behind him.

It's only at that moment that I realize that I'm about to be alone in Caleb's apartment for two days. The thought is mildly terrifying, so I grab my boxing bag from the corner and head out to Anthony's. This terror is nothing a little hitting a heavy bag can't fix.

"Your form is a bit off today, Cass," says Anthony as I take another possibly slightly overly aggressive swing at the bag.

I pause. My fight is in two weeks, and I need to be on my A game if I don't want to have my ass kicked.

"Sorry, I'm a bit distracted today," I say before taking a swig of my water.

"Caleb's in L.A., right?"

"Um… yes?" I'm not sure what that has to do with my boxing form.

"Will he be here for the fight?"

"The game schedule for the third round of the playoffs isn't set yet, but hopefully, yes," I say. "Why?"

Anthony looks me right in the face and says, "You're always a bit off when he's not around. He pushes you. Ever since you gave him that black eye, it's like you're connected or something."

Well, this is news to me, and I'm not exactly sure how I feel about it. On the one hand, there's no one I'd rather be connected to. On the other hand, I really hate that it could negatively impact my abilities in the ring. And I hate that it's something I'm not aware of, let alone in control of.

"Look," Anthony continues, "all athletes have routines. Caleb's part of yours. There's no shame in that."

"But if it's hurting what I'm able to do…"

"I'm going to stop you right there," Anthony interrupts. "Caleb has helped you immensely. There's no world in which you're as good of a fighter, or, dare I say, as good of a person, without him."

I pull off my gloves and start to undo my hand wraps. I think back over the past few years. How much more I came to the gym because Caleb was coming too. How much extra I sparred because he was there to help me. How much I looked forward to our time at the bar after a class. Not just because of boxing but because of Caleb. Because I wanted to spend time with him. Not just as my best friend, I realize. But because he's him and I'm me, it was always going to be inevitable.

Holy shit.

Holy shit.

No. Nope. No.

I cannot be in love with Caleb Mack.

We've barely even started dating!

But, fuck me. I am. I probably always have been.

I'm in love with Caleb.

… Shit.

The fact that I have to wait another thirty-six hours to see Caleb is going to kill me. I don't even know what I'm going to say to him, but I know that if I don't see him soon, I'm going to burst into flames as hot as the sun.

That being said, I am not above using the fact that he's gone to my advantage. He's been eating extra healthy with the playoffs, and I've been trying to be supportive by doing the same, but damn, a girl needs her Chinese takeout with at least some regularity. I open the door of the condo, *Caleb's* condo, I remind myself, and thank the delivery driver for my spicy chicken.

There are other playoff games on tonight that will help dictate who the Blizzards play in the next round, assuming they make it, so I flip on—*Caleb's*—massive flat-screen TV and settle in for a night of hockey and fried food. Two of my favorite things. I even let myself steal one of Caleb's practice sweatshirts, so I'm extra cozy.

All of this is supposed to be a distraction because, internally, my brain feels like it's on fire. It's moving so fast. What if I'm wrong? What if Caleb doesn't feel as strongly? What if I ruin this like I've managed to ruin every short-lived relationship I've ever been in? The questions swirl and swirl through my brain as I chomp into an egg roll.

Of course, my phone picks my latest panic moment to ring, and it's Caleb on FaceTime. I quickly finish chewing and swipe to answer.

"Hey," I say.

"Hey, you!"

He's lying in a hotel bed, shirtless, and I can't help but notice, with a big grin on his face.

"How was the flight?" I ask, taking another bite of my egg roll.

"Pretty good. I got my own row again. Oh my god, is that an egg roll?" he asks, almost salivating as he does.

I giggle. Yes, Caleb Mack has reduced me to a giggling idiot.

"That sounds so good," he continues.

"We'll do a three-day sampling of all the fried food in the city after you win the Stanley Cup."

"And you'll wear my jersey the whole time?" he asks with a glimmer in his eyes.

"I'll wear whatever you want," I say with a knowing tone.

He laughs his sweetest, warmest laugh. "Don't threaten me with a good time, baby. Wait, are you wearing my hoodie?"

Shit.

I forgot I had it on.

"Um... maybe?" I say.

"Do you miss me, Lilac?"

I look away from the screen and mumble, "Shut up" under my breath.

"Nope, I think you miss me," he says.

"Of course I miss you, you big dummy," I basically yell. Then I quietly say, "I always miss you when you're on a trip."

Caleb gets a knowing look on his face. "Always?"

"Shut up," I mumble again.

"Alright, I'll change the subject, but just know that this is definitely going to my head."

I can't help but giggle again. Goddammit.

"How was training today?" he asks.

He clearly knows how to distract me because boxing is one of the few things that I can talk about for what feels like forever without getting bored. Except training today wasn't great for obvious reasons, and I don't really want to think about it.

"Meh," I say.

"What do you mean, 'meh'? Did you get hurt or something?"

No, I just realized that if you're not here, my entire equilibrium is off, and I hate that I need you, but I do, and also, I think I've been in love with you for like a year? I think.

"No, I was just off today, I guess," I say instead, eyes once again avoiding the screen.

"Well, you, on an off day, could still kick my ass," he says earnestly. I still don't look at the screen. "Hey," he continues. "I know you hate when I ask this, but are you okay?"

I finally face the camera again but can't seem to find the words to explain what's going on with me without telling him I'm in love with him over FaceTime, which is not how I want that conversation to go.

"Cassie?" he asks.

I noticed that he didn't say 'baby' or call me a flower this time, and his tone was more serious than I'd like.

"I'm okay," I say. "Just a weird day. But you have a big game tomorrow; you need to go to sleep."

"You're probably right," he says, looking toward his watch. "But only if you promise me you're really okay."

"I'm okay."

And I mean it because the look on Caleb's face is so kind and sweet, and it honestly does make me feel better just to talk to him.

"Okay. Call me if you need me."

I feel a smile spread across my face because I know he really means it. "I will. Goodnight, baby."

"Goodnight, baby."

I'd like to say that seeing Caleb after my realization today freaked me out. I'd like to say that it made my fear worse because that would mean that I'm being a logical fucking human. But as soon as his face filled my screen, something inside me softened, and I honestly don't know if I've ever felt more calm. Calm isn't exactly my general state of being.

I turn on the Dallas v. Seattle game and eat my entire container of spicy chicken, knowing that Caleb is miles away but also sort of closer than ever.

CHAPTER 34
CALEB
THE NEXT MORNING

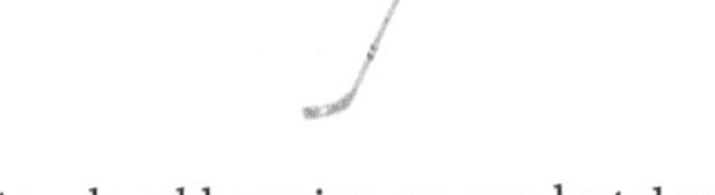

I wake up to a loud banging on my hotel room door.

"Mack! Wake up!"

I lean over to check the time. It's 6:30 a.m., and we don't have to be at the arena for another few hours, and I'm not exactly a morning person. Just when Greggs and King were growing on me... they had to wake me up at an ungodly hour.

"Hang on!" I holler as I stumble out of bed and manage to avoid tripping over my suitcase on my way to the door.

I swing the door open to find Greggs and King standing in the hallway, fully dressed and ready for the day. "What is wrong with you guys?" I ask as I self-consciously try to adjust my unwieldy hair with one hand and cover my yawn with the other.

"Nothing?" says King like this is a perfectly reasonable interaction to be having before the sun is up. "We're taking you on our pre-away-game ritual."

My brain is still a bit fuzzy, but regardless, I'm a little touched and shocked that they continue to want to hang out with me after the whole panic attack thing, so I hold the door open for them and walk toward my bathroom to get ready.

"Let me get showered," I say. "Make yourselves at home."

I don't know what I expected, but I would not have guessed that Greggs and King's pre-away-game ritual would be so wholesome. We're seated in a booth of a hole-in-the-wall diner a few blocks from the hotel.

"So your ritual is that you… sneak away to eat a greasy breakfast?" I ask as I take a sip of my coffee. They didn't even mock me for adding a boatload of cream and sugar to it.

"We, well…" King hesitates.

"Will you stop being bashful about this? My therapist says it's toxic," says Greggs.

I have exactly zero clue what's going on, so I just look at King expectantly.

King rolls his eyes before turning back to me and says, "We like to set aside away games for our friendship."

"Okay? And why is that weird?" I ask.

"Because we're supposed to be macho hockey players," says Greggs. "And friend dates are 'for chicks,' according to this guy."

"Friend dates?" I say.

"We just hang out, sober, and talk," says King, clearly trying to downplay whatever… this is.

"That sounds… nice?" It sounds like what I do with Cassie most days of the week, actually.

"It is nice," says Greggs. "And we want you to join us."

"On a trial basis," says King sternly. "There are rules."

"Rules?" I ask.

Greggs clears his throat. "We don't tell the other guys

where we are or what we do. What's said here stays here, chicks included. And we have to be honest."

"Do you agree to the rules?" asks King.

"Um… sure?"

"You have to say yes." King is being really intense about this whole thing.

"Okay, fine. Yes. I agree."

Our server appears with our egg white omelets (we still have to be healthy even if we're eating at a diner with the playoffs going on) and more coffee. I take a huge bite and hope that getting out of bed this morning wasn't a huge mistake.

"Alright, Thomas, you're up first," says Greggs to King. It actually takes me a second to remember that King's first name is Thomas because no one ever uses it. "How are you?"

King takes a long swig of his coffee, followed by a deep breath. "I don't know, man. I guess I've just been thinking a lot about what I want. This isn't it. Well, not all of it, anyway. I don't want a bunch of first dates that go nowhere. I want the real thing. And I know it goes against my whole brand or whatever, but I don't care anymore. The problem is, I have no clue how to go about changing or getting a woman to take me seriously."

Well, that was… a lot. I'm shocked to hear King wants to be in a serious relationship. He's very well known to be a bit of a player. But I guess I haven't tried to get to know him as well as I probably should have.

"There," he says after taking a sip of his coffee. "That's how I'm doing. How are you doing, Mitch?"

I turn my attention to Greggs. "I'm actually doing pretty well. I'm at peace with how the season is going, and I'm not in a particularly existential place right now, which is weird."

"Since you asked me to check in on this… Have you been taking your meds?" asks King.

"Yeah, I have been," Greggs says. "Thanks for checking."

They fist bump. About Greggs taking his bipolar mood stabilizer... I think? What? Is? Happening? I mean, I obviously support Greggs taking his meds and everything. I've just never heard two hockey players be so open about stuff like that before. These guys really are surprising me today.

"Alright, Caleb. Your turn. How are you?" asks Greggs.

"I'm... fine?" I say like it's a question because I honestly don't know how to answer that question after the deep admissions of my teammates.

"Be serious, Caleb. How are you, really?" Greggs asks again.

I take a sip of my coffee and think about my answer. A real one that will make Greggs stop asking me questions.

"Really? Well, I guess I'm struggling a bit with balancing hockey and this whole test-dating thing with Cassie. Lance's fight with Stella the other day really got in my head. Things with Cassie are kinda awesome, though, and I want to try to make it work, I think."

"Nice! Great job sharing for the first time," says Greggs as he and King high-five each other before turning to me, palms outstretched, eagerly hoping I won't leave them hanging.

I sheepishly high-five them both and turn back to my omelet, hoping we aren't making too much of a scene in this quiet diner.

The next hour is filled with similarly deep questions and conversation. I do my best to share honestly because these guys have opened up their friendship to me, and I feel like I at least owe them that much. I'm not too big to admit that I don't end up hating it. We depart the diner and head to the arena, ready to take on both L.A. and our lives—as a team.

CHAPTER 35
CASSIE

I walk into the bar to find Hazel and Stacey already sitting with a seat saved between them. There's a guy talking Stacey's ear off, and Hazel is giggling to herself about something on her phone.

"Hey!" I yell over the music as I approach them.

"Hi!" Hazel says, jumping out of her stool to give me a hug.

Stacey, like myself, isn't much of a hugger, but she holds up what appears to be a Diet Coke and says, "Got this for you."

"Thank you," I say, taking a sip. "What are you laughing at?"

"Oh, nothing. Just a funny tweet about Thomas King," Hazel says.

"What did he do now?" I ask, a bit worried about King's latest escapades being online again.

He has a reputation as a player, but I think he's actually a really good guy below all of that. He's certainly helped Caleb come out of his shell lately.

"Just another date gone wrong, it sounds like," she says. She holds up a photo of a woman throwing a martini all over King.

"Yikes," I say.

"Not all hockey players are like Caleb," says Stacey. I know it's supposed to be a dig at Greggs, but I can't say I disagree.

Caleb is… special.

I take my seat and pull out my phone to shoot off a quick heart emoji to Caleb for good luck before the game. My finger hovers over the send button, unsure if I should hit it. On the one hand, I've sent Caleb this exact emoji many times. On the other hand, it feels like it has a different meaning now, and I don't want to freak Caleb out by sending it prematurely. Finally, I suck down my fear and tap the button. I can always say it was a typo.

Immediately, my phone buzzes with a response. It's two heart emojis back. My anxiousness settles down, and my heart swells when I see it, especially knowing that the game starts in just a few minutes and he's probably busy getting prepared.

A few moments later, the TVs all change over to the Blizzards' game. If we win tonight, we go onto round three of the playoffs, and I know we don't technically have to win tonight for that to happen, but I'm still so nervous for Caleb regardless. The Blizzards take the ice, and the puck is about to drop when Stacey leans over to me.

"So, how are things going with Caleb?" she asks.

"Really good," I say because I can't help but tell the truth. "Which kind of blows my mind a little."

"Why? Caleb seems great?" asks Hazel.

"Oh, he is. I was worried about myself," I admit.

Stacey nods along. "I can understand that. I'm not much of a relationship person either."

I open my mouth to protest. To say that that's not the reason. But isn't it? I've never really dated. I've barely even had friends for most of my adult life. I even keep my parents at arm's length.

Caleb's always just been... Caleb, though. Something about him broke through, and I can't help but be myself with him. At first, it was annoying, then it was terrifying. Now, I have to admit it's really lovely. And it's the only reason I even considered our whole test-dating arrangement.

I turn my attention to the TV nearest to our section of the bar because Caleb's face is filling the screen. The commentators are talking about what an impressive season he's had and how focused he clearly is. I've seen it, too. He's always been good, but this season has been something else. Pride fills my whole being when they mention he'll be a top choice for MVP if the Blizzards win the Stanley Cup.

My pride doesn't drop for a second throughout the entire first period because every minute that he's on the ice, he's on fire. I've truly never seen him play like this before. He's aggressive but not making penalties. He's doing all the right things. Between King and Lance, our offense is doing all the right things, and Greggs is playing just as well as Caleb tonight. You can feel the air in the bar change throughout the evening. There's a clear hope in the fanbase that this is the year, which, after last year's injuries, would really be something.

We're up by three near the end of the third period, and L.A. has pulled their goalie in an attempt to even the score, but it does them no good. Caleb gets possession of the puck, weaves between L.A. players like it's the easiest thing in the world, and makes the final score seven to three. Greggs rushes over to him and gives him a massive hug, lifting him off the ground slightly. Even Stacey seems amused by the gesture because I hear a slight giggle escape from her before she can stop herself.

The TVs all switch over to the commentators, and the bar begins to empty. We decide to have another drink before leaving, and I find myself feeling so damn comfortable with these women. For the first time since I was a kid, I think I might actually have female friends. I'm not entirely sure how not to screw it up, but I actually care enough to try this time, so I guess I'll start there.

Once I'm back at Caleb's condo, my phone rings, and Caleb's face fills my screen on FaceTime.

"Hey, you," I say as I answer.

"Hey, baby," he yells. Wherever he is, the place is loud, but he doesn't seem bothered by it for once.

King pops into the frame and yells, "Cassie! Hi!"

I laugh. "Hi, Thomas."

"We made Caleb come out with us, and he's not being a miserable dork for once!" King says.

"Hey! That's *my* miserable dork you're talking about," I say it without even thinking, and I'm suddenly terrified of it.

"Told you," King fake whispers in Caleb's ear before disappearing from the screen.

"What did he tell you?" I ask.

Caleb's cheeks turn even redder than usual as he mumbles, "King thinks you like me."

Oh, if only King knew. And if only I knew how to handle it.

"I do like you, Caleb," I say.

"But do you *like like* me?"

I can't help but laugh because Caleb is clearly a little tipsy, and it's adorable.

"Yes, baby. I *like like* you. Now go have fun with your friends."

Caleb's face scrunches up momentarily at the mention of the word 'friends,' but he recovers quickly and gives me a nod. "Okay. I'll see you after school tomorrow for our date."

"Goodnight, baby," I say.

"Goodnight, baby."

CHAPTER 36
CALEB
THE NEXT DAY

open my condo door feeling a little exhausted from this playoff run but a lot excited to see Cassie. Tonight is our third date, and I have the perfect plan. Cassie has a thing about county fairs; it might seem a bit whimsical for her, but she loves them for some reason. When I saw that there was one in a local suburb, I knew it was what we had to do for this date.

I open the door, almost expecting to see Cassie sitting on my couch, but when I walk in, she's nowhere to be seen.

"Lotus?" I call out.

"One second!" she hollers back.

I set down my duffle on the floor and cross to the kitchen to make a coffee. It might be four o'clock in the afternoon, but I stayed out too late with the team to be what Cassie deserves without some caffeine.

"Hey you," she says from behind me as I stir cream into

my mug. I turn to see her smiling in her usual jeans and sneakers.

"Hey," I say, closing the space between us.

I envelope her into my arms and breathe her in. Gosh, I missed her. And now I have her for almost a whole week until the next round of the playoffs starts.

"I missed you," she mumbles into my chest, and I swear it makes my heart soar all the way to the sun.

I kiss her forehead and whisper, "I missed you too. Are you ready for our date tonight?"

"Yes! I'm so excited!" She even bounces a little on her heels as she says it, which she only does when she's really, truly excited.

"You just want nachos."

"And funnel cake!" she adds.

"Alright, let me get changed and chug this coffee, and we can get going."

"Ohmygodthisissodelicious," she says as she shoves more funnel cake into her mouth.

Taking Cassie to this fair was definitely the right decision. So far, she's eaten something from every stand we've passed, and we've barely made it past the front entrance.

"Oh hell yes!" she says. She hands me her funnel cake and basically bounces toward the High Striker. "Hello, good sir," she says to the attendant. "What's my prize if I get it all the way to the top?"

"Anything you want," the clearly very bored teenager says in response.

"Amazing! Caleb, give this man three tickets, please."

I shove my hand in my pocket and fish out the tickets while balancing the multiple food items Cassie has me holding.

"You don't want more than one try?" the attendant asks.

Oh boy, here we go.

"Do I look like I need more than one?" demands Cassie.

"Well, um…" the kid mumbles.

"Hammer, please," she says as she holds her hand out impatiently.

The kid hands her the hammer, and she approaches the bell. She raises the hammer triumphantly above her head and smashes it into the base of the bell. The sensor rises up quickly and reaches the top with a ding.

"What the…" the kid says while I basically laugh my butt off. There's nothing better than watching a man underestimate Cassie.

"So, I can have anything, right?" says Cassie with a smirk. "I want that." She points to a teddy bear near the very top of the stand.

The kid ducks down toward a bin, presumably to pull out an identical bear. Cassie coughs dramatically and says, "No, no. I want that one."

"That exact one?" the kid asks, deflated.

"Yep. You can reach it. I believe in you."

He winds up having to use a stool to reach it. He lets out a sigh as he hands it over to Cassie, who is completely elated by the entire interaction.

"Have a wonderful night," she says with a nod before marching away, teddy bear in tow.

We wander lazily through the fair, hand in hand, making a list of all the rides we want to go on and all the snacks Cassie wants to eat. We settle on a ride that looks like a giant spider as our first choice, and even though Cassie is the one who's been eating all the food, I feel mildly ill afterward.

"You know what will help you feel better?" Cassie asks.

"What?"

"Cotton candy!" she says with a bounce.

"Oh really?" I chuckle.

"Yep! It's a scientific fact. Cotton candy fixes everything."

How is she so gosh darn adorable?

"Well, in that case, let's go get some," I say.

We walk through the fair and find a cotton candy stand with a few different flavor options. Cassie chooses blue for both of us, despite my protests about our teeth turning blue. She's sitting on a bench, pulling small pieces of her cotton candy off of the stick and placing it dramatically into her mouth. I pull out my phone to take a photo because Cassie is just being too cute, and I want to remember this night forever.

"Don't you dare post that," she says moments after I take what might now be my phone background photo.

"Well, I wasn't going to, but now that you mention it…"

I load the photo onto my Instagram story and get ready to share it with my close friends, which is basically just the team, Cassie, and my mom. But then my finger hovers over sharing it with all of my followers, and I pause.

"Caleb, I will kill you," she says, inching toward me. "You have, like, half a million followers."

She reaches out to try to take my phone, and I stand quickly, knowing she won't be able to reach me even if she tries.

She tries.

She tries by climbing up my body like a koala.

"Give me the phone, Caleb Mack!"

"Shhhhh," I say, suddenly fearful that someone will recognize me and put me into an anxious spiral on our date night.

"Sorry!" she squeals. "But that's what you get!"

I extend my arm far above my body and post the photo before she can stop me. I've shared photos of Cassie before, and hockey Twitter always seems to lose its collective mind about it for some reason. I doubt this will be any different, but the world needs to see how gorgeous my… whatever she is to me… is.

She plops down on the bench and lets out an over-the-top sigh before pulling out her phone.

"At least you didn't tag me this time," she says. Then she looks up at me with a big grin, and I know she's not actually mad. She might even be a little happy about it for some reason.

"Did you even look at the photo?" I ask.

"Yes, I did. And you captured my obsession with this cotton candy perfectly, so I've decided I'm okay with it."

"No one is going to be looking at the cotton candy, Magnolia."

She looks up at me with a genuinely confused look on her face. "What do you mean?"

I take her hand and pull her close to me. I rest my hands on the space where her jeans meet her crop top. "I mean…" I lean down to kiss her nose. "You are stunning."

Her cheeks turn a soft shade of pink. "Oh shush."

"Nope. I've never told you that before, and it's a crime. Ever since you literally knocked the wind out of me when we first fought, you've been taking my breath away."

Her eyes grow wide, and it seems like she wants to say something. But instead, she rises to her tiptoes. Our noses fall together, and the entire fair goes silent. It's just our breath and her hands on my chest. Then, Cassie Flowers gives me a kiss. No. Not just a kiss. It's the kind of kiss that changes the trajectory of your life.

When we part just a bit, I say, "You're incredible, Cassie," and she goes right back to kissing me.

I can feel the words she's trying to say in her kiss, I think. And I think the wooing attempts I've made have actually worked.

"I'd ask if you want to get out of here," she says after we finally stop making out like teenagers at a county fair. "But I really want to kiss you at the top of the Ferris wheel."

We ride to the top and the wheel pauses. Cassie leans over to me and says, "I believe I was promised a kiss."

So I kiss her. It's short but sweet and cozy, and I want

nothing more than to keep kissing her. But the Ferris wheel lurches forward, and we're back on the ground before I can. When we reach the bottom, she takes my hand and guides me back toward the car.

"Let's go home," she says as we reach the car.

All night, her three-date rule has hung in the air. I'd never assume she'd just sleep with me because of that. Cassie doesn't do anything she doesn't want to do, and I certainly wouldn't pressure her. But when she gives me a knowing look in the elevator on the ride up to the condo, I'm fairly certain I know what's about to happen.

When the door to my condo closes behind us, neither of us says anything at first. We just kick off our shoes like we have so many times before, and Cassie turns around to face me, taking a step back. She slips her t-shirt over her head to reveal the sexiest bra I've ever seen. She may have been casually dressed for the fair, but underneath, I can tell she was planning on this, and it's reassuring to know that it's not just me who wants it. Then, she unbuttons the top of her jeans and shimmies out of them slowly, showing me the panties that match her bra.

I'm already stiffening against my jeans, and we haven't even touched yet. I quickly slide my t-shirt over my head and kick off my jeans. It's taking every ounce of my control not to pick her up and carry her to my bedroom, but I want her to lead this.

Cassie reaches out for my hand, turns, and takes a tentative step toward the bedroom. It's a good thing she's the one leading me this time because I'm at a total loss when I see her from behind. Her hair flows loosely down her back and stops just before the bra clasp I so desperately want to undo while her hips sway freely from side to side as she guides us down the hall.

When we reach the bedroom, she gently pulls me onto the bed, placing herself directly below me. I grind my hips into her gently, and she lets out the most erotic sigh I've ever heard. Then her hands are in my hair, her hips are grinding back up against mine, and her lips are on mine.

I reach behind her to undo her bra and watch her amazing tits fall free. When we first hooked up, I told her to play with them herself, which was insanely sexy, but I didn't even get to touch them. The whole thing was quick and hot as heck, but this time, I want to take my time exploring every inch of her.

I bring my lips to her ear and ask, "Are you sure?" before continuing.

"Positive," she says with a nod and a quick kiss just below my ear.

I take a sharp inhale at the contact and let my tongue slide down her neck to her collarbone before peppering her shoulder with a few sweet kisses. When I finally reach her chest, she's full-on wiggling below me, clearly wanting more. I slide her nipple into my mouth and give it a long suck while I reach between her legs. I move my hand inside her panties and find her sensitive spot, circling it with my finger slowly. I want to take my time with her, and I want to drive her a little bit crazy while I do. When her breath starts to pick up, I bring my body lower, dragging my tongue down from her chest to her stomach and eventually between her legs.

"C-Caleb," she moans with a quick breath when my tongue starts to swirl her while I slide one finger and then two inside her.

She's never said my name like this, and I swear I could hear it a million times, and it would never get old. I look up at her to see hands on her tits while her hips move against my mouth. It's the sexiest thing I've ever seen. She continues to thrust into my mouth while I work my fingers inside of her, eventually moaning out my name when she comes.

I expect her to lay back and rest or to take a moment before deciding to do anything else. I definitely don't expect her to pull me up and shove me onto my back before crawling on top of me and sliding down my body. Before I know it, her head is between my legs, and her tongue is licking up me. She holds eye contact with me the whole time, and now *this* is the sexiest thing I've ever seen. The sensation is already too much to bear, and I know I'm not going to last long with Cassie's beautiful face looking up at me while she slides her mouth up and down me. I pull her hair back with one hand and cup her cheek with the other while she moves until I'm so close.

"Stop," I say with a pant. "I'm too close, and I don't want this to end yet."

A smile spreads across her gorgeous face, and she crawls back up me, settling her hips on top of mine.

"Condom?" she asks.

I reach for the bedside drawer and pull one out to hand to her. She rips it open with her teeth, and I think I might be about to die of pure bliss. But then she's sliding it on me, and I'm definitely about to.

"Ready?" she asks, and all I can do is nod because I'm completely at a loss for words as the woman of my dreams mounts me and slides down.

I thrust up into her because I can't help it, and she lets out a moan. Her hands brace on my chest as our hips move together, and I let my fingers squeeze at her nipples.

"Caleb," she moans again.

"Yes, baby. I love it when you say my name like that."

"Caleb," she says again, the moan cutting through my name.

I was already close, and now I feel like I'm about to lose it. I think she might be close, too, because she's letting out these sexy little moans, and her hands are squeezing my chest.

"I'm close again," she says. I feel her tighten around me, and it's all I need to be able to let go of my release.

"Cassie," I moan as I come, seeing nothing but stars as I do.

When we both finally return to earth, she rolls off me and snuggles into my side.

"Fuck, baby," I say, and she starts to giggle. "What?"

"You never swear."

"I swear!" I say, even though I know I don't. I couldn't really tell you why. I just never have much.

"No, you don't," she says.

"Well, you do wild things to me, baby," I say, reaching out to kiss her.

Our lips linger together for a long moment before Cassie gives a satisfied sigh. "I'm sleepy."

I get up quickly to discard the condom and put back on my boxers because I can't seem to sleep totally naked. When I return to the bedroom, Cassie is curled up wearing my Blizzards hoodie and nothing else. She looks cozy and sexy, and all I want is to envelope her in my arms for the rest of the night. I crawl into bed and settle in next to her, pulling her back into my chest and giving her neck a kiss.

I swear I could repeat this night over and over again for the rest of my life, and it would never get old.

CHAPTER 37
CASSIE
THE NEXT MORNING

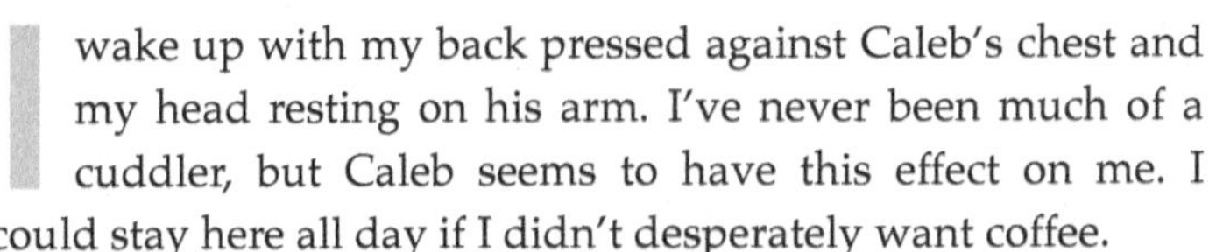

I wake up with my back pressed against Caleb's chest and my head resting on his arm. I've never been much of a cuddler, but Caleb seems to have this effect on me. I could stay here all day if I didn't desperately want coffee.

I turn my body around in Caleb's arms, and when we come face to face, I see the most adorable thing I've ever seen. Caleb's already usually unruly hair is even more all over the place, and his rosy cheeks move upwards into a grin as he opens his eyes.

"Good morning, baby," he says, lifting his head to drop a kiss on my shoulder. "Do you want coffee?"

"How did you know?"

"Because it's the morning, and you're you, obviously."

I feel a grin spread across my face as I say, "Yes, please."

He gives me another kiss, this one on my nose before he rolls out of bed. I let myself appreciate the view as he walks out of the bedroom before I get out of bed to join him in the kitchen. There's something exceptional about his ass, and I'm not ashamed of enjoying it a bit, especially not after last night.

I wanted Caleb so badly the whole time we were at the fair. I'm not surprised that I basically climbed him like a tree the moment we got back to his condo. I'm actually surprised I made it to date three, given how completely sexy he is. But it meant a lot to me that he wanted to follow that rule, just like I followed his rules of trying three dates.

Which brings us to this morning. We've officially had three dates, so now what? Do we just... continue going like normal? Do we go back to being friends? After last night, I don't see how that's possible, not because it changed things for us. We honestly still feel like *us*. It's not possible because I can't imagine a world in which I'm not in love with Caleb Mack. And while I'm sure he's not there yet, maybe he will be someday.

Then again, there are two people involved in this decision. What if Caleb decides he doesn't want to keep going? Oh God, what if he's decided he wants nothing to do with me now? I know he promised he wouldn't do that, but sex changes people sometimes. Shit. Shit. Shit. What have I done?

"Coffee's ready!" he hollers from down the hall.

I sit at the edge of the bed and try to gather up the courage to go down the hall and face him.

"Snapdragon?" he yells.

I can do this.

"Coming!" I holler back.

I stand, pull Caleb's massive sweatshirt down as low as it will go, and make my way to the kitchen. When I get there, there's a black coffee sitting on the edge of the island, and Caleb's mixing cream and sugar into his own mug.

"So," he says as I raise my coffee to my lips and take a sip.

"So," I say back. "I'm not sure what to say right now."

God, I hope last night doesn't turn into the biggest mistake of my life.

"Just say how you're feeling," says Caleb. "I'll still be here, no matter what."

He takes a sip of his coffee, and I try to gather my thoughts. Finally, they all seem to come out at once as I say, "I really like you, and I really like this, and I want to keep going if you want to keep going, but also no pressure because I know I'm a lot and I just want you in my life and I'm so scared of losing you, please make me stop talking…"

Caleb rounds the corner of the island and places his hands on my shoulders.

"Baby," he says. "I really like you too. And I really like this. And I want to keep going too."

"Really?" I can't quite believe I'm so lucky.

"I'm in this, baby," he says. "Fully. There's nothing you could say that would make me not want you in my life, and I'll take whatever form that comes in, but I'd really like for us to be together."

"Together," I repeat. "Like a couple?"

"Like whatever you want us to be. But yes, I do mean like a couple."

"I'd like that," I say. *I'd like nothing more.*

He lifts my chin with his hand, and I rise on my tip toes to bring my mouth to his. The kiss is long and sweet and perfect, and when it's over, I lower my heels to the ground and rest my head against his chest, letting him hold me tight.

"Are you ready for our fourth date?" he asks after a quiet moment.

"Oh shit," I say, remembering his idea of skating. "I'm going to make a fool out of myself."

"As someone who literally got a black eye from you the first time we met, I'd say I still have that covered. You'll be great," he says with far too much confidence in me.

I am not great.

I'm sure I must look like a baby giraffe taking its first steps with how wobbly my legs are as I step from skate to skate on the Blizzards' practice rink. Caleb's doing literal laps around me while I attempt to get my footing. The only thing making this even somewhat bearable is the giant smile on Caleb's face. At least one of us is having fun.

"How do you make this look so easy?" I ask as I try to find my center and balance.

"I've skated since I could walk. You'll get the hang of it."

He starts to skate backward and reaches out for my hands. Having him there makes me feel a bit steadier, which I guess is always the case, skating or otherwise. I start to glide from foot to foot, taking longer and longer strides as Caleb guides me around the rink in a circle.

"You're doing great," he says, pulling me along just a bit faster.

I actually don't hate this now that I'm getting the hang of it. At one point, I start to lean back too far, and Caleb guides my body back into the right position so I don't fall. Eventually, he even carefully lets go of my hands, and I'm able to stay upright without falling over. It's kind of fun and freeing, just gliding across the ice.

"You're honesty a natural," he says as we sit on the bench. "I can't believe you didn't fall."

"You held onto me most of the time," I say, unlacing my skates and sliding my aching feet from them.

"That doesn't mean much, other than if you fall, I'm falling with you."

If you fall, I'm falling with you, I repeat in my head.

I don't hate the sound of that.

CHAPTER 38
CALEB
THE NEXT DAY

'm sitting on the couch, watching some tape of Dallas, the next team we'll be facing in the playoffs, and icing my hip, which has been bothering me a bit. Cassie is in my armchair just across the coffee table. She has a romance novel in her lap, and every few minutes, she either squeals or kicks her feet excitedly. Who knew she was such a lively reader? The feet kicking is why she's in the chair and not sharing the couch with me. She almost kicked me in the nuts earlier this morning and decided to move, despite my protests, to avoid injuring me.

I feel guilty that I'm not reading with Cassie. But as soon as we found out that we were playing Dallas, I had to shift my attention to preparing. Cassie says she doesn't mind, but that doesn't make me feel any better about not being able to give her a normal Sunday morning with her boyfriend.

At least whenever she gets up to refill her coffee or grab a snack, she saunters over to me first to give me a kiss. It's really just a normal day of us hanging out but with something more added in.

That something more means that I got to hold her hand yesterday while we skated without her getting nervous. It means that she kissed me in the middle of our movie last night, completely out of the blue. It also means that I can walk over to her right now, pick her up out of her chair, and carry her to the bedroom. Which I'd honestly love to do if she didn't seem like she was enjoying herself so much and if I didn't have work to do. I have to force myself to study Dallas' star forward instead of the gorgeous woman in my living room.

"I should really go train for a bit," she says as she closes her book a few minutes later. But she doesn't stand up.

"Do you want me to go with you?" I ask because I think maybe she doesn't want to leave me here.

"You can't spar with me right now with the playoffs. I'm just going to hit a bag for a bit."

"I could still go with you. I'll just use the treadmill for a bit or maybe hit a bag too. I need to get some cardio in anyway."

"You really want to?" she asks.

"Spend more time with you? Yes, yes, I do."

We walk into the *fight* side of Anthony's Fight and Flight as the class wraps up. I take a deep breath, ready to brace for the impact of having to talk to people while they pack up, and Cassie and I get ready. Cassie and I have mostly kept to ourselves here, but I recognize a few people taking off their hand wraps, and I know they're going to want to talk about the playoffs.

I always clam up when random people want to talk about hockey with me. I worry that I'll get too detailed or let something slip I shouldn't. I keep my head down and walk to the corner locker in the back of the gym. I'm not sure why I was worried because everyone seemed to respect my space, even if one or two of them were staring.

What bothers me more is that several guys are completely ogling Cassie as she takes off her sweatshirt to reveal a sports bra and her impressive abs. She's really been working hard lately, and it definitely shows. She looks so strong and confident as she wraps her hands and starts to warm up. One of the guys says something I can't make out under his breath, and while I can't tell exactly what he said, his eyes say enough.

I grab my hand wraps and gloves from my bag and march over to Cassie. Immediately, I scoop her into my arms. I can admit I'm a possessive a-hole, but I don't care.

"Is this okay?" I whisper as I pull her close.

She giggles and gives me a nod before I crash my mouth down to hers. It's quick and warm, and I completely forget about the guys by the end of it because there's just Cassie and me, and our lips dancing against the world. When we come apart, I can't help but look down at her with what I'm sure is a big, dopey grin on my face. Because she's mine, and I can't think of anything more grin-inducing than that. I know she still might panic at some point. You don't just change from a committment-phobe to a relationship person overnight, but I think I'm ready to handle it; however it happens.

After a few moments of staring at each other while I hold her in my arms like the lovestruck man I am, we each choose a heavy bag to work out on. Cassie plugs her phone into the sound system, and her pump-up playlist radiates through the room. Now it's just us, the bags, and our sweat as we hook, jab, and uppercut our way through the workout series Cassie put together for us on the ride over here.

Sometimes, people think I'm the athlete between the two of us, but those people have clearly never seen Cassie in the boxing gym. She's an absolute force, and I'm in awe during our final round when she freestyles and adds in some kicks 'for fun.' It might sound intense, and it is, but she's also so graceful as she does it. It honestly looks more like dancing than fighting.

Our final round comes to an end and Cassie dramatically

collapses on the floor. I sit next to her and stretch while we both catch our breath, so I'm not quite as sore in the morning. Between this and practice this morning, though, I will definitely be feeling it. Especially in my hip.

"That was great," she says, genuinely thrilled that she just pushed her body so hard.

Don't get me wrong, I enjoy boxing, but Cassie's love for it is something else. Her drive and determination are some of the reasons I was so drawn to her in the beginning. It's rare that I meet someone who cares as much about something as I care about hockey. It might be part of the reason we clicked so quickly. I love seeing her here, fully in her element. I hope I don't have to be away for a game during her fight. It would break me to know that she was finally following that dream without me by her side.

Fight and Flight isn't exactly known for its healthy food, so we head home together and make dinner. We eat on my couch while we watch a home improvement show and critique the design choices.

As I'm falling asleep with Cassie in my arms, I feel this overwhelming sense of gratitude. I have to hold on to this moment forever so I don't ever forget how dang lucky I am.

CHAPTER 39
CASSIE
THE NEXT MORNING

wake up to find the rest of Caleb's bed empty. I know Caleb has an early interview today, so I'm not surprised, but it still feels achingly lonely to wake up alone for the first time in a few days. I lay in bed for a few minutes, scrolling through Instagram before I decide to be an adult and seize the day or whatever.

I decided to make a cup of coffee, and I truly thought I was alone, so I nearly slam into a wall when I see Caleb at the kitchen island.

He doesn't turn around despite my shrieking. He doesn't move at all. He's hunched over, mumbling something to himself. I walk over slowly and open my mouth to ask him what he's saying, but he turns his head slightly toward me and says, "I have an interview this morning."

"I know," I say. "You mentioned it last night."

I can see his hands shaking out of the corner of my eye, and I think I realize what's happening. Caleb hates crowds, but he hates one-on-one conversations with people he doesn't know even more. I can't imagine the impact of adding in the fact that millions of people could be reading or watching what he says.

"You haven't met this reporter before, have you?" I ask.

He shakes his head no and looks down at his untouched coffee. His breathing starts to get more labored, and I'm not exactly sure what I'm dealing with here, but I don't think it's good.

"Caleb, are you okay?"

I place a hand on his back. He leans into my hand, which tells me maybe it's helping, so I place my other hand on his thigh in an attempt to center him.

"This happens sometimes," he says, so faintly I almost can't hear it.

I know that by 'this,' he means panic attacks because he said he had one the night of the gala. He said that Greggs and King helped him get through it. I wish I knew what they did because I'm at a complete loss. I've had students with anxiety, but this is a completely different situation. I think my touching his back might be helping him, though, so I wrap my arms around him.

"Take a deep breath," I say.

He doesn't at first. His breaths are still short and labored. Eventually, he shakes his head and manages to take a deep breath.

"Hold it," I say, strengthening my arms around him. "Now let it out."

I squeeze my arms around him as tight as I can. When I loosen my arms around him, his breathing seems a bit more normal, and he looks slightly less terrified than he had when I walked in.

He looks over at me. "Thanks."

His usually rosy cheeks are even more red with embarrassment.

"Did that help?"

He gives me a strong nod but doesn't say anything. I can tell he wants quiet right now, so I pour myself a cup of coffee and sit down next to him. I take his hand and interlace his fingers with mine, placing our hands on the counter. He looks down at our hands with an amazed expression on his face, like he can't quite believe that I'm really in his kitchen holding his hand. I guess I can't quite believe it either. The past few weeks have been a complete whirlwind in the best way, but we're still us. Caleb still has anxiety. And lord knows I have my own shit to deal with too.

But I want to help him in what little ways I can. I might not be able to fix this, but I can be here, and I can hold his hand, and I can do small things to make life a little bit less jarring for him. I make a mental note to order him a weighted blanket because if my squeezing him helped, that might too when I'm not around.

"When is your interview?" I ask, hoping that bringing it up doesn't make him spiral again.

He looks over at me with a soft smile. "It's in about thirty minutes. I should get going," he says.

"Do you want me to come with you?"

"Don't you have school?"

"I can call in sick. I don't mind."

"It's okay, Stacey is meeting me there. The interview is about the nonprofit."

I feel relief wash over me, knowing that Stacey will be there. She might be a bit intense, but she's a familiar face, and Caleb seems to like her. It should help him to have her there in case he needs to cut the interview short or gets really stuck on a question.

"Call me if you need me. I can always be the cool teacher and put a movie on," I say.

He lets out a low chuckle and puts his arm around my waist, pulling me to his side. "Thank you, baby."

I let my head fall to his shoulder. "I've got you, Caleb. I've always got you."

He kisses the top of my head before standing up and walking toward the front door with only a bit of hesitation.

"I believe in you," I holler as he opens up the door.

He turns to me and flashes me a small but genuine smile. As soon as the door shuts behind him, I pull out my computer and place an order for a weighted blanket. It'll be the perfect surprise for him, I just know it.

CHAPTER 40
CALEB

arrive at the coffee shop where I'm meeting Stacey and the reporter a few minutes early. It's an old trick I learned a long time ago to make interviews a little less intimidating. If the reporters have to approach me and I already feel comfortable in the room, I feel much more confident.

I should probably be embarrassed by how Cassie found me this morning, but I'm not. Cassie knows me better than anyone, and Dr. Chells has been helping me realize that I have nothing to be ashamed of, even if it feels super shameful at the moment. When Cassie came into the kitchen this morning, I was actually relieved. It meant that I didn't have to fight through the anxiety alone. I'm getting better at that, but it's still nice to have someone I love and trust there with me.

I order a coffee and settle into a table in the corner. I read the start of a new fantasy book on my phone, just as a distraction, and a few moments later, Stacey walks through the door. I give her a short wave.

"Hey, Caleb," she says with a kind smile. I realize I haven't seen her smile like this before, probably because I'm usually with her when Greggs is around. "How are you feeling about the interview?"

"I feel good," I say, and it's mostly true. Cassie's help this morning gave me the confidence I needed to be able to do this and do it well, I think.

"Do you remember your talking points?" she asks as she takes the seat next to me.

I repeat them in my head for good measure and nod.

"You're going to be great," she says. "Oh, here's Gretchen now."

Gretchen, the reporter from the local culture magazine, is younger than I imagined. She's maybe a few years older than Cassie. I stand to greet her and hold out my hand. I note it isn't shaking this time, which it normally would be.

We shake, and she introduces herself before getting her and Stacey coffees.

"Gretchen is great, and you're ready," says Stacey under her breath as Gretchen waits for the coffee.

Once Gretchen had returned, placed a recorder on the table, and pulled out a notepad, my heart started to beat a bit faster.

I've got you, Caleb.

I repeat Cassie's words like a mantra as I shift nervously in my chair. *I've got you, I've got you, I've got you.*

"So," Gretchen starts. "Caleb, tell me about *Smashing Barriers*."

"*Smashing Barriers* is a nonprofit I started to help increase access to hockey in less affluent and marginalized communities. Our goal is to help kids be able to play team sports without the large financial burden that usually comes with hockey."

"Tell me more about that," Gretchen says. "Why is hockey so expensive?"

Stacey and I practiced this one, so I launch immediately into my answer. "Well, for one, you need a lot of equipment to get started. We're talking hundreds of dollars just to make sure you're able to play safely. And that's before all of the fees. Hockey isn't played in schools here. It's only a club sport, so only kids who can afford it are able to play."

"What made you realize this was a big enough issue to warrant a nonprofit?" Gretchen asks.

This question takes me a bit off guard, so I pause for a second before deciding to settle on just telling the truth.

"I'll be honest, I didn't just realize it one day. I've sort of always known. My own parents talked about the impact the cost of my playing had on them financially. I had a friend growing up who had to quit because his family couldn't afford for him to continue. But I've spent some time with some kids this season, and seeing the issue up close really made it hit home for me. It made me realize I couldn't sit on the bench anymore. I had to get on the ice and put some skin in the game."

"I'll bet your parents are proud of you. In your speech at the gala, you mentioned a woman named Cassie who helped you with this. Are you comfortable telling me more about her?" Gretchen asks.

"Cassie is, well, she's my girlfriend," I say. "I think."

I look over to Stacey to see her eyes go wide. Suddenly, my palms are sweaty because I definitely didn't expect this coming up, and I'm not sure Cassie is ready to be outed as my girlfriend in a magazine.

"Sorry, can we not include that?" I ask.

"Of course," says Gretchen. "Is there anything you'd like to say about her? If not, we can go on to the next question." She doesn't seem upset in the slightest, which is a relief.

"That's okay. What I said at the gala was true. None of it would have been possible without her, Greggs, King, and, of course, Stacey." I look over to Stacey with an appreciative smile. "I've got a really supportive group of people around me, and I'm so grateful for their help."

"Perfect, that's great," Gretchen says. "Anything else you'd like to add?"

I look over at Stacey, and she gives me an encouraging nod.

"Yes," I say. "If folks want to learn more about *Smashing Barriers*, they should visit our website, where they can see real stories of the impact our work is having. That's also where folks can contribute to the cause if they're so inclined."

Gretchen reaches for the recorder and shuts it off. "That was great," she says. "I've got the photos from the gala, but I'd love to get some of you playing with some kids. Can we schedule that with our photographer?"

I think about it for a second. I hate the idea of using these kids for publicity. But it's for the cause, and I honestly think that Ralph and his friends would think it was cool. Finally, I nod and say, "We'll have to check with their parents, of course, but I'm okay with it if Stacey is. We'll have to schedule it after the playoffs, though."

"I love the idea," says Stacey. "I'll reach out to get something scheduled, Gretchen."

"Perfect," Gretchen says as she stands up. I join her, and we shake hands again. "Really great meeting you, Mr. Mack."

"You too," I say.

It doesn't even feel like a lie when it comes out of my mouth because, for the first time ever, I didn't feel like a bumbling idiot during an interview.

Once the door to the coffee shop closes behind Gretchen, Stacey turns to me. "You were great! And I won't even ask about that Cassie thing because I'm so happy with how that went."

I let out a little laugh. "I appreciate that."

"I'll follow up today about getting the photos scheduled,

and the story should be ready to run next month," she says. "It'll be perfect timing after your Stanley Cup win."

"Let's not get ahead of ourselves," I say. "We've got a long way to go."

"I might work for you, but I'm first and foremost a Blizzards fan, so you better have faith in yourself, Mack," she says sternly.

"I have faith in the whole team," I say confidently. "I'm just a little superstitious after last season."

I think back to how our injuries finally caught up with us in the first round of the playoffs. In a season we were supposed to go all the way, we didn't even make it past game six of the first round.

"I have faith too," she says with that same kind smile from before. "I've got to get going. I have a million emails to answer. I'll talk to you soon."

I'm walking back to my car when my phone buzzes with an email from the NHL Players' Association.

Subject: Third Round Schedule: Colorado vs. Dallas

I take a deep breath as I click to open the email. *Please don't be away during Cassie's fight. Please don't be away during Cassie's fight. Please don't be away during Cassie's fight.*

My eyes scan to next weekend and…

Crap.

It takes me at least a full minute to realize I've basically collapsed against my car. Cassie is going to be crushed. She won't show it. She'll say she's fine. But I know better. And I *want* to be there. I curse again under my breath and aggressively pull the door to my SUV open. I'll have to figure out a way to make this up to her. I pull out my phone to text her. She'll be in school, but I want her to hear it from me before the schedule is public.

Caleb: I just got the schedule for round three…

She must be on her break period because she replies right away.

Cassie: That "…" is making me nervous. What's wrong?

Caleb: We'll be on the flight to Dallas during your fight.

Caleb: I'm so sorry, baby.

Caleb: I feel awful.

The dots that show that she's typing appear and disappear a few times before her reply comes through.

Cassie: It's okay, we knew this might happen. You can make it up to me.

Caleb: Any ideas of how I can do that?

Cassie: Win.

Cassie: And then I want center-ice seats for the Stanley Cup Final.

I feel sick to my stomach as I settle into my car. This is exactly what I was afraid would happen if I committed to Cassie. It's been less than a week of us being officially together, and I'm already hurting her. She deserves someone who can be there. She deserves so much more than I can give her, but I'm too selfish to let her go now that I have her. I'm in love with her, and as much as I wish I could walk away and give her a chance to be with the kind of person she's worthy of, I can't stomach the thought of losing her. What if this leads to her freaking out? I have to reassure her by acting normal, or she'll know *I'm* the one who's panicking, and then I'll definitely lose her. I type out a response and hit send before I can stop myself.

Caleb: You got it, baby.

CHAPTER 41
CASSIE
A FEW DAYS LATER

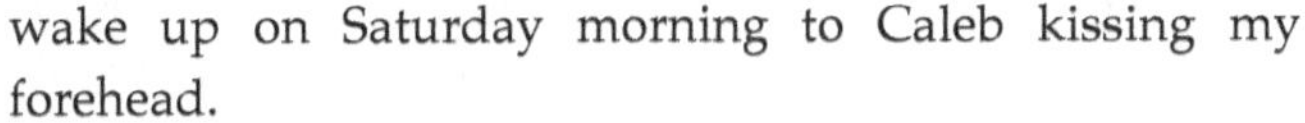

wake up on Saturday morning to Caleb kissing my forehead.

"I've gotta get going," he says, the sadness permeating his voice.

I roll over to see him standing next to the bed, duffle in hand.

"It's okay, baby. I really, really do understand," I say.

And I do. I mean, I can't expect him to skip a playoff game for crying out loud. He's gone above and beyond in comparison to what I would have expected him to be able to do during the playoffs, so as much as I wish he was going to be here today, I know how lucky I am.

"I'll see you tomorrow morning," he says, kissing my forehead again and walking slowly out of the bedroom.

When I hear the front door shut, I decide I should probably get my head in the game and get over to the gym. I put my pump-up playlist on Caleb's Bluetooth speaker and decide to make a cup of coffee.

I'm greeted by a bouquet of flowers. They're peonies, I notice. There's a card sticking out of the top. I open the mini envelope to find a note in Caleb's messy handwriting that says, *To my favorite Flower. Kick some ass today. Love, Caleb*

A smile spreads across my face. He must have woken up so early to get these. Once my coffee is ready, I place the card in the pocket of my gym bag and make my way to the bathroom to shower and get ready for my fight.

The fight isn't at *Anthony's*; it's at another, bigger gym in town. When I walk in the front door, I'm immediately overwhelmed by the sheer number of people. I know they aren't all here for my fight, but I'm still a little bit terrified. I've never fought in front of a crowd before, and the idea is suddenly making me sick to my stomach.

I find myself aching for Caleb. Which is ridiculous. I boxed before I even met him. I can do this without him here. Still, I pull out my phone and send him a quick selfie of my scared face.

Cassie: There are so many people here.

Caleb: You've got this. Here, I made you a playlist. Just put on your headphones and ignore them.

A link to the playlist comes through, and I'm already calming down before I even put my headphones on. Caleb might not be here, but knowing he's in my corner, even from afar, makes me feel so much better.

Once I've signed in and been weighed, I make my way across the gym to the warm-up area. I find Anthony there, and he walks me through how the rest of the day will be going. My fight isn't slated to start for another hour, so I slide on my headphones and click on Caleb's playlist link. *Eye of the Tiger* comes on, and I immediately start laughing. He would absolutely pick the cheesiest possible song to start off a boxing playlist, and I love it.

I try to ignore the clock and focus on the music, warming up, and my breath. I've trained my ass off for this, and I know I'm as ready as I can be. Anthony taps my shoulder when my name is called, and I make my way to the ring. I don't remove my headphones until the last possible second, letting the music and Caleb guide me through the last few moments of calm before the storm.

I step into the ring and shake hands with the woman I'll be fighting. We're in the same weight class, but she's a bit taller than me, so I mentally adjust accordingly and get my gloves on. The announcer walks through the rules, and all at once, I hear the bell ding.

The next three minutes are a sea of hooks, jabs, and uppercuts as we each try to take the other out. The woman I'm fighting is incredibly good, but I'm able to hold my own enough that neither of us lands a knockout in the first round.

We take a one-minute break where Anthony pumps me up and fuels me with water, and then we're off again.

I take a few unnecessary hits, each one more frustrating than the last. By the time the round is over, I'm starting to feel a bit exhausted, and I might be bleeding a bit on my cheek.

Anthony tries to fire me up again, but I honestly don't hear a word he says. I repeat the lyrics to *Eye of the Tiger* over and over again, hoping that Caleb's virtual presence will somehow help, but it doesn't seem to be breaking through to the rest of my body because I enter the third round feeling fairly useless.

I take a knockout punch in the first minute of the third round, and I can't get back up fast enough. The bell dings, and it's over. I'm out. I lost.

Anthony helps me to my feet as soon as he's allowed and gets me out of the ring.

"I know you don't want to hear this right now, but I'm really proud of you," he says.

"Thanks," I say under my breath, body still reeling from the fight.

I sit down on a bench and rip off my gloves. I start to undo my hand wraps as I reckon with what happened. I'd been so prepared; I worked so hard to make sure I was ready, and I got knocked out in three rounds. I know it was my first fight, but it doesn't matter. I should have done better.

My mind wanders back to the last time I was off my game. Caleb was out of town for an away game, and Anthony noticed. I thought he was crazy for thinking that Caleb's presence had so much control over me at the time, but maybe he was on to something. Because here I am, alone at my fight after losing miserably.

My first instinct is to call Caleb, but then I'm giving into Anthony's notion that I need Caleb. I can't spend half of my life sucking at everything I care about while Caleb is on the road.

I pack up my things and head for the door, barely saying goodbye to Anthony on my way out. Once I'm in my car, I don't know where to go. I'd have Caleb's condo completely to myself, right? Now, while I want to be alone, I know I'll feel his absence, and I'm trying my best not to be irrationally upset with him. It's not his fault I've grown too attached. I've never relied on anyone before. I don't know why I thought that I could now. It was clearly a mistake.

Without realizing how I got there, my car is suddenly outside of Washington Park, the park in the center of my favorite neighborhood. It's filled with running paths and bike paths and lakes and playgrounds, and I love it. I'm still in my workout clothes, so a little run doesn't seem like the worst idea in the world right now, even if I might still be bleeding a bit on my face. I get out of my car, leave my phone behind, and take off running before I even reach a designated path. I just need to be alone, and I need to get away from my own thoughts.

I run, and I run until I can barely breathe. When I finally have to stop for a break lest I pass out, my brain catches up with me, and I'm forced to think through what happened. Yes, I lost. But it was my first fight ever. Just because it was an amateur fight doesn't mean the other fighter wasn't more experienced than me. Back when I took my first swing at a bag, I never dreamed I'd be able to even fight another person, let alone make it three rounds. There will be more fights because deep down, as much as I want to right now, I know I'm not going to stop trying.

After a few miles in the crisp spring air, I feel a bit better. I still have no idea what to do about my reliance on Caleb, but the loss doesn't feel quite so fresh and painful. I can see my life beyond today, which I honestly hadn't been thinking about, and it's not all that bad. I've got Ralph's final game of the season next week. I've got book club with Hazel coming up soon. There's more to life than training, and mine doesn't totally suck.

Absent from my thoughts, for the most part, though, is Caleb. It's too scary and too painful to think about what all of this means for us. He's been my rock throughout this process, and he was so sweet today before the fight. I don't know how to tell him that I lost.

I spend hours in the park. I tell myself it's because I want the time outside and completely ignore the fact that I'm clearly avoiding going back to Caleb's condo. When it finally gets dark, I have no choice but to go back. I take the long route downtown and stop for ice cream on the way. Hell, I've earned it. When I finally open the door to Caleb's condo, the scent of the flowers fills the space. I sit down on the couch, and for the first time all day, I allow myself to cry.

CHAPTER 42
CALEB

When we land in Dallas, I immediately pull out my phone to see how Cassie's fight went, but the only messages I have are from my mom, wishing me luck with the game tomorrow. I restart my phone, assuming Cassie's text just hasn't come through yet, but once it's back on, there's still nothing. I pull up Cassie's number and hit send, but the call goes directly to voicemail. I have to shove my phone in my bag because it's time for us to get off the plane and get to our hotel, but I'm sure Cassie will call back soon.

Except she doesn't. It's been hours since we landed, and I'm sitting in the hotel restaurant at a table by myself, eating a mediocre salad. I keep glancing at my phone, expecting to see a text or missed call. I didn't hear a ring, but nothing happened. It's just silence, and I'm starting to get worried. Not because Cassie can't take care of herself, she absolutely can, but because the silence makes me think something happened. Cassie never lets her phone go to voicemail unless she's teaching or at the gym, and I know her fight ended hours ago. I've called her three times now, and each one has gone directly to voicemail. I decide to shoot her a text, even if what I really want is to hear her voice. At least she'll know I'm thinking of her. Especially if what I think happened did, in fact, happen.

Caleb: Hey, baby. Just want to be sure you're okay. Call me when you can.

The text goes through, so I know that she at least got it, even if she doesn't see it right away. I really don't know what to do. I don't even know what happened for sure. I decide to call it a night early and head up to my room. The last thing I want is to hang out with my teammates right now, and I'm sure some of them will show up in this restaurant soon.

Once I'm showered and in bed, I cave and text Anthony. I want to let Cassie be the one to tell me what's going on, but I'm getting really worried, and I need to be sure she's okay.

Caleb: Hey, just wanted to see if Cassie is okay.

Immediately, three dots appear, showing Anthony is writing his reply, and a few seconds later, his text buzzes through.

Anthony: She didn't tell you?

Caleb: I haven't heard from her since I got to Dallas. I'm a bit worried.

Anthony: She's okay, and she did great, but she lost. Knowing Cassie, she probably just needs some time alone.

Caleb: Okay, thanks for letting me know.

I know Anthony is right. This is a very Cassie way to react to a loss. So I shouldn't take it personally. But to be honest, I feel like crap. If I'd been there, she wouldn't have been able to run away. We would have gone for a walk, gotten ice cream, or watched a movie together to get her mind off of it. I would have been able to help. But I can't help if I'm not there. And, like it or not, I won't be there for a large part of her life. Cassie is independent and totally capable of taking care of herself, but that doesn't mean I don't *want* to be there. And it doesn't mean she doesn't deserve someone who *can* be.

I don't know what to do. I thought I could handle it all—hockey and a relationship and all that comes with it—but maybe I can't. Maybe hockey just owns too much of me. But I owe it to Cassie not to make any rash decisions. And I owe it to my team to give these playoffs my all. I guess I just have to keep trying, and right now, I have a game tomorrow that I need to focus on. So I set my alarm on my phone and call down to the front desk to set up a backup wake-up call. Once I'm settled in bed, I shoot off a quick text to Cassie. I may not know what to do, but she's still my best friend, and I still want to be there for her as much as I can manage.

Caleb: Anthony told me about the fight. I'm so sorry. I'm here whenever you're ready to talk.

CHAPTER 43
CASSIE
TWO DAYS LATER

wake up in Caleb's condo alone. I hate that I long to be in his arms when my eyes flutter open because I know I'm already too reliant on him, but my heart betrays me, and I do. I want him here. I want to talk to him, to be reassured by him. So why can't I bring myself to call or text him back?

I've always been independent. I've always put keeping myself safe and secure above all else. I've never wanted to date. But now that we're doing this, I don't want to stop. And yet, I can't seem to find the words to talk to Caleb. I know he'll be back soon; his flight home from Dallas was already scheduled to land. I have to figure out how I'm going to explain ignoring him for thirty-six hours. Then again, he only called me a couple of times and sent me a few texts. I didn't hear from him at all yesterday. Maybe it's because of the play-offs. Because I'd hate for him to be upset with me after everything else that's happened. I don't think I could handle that.

I make my way to the kitchen to make myself a cup of

coffee. As it brews, I go through my phone notifications from overnight. My breath hitches in my chest when I see a text from my landlord.

Evil Landlord: Apartment is fixed. Feel free to move back in whenever.

The fact that this man didn't even apologize for all the trouble he's caused me is neither here nor there because now I have a whole new set of problems. I can't just stay here with Caleb when my apartment is perfectly fine to live in. Caleb's condo is great, but it's also his condo. I'm not sure he'd even want me here, knowing I have my own place again. This whole thing is still so new and honestly so complicated that I don't think it would be smart of us to continue playing house. I see him more when I'm here, but I'm honestly not sure that's a good thing. What it really means is that I'm becoming more reliant on him, and that's not safe. My own apartment is safe. My life before we started this whole thing was safe. Alone is safe. My phone buzzes on the counter as the coffee pot finishes brewing my cup.

Unknown: Hey Cassie! It's Stella, Grant Lance's wife. I heard we might need to make you a WAG jacket for the rest of the playoffs and just wanted to get your sizing information. Let me know! See you in the family section soon!

I drop my phone on the counter and try to wrap my mind around that text. They want to make me a WAG jacket? How does Stella know Caleb and I are together? Are we even at that level yet? I don't know, but I do know that I'm not ready to waltz into the Blizzards' arena wearing a bejeweled jacket with Caleb's name and number on it. The idea actually makes me want to vomit a little bit.

Before I can think of what to say to Stella, I basically run to the bedroom and pull open the drawer Caleb cleared out for my things. I pull out all my clothes before digging under the bed to find my duffle bag. I toss the clothes in the bag and quickly move onto the bathroom, where I clear off my—no,

Caleb's—shelf and throw my toiletries into the duffle. I carry everything to the living room and put it on the couch while I search for my shoes.

I'm back in the bedroom when I hear a key in the lock of the front door. I hear the door creak open and Caleb's voice call out, "Snowdrop?" in a timid voice.

I take a deep breath and try to center myself. I'm an adult. I can handle having this conversation. I round the corner of the bedroom into the hallway slowly, mentally preparing to see Caleb.

I was not prepared. He's standing in the doorway looking as gorgeous as ever, a small smile on his face. He's sweet and kind and perfect, and I don't know what to do. I love him. It's never been more clear to me than it is at this moment. But that doesn't mean I'm capable of this. It doesn't mean I deserve him, either.

"Hey," I say as I walk toward him.

"Hey, baby," he says, taking a step forward and placing his bag on the floor. He looks to the couch, presumably to take a seat on it, and that's when he sees it.

"What's this?" he asks, motioning to my bag on the couch.

"My apartment is fixed. It's time for me to go home."

He looks at me, then the bag, then at me again. "Can we talk about this? We haven't spoken in two days."

I walk toward him, eager to somehow wipe the hurt from his face but unsure of how to do it. "I know. And I'm sorry about that. But I have to go. You have a game tomorrow to prepare for."

"I know I do," he says with a sigh. "But I need to know what's happening right now. With us."

"Nothing is happening. I just need to go home."

It's not entirely true. The truth is that I don't know what's happening with us. But he deserves for me not to make any rash decisions, and he deserves so much more than what I'm doing right now, too. But every bone in my body is telling me to run, and I can't stop myself. At least not fully.

"Okay," he says.

I should be relieved, but instead, I feel like he just punched me in the gut.

"What?" I ask.

"Okay," he says again. "If you really feel like you need to leave, I'm not going to stop you." I thought he'd at least fight me on this. Why is he giving up so easily? "Cassie," he says, my real name sounding all sorts of wrong coming out of his mouth in that tone. "We just started dating. It makes sense for you to go back."

It sort of seems like he's trying to convince himself as he says it, but I already know he's right. This is still new, and it feels fragile in a weird sort of way. My leaving means we'll both be able to focus on what we need to, and I'll be able to figure out what to do about us.

I nod and take another step toward him. "If you're sure." I reach for his hand. He takes mine and gives it a squeeze, just like he had so many times before we even started dating.

"I'm sure," he says.

CHAPTER 44
CALEB

load Cassie's few bags into the back of my SUV and close the hatch. The moment I saw her bag on the couch, I knew I had to let her go. I keep telling myself I haven't lost her, that we're still us, but that doesn't mean it doesn't sting seeing her leave so easily. Even if I've been struggling to figure out hockey and us, I love her, and knowing she would have left without even saying anything if I hadn't gotten home when I did feels like crap.

I get into the SUV, and we drive back to her place in silence. I insist on making sure everything is safe, and Cassie reluctantly agrees so at least I can help her get settled back in.

Once we arrive outside her apartment, we unload the trunk and carry her bags up the stairs. She didn't have much at my place, so it only took us one trip.

When I finish placing her things on her bed, she turns to me and says, "Well…"

"Well?"

"I don't know how to do this."

"Do what?" I ask.

"Whatever happens next," she says. "I don't know what we're doing."

I take a step toward her, wanting so badly to close the distance between us completely. To kiss her and somehow make it all better. But the truth is, I don't know what we're doing either. I know I'm in love with her. I know I want to be with her. I just don't know *how*.

"Me either, baby," I say, testing out the nickname. It still feels right on my lips when I'm saying it to her, which is reassuring. She seems to soften when I say it, too.

"Can we figure it out?" she asks, taking a step toward me.

"I promised you that, no matter what happens, I'll always be here. That's still true. I'm not going anywhere. We just have to take this one step at a time."

I don't know what the next step is, though. I have a home game tomorrow, and then it's back on the road. But that's how this is always going to be, at least until I retire. And I'm only twenty-three. I can't exactly expect Cassie to wait for me for the next decade of my career to figure out what the next step is.

"Don't you have to get to practice?" Cassie asks.

I look down at my watch and discover I'm going to be late if I don't leave now. "I do," I say. "I'll see you..." I pause because I don't actually know when I'll be able to see her again. "Soon."

I close the space between us and give her a quick peck on the cheek. It's nothing like the kisses we've shared before. It's quick, devoid of emotion, and a bit sad. But it's all I can manage right now.

"Bye, baby," she says with a soft smile that could rip my heart out.

I can't believe I'm just leaving her in her apartment right

now for practice. It feels like I'm giving up on us, even if I just said I'm not.

But I don't know what else to do, so I say, "Bye, baby," with a dumb wave and walk out of her bedroom and through her apartment door.

Grant Lance isn't an angry person. He's been in a few fights over the years, but they've been rare and justified, in my opinion. So when I walk into the dressing room at the practice arena to get ready for our ice time, I'm more than a bit surprised to see him throwing a chair into the wall. I don't say anything. I just swerve out of range of his apparent rath and make my way to my stall.

Greggs is sitting at his stall next to mine, staring at Lance but not saying a word. I look at him, eager for some kind of an explanation, but he just shrugs at me. Eventually, King walks over to us and says, "Something happened with Stella," in a hushed tone.

"Is the baby okay?" I ask.

"No!" Grant yells from across the room. Evidently, he heard me. Crap. "The baby is breach, and Stella is freaking out, and I'm stuck here with you baboons instead of with my wife and our soon-to-be child at the doctor's office."

I know nothing about babies or pregnancy, so I'm not sure exactly what Grant means, but I can tell it's important. I walk over to him and, despite every macho instinct I have whilst being in a hockey locker room, I wrap my arms around him. He stiffens at first as if he's surprised I'm hugging him, which, to be fair, I am too. Eventually, he softens and returns the hug.

"This is really hard," Grant says, pulling out of the hug but not moving away from me. "I've seen other guys go through it, but I never understood. Not really."

"I know it's hard," I say. "But if anyone can do it, it's you.

You're the best captain I've ever had, and you're going to be an even better father."

"Really?" he asks. He's usually so self-assured. This must really be getting to him.

"Really," I say.

I mean it, too. Grant is a fantastic captain, and I can tell he'll be a great dad, even if he's not able to be around as much as he would like right now.

Is that true for me too? Can I be the kind of partner and father I want to be while still living out my dream? Or will I wind up like so many other players: a part-time father, likely divorced, and virtually alone? This is why I always figured I'd wait to be with anyone until after I finished my hockey career. But I can't expect Cassie to wait that long for me. I have to figure this out.

"Thanks, man," Grant says, patting me on the back in the way men do when they don't want to actually show affection. "I needed that."

"No problem. You'll figure it out," I say.

And I will, too, because I have no other choice. I owe Cassie at least that much.

CHAPTER 45
CASSIE
FOUR DAYS LATER

The Blizzards won their home game a few days ago, and right now, they're on their way to winning this away game. Just one more home game, and then if they win this series, they go to the Stanley Cup. It's everything Caleb has been working for, and I'm so proud of him.

That means that my feeling like shit right now not only isn't justified, it's ridiculous. Ever since I moved back into my apartment, things have been a little weird, and I miss him. But I have to remember that not only is he out there following his dream, but also that I chose to leave. I could be sitting in his condo right now, but I ran away, and even though we're still a couple, he feels further away than he ever has before.

I watch the Blizzards eke out a win in overtime on my tiny little TV. Once Caleb is off the ice and walking back to the dressing room, I pull out my phone to text him.

Cassie: Congrats! You played great. Especially in OT! See you tomorrow?

I scroll through Instagram, waiting for a reply for a few minutes, but nothing comes through. I have a long day of work tomorrow—parent-teacher conferences will last late into the evening. I shoot Caleb a quick heart emoji and get ready for bed. I'm sure he'll get back to me once I'm asleep.

I was right about it being a long day; conferences were scheduled one on top of the other, and I'm exhausted. Seeing Hazel in the hallway is definitely a sight for sore eyes. I give her a quick wave and cross the hall toward her.

"Hey!" I say. "Where's Ralph?"

"Who knows." She laughs. "I think he wandered off with a friend somewhere."

"How did his conferences go?"

A smile spreads across Hazel's face. "Really good, actually. I can't thank you enough for bringing Caleb into his life; I think it's really helping him."

"I'm so glad," I say. "That's exactly why I did it."

"Speaking of Caleb, how's he doing with the playoffs?"

"He's doing okay. I think. Actually, I don't know. I moved back into my apartment, and I'm not sure how he's doing. We haven't been able to talk much."

Hazel nods. "I don't envy you. I wouldn't want to start a new relationship in the middle of something that intense. But you guys will figure it out."

"Yeah."

I don't say anything else because I'm not entirely convinced that we will. I love Caleb, but I love my independence. I know Caleb respects that because he didn't argue when I said I had to leave, but I don't know how to be the person he deserves. That, on top of the playoff stress, has become a lot to manage.

I give Hazel a hug and head back to my classroom. I have a few more conferences to get through before I can leave, and

I want to be sure I have time to talk to Caleb. He'll be so excited to hear about Ralph doing so well in school.

Once I'm finished with conferences and in my car, I pull out my phone to dial Caleb's number. He never replied to my text about hanging out tonight, but I figure if he's free, he'll answer.

"Hello," an out of breath Caleb says as I start my car.

"Hey, baby."

"Oh," he breathes. "Hey."

I can't tell what he's doing, but he seems like he might be busy, so I ask, "What are you up to?"

"I'm just at the practice rink, working."

"Oh, okay."

I didn't think he had practice today, but he must be working on his own. "I just wanted to share some good news."

"What's up?"

"We had parent-teacher conferences today, and I ran into Hazel. She said Ralph's doing much better in school. She thinks it's because you worked with him during the regular season."

"I'm really glad to hear that," he says. "He's a great kid."

"Yeah, he is. Well…" I pause. I want so much to keep talking to him, but I know he's at the rink, and he probably needs to keep working. "I'll let you go. I just wanted to let you know."

"Thanks, baby," he says. "I'll see you soon."

"Sounds good," I say. "Goodnight."

The line goes dead, and I drive home in silence. Why am I so sad? I like being alone. I like my independence. Have I really become so reliant on Caleb that I can't even handle one night alone anymore? That can't be good. Not at all. So, I spend the rest of the night on the couch by myself, trying to ignore the aching feeling in my chest, hoping that this annoying attachment I feel to him dissipates soon.

CHAPTER 46
CALEB
TWO DAYS LATER

'm still at the rink after our optional ice time in Boston. Everyone else has left, and the Zamboni is waiting to smooth over the ice, but my shot is off, and I'm not leaving this rink until I fix it.

My shot's not the only thing that's off, though. Cassie sounds weird whenever we talk. Ever since we won the third round of the playoffs and moved on to the Stanley Cup, she's sounded almost sad. If we were still just friends, I'd march over to her apartment as soon as we land tomorrow and demand to know what's wrong, but I think it might have something to do with me, and I don't want to risk losing her right now. Not while I'm still trying to figure out what to do about my feelings for her and how much they don't fit into my life. How much I can't be the person she deserves.

My phone buzzes with a text. It's from Cassie.

Cassie: Good luck tomorrow, baby. I'll be watching with Hazel and Stacey!

Caleb: That sounds fun! Tell them I say hello.

Cassie: Any fun plans for the rest of the day?

Caleb: Still at the practice rink here. Going to bed early, I think.

Cassie: Sweet dreams.

Caleb: You too, baby.

I've been trying to do my best to be attentive when she texts and calls, but we haven't been able to hang out much since she moved back to her own apartment. She's been busy with the end of the school year, and I've been busy with the playoffs. It means we're basically a long-distance couple right now, and I hate it. I want her there when I get home from a trip. I want her in my arms when I wake up in the morning. I hate waking up alone, knowing she's across town doing the same.

I take another shot, and it finally goes into the net. I sigh with relief and skate off the ice, waving to the crew so that they can start clearing it. Once I'm changed out of my gear and heading back to the hotel, I get another text. This one is in my group chat with Greggs and King.

Greggs: Don't forget about breakfast tomorrow!

King: Like you'd let me.

Ugh. I do not feel like getting all emotional right now. I just want to focus on the Stanley Cup. We're so close, I can taste it. Just four more wins, and it'll be ours. Boston is a tough team, and I'm worried about their top line in particular, but I still think we can do it.

I shove my phone in my pocket and hope that maybe Greggs will forget about inviting me in the morning so I can get some extra sleep.

Greggs does not forget. There's a loud banging on my door at promptly six o'clock in the morning. Lucky for me, I'm already awake. As much as I dread having to bare my soul to my teammates right now, I realize I actually haven't minded starting my game days a bit earlier, and eating a healthy breakfast will give me good energy for the game tonight. When I open the door, Greggs and King look shocked.

"What?" I say.

"Nothing," says King. "We're just used to having to drag sleeping beauty out of bed."

"I'm starving," I say. "Let's go."

Once we're at the local brunch spot King picked out, I place an order for an omelet and brace myself for what's about to come.

"Okay. Someone ask me how I am," I say, eager to get this over with.

"That's not how this works, Mack," says King.

"Shut up, Thomas." Greggs gives King a shove. "He actually wants to share. How are you, Caleb?"

"I'm good," I say.

After a few moments of silence, Greggs says, "And…?"

"And that's it," I say. "I'm good."

King gives me a dubious look, and Greggs just shakes his head.

"We're all under a lot of pressure right now, so I'll let this slide today," says Greggs.

"I won't!" says King. "Every away game, I've embarrassed myself in front of you for, like, two years now. Caleb doesn't get to hide just because he's currently being a moron and doesn't want to admit it."

"How am I being a moron?"

"When's the last time you saw Cassie?" King asks.

I have to stop and think. I guess it's been a week now. That's the longest I've ever gone without seeing her. No wonder she feels so distant.

"About a week," I say. "But I've been busy. Obviously."

"When's the last time you called her?" Greggs asks.

"We talked last night for a bit."

"That's not what I asked. I asked when did *you* call *her*."

Oh.

Well.

"I… uh…" I fumble.

"Exactly my point," says Greggs.

"What do you mean?"

"You're avoiding her," King says.

"I am not avoiding her. I'm just busy."

"So busy that you can't pick up the phone and let her know you're thinking about her?" Greggs asks.

"You know how it is," I say. "I have to stay focused."

"Since when is Cassie a distraction?" asks King. "From what I can tell, she's been nothing but supportive of you and hockey."

Okay, that's actually a good point. Cassie's never once made me feel bad about any of this. She's always checking in to see how practice went or letting me know how proud she is of me. Why am I so worried about upsetting her?

"Well, I, uh…" I start. "I guess I don't feel like she should be supportive of it."

"And why is that?" Greggs asks while King nods along.

"Because… Because it's hard to be a WAG."

"Well, of course it is," says King. "But has Cassie ever actually told you that any of this bothers her?"

"Well… no," I say. "But it has to, right? I mean, I miss the crap out of her when we're at away games. Do you think she doesn't really feel the same way?"

"That's not what I'm saying at all," says King. "I'm sure she misses you. But maybe she's okay with missing you. It's not like Cassie is new to all of this. I don't think you're giving her enough credit."

Maybe I'm not. Cassie does know how all of this goes; she's been friends with me for a long time. Maybe she'll really be okay with it. Maybe I'm looking for excuses.

"I'm scared," I say, not realizing I said it out loud.

Greggs nods for a moment in silence while King takes a bite of his omelet.

"Scared of what?" Greggs finally asks.

"That I'm not good enough for her," I admit. "That she's going to leave. And then I won't just be single. I'll have lost my best friend."

"Ding, ding, ding," sings King with a mouth half-full of food.

A grin spreads across Greggs' face. "And this, my friends, is what we call 'self-sabotage.'"

I know he's right the moment he says it. I've been avoiding Cassie because I don't think I can be good enough for her. It's not just about my hockey schedule. It's about *me*. I have to talk to Cassie. I have to make this right. But I can't just do it over the phone. That's not good enough. I pull out my phone and type out a text to her.

Caleb: Good morning from Boston! I've got optional practice tomorrow afternoon when we get back that I should do, but then can we get together? Maybe for dinner before Ralph's game? I miss you.

I miss you so much, I think.

I'll fix this. I'll make sure she knows she can count on me, even when I'm not able to be there in person. I'll let her know the kind of partner I'm capable of being.

I just hope I'm not too late.

CHAPTER 47
CASSIE
THE NEXT AFTERNOON

'm packing up my desk in my classroom, eager to get home and get ready for my date with Caleb. I haven't seen him in over a week, and we've barely been able to talk or text. Things have felt a little weird, but tonight, we're having an early dinner. I hope that seeing him in person will help me get over the fears that have been festering since I moved back into my own place. The ones telling me that I'm not capable of being with anyone, and especially that I'm not good enough for him.

My phone buzzes with a call from Hazel. I send her to voicemail, knowing that I'll be seeing her in a few hours at Ralph's game anyway. But then it rings again when I reach my car, so I answer while attempting to balance the papers I need to grade and get into my car.

"Hello?" she asks before I can even get a word out.

"Hey, Hazel! What's up?"

"Ralph is missing," she says. "He didn't come home from

school, and he's not answering his phone. I have no idea where he is. The police said to stay home in case he comes back here, but I'm freaking the fuck out, and I don't know what to do."

"Okay," I say. "Take a deep breath. I'll call Caleb. We'll go find him."

"Thank you," she says.

I hang up before either of us can say goodbye and dial Caleb's number while I start my car. It goes directly to voicemail. I let out an audible groan because while he's sent me to voicemail more than a few times over the past few weeks, right now, I really need him to answer.

I text him before turning on my navigation to the Blizzards' practice rink. If I can't reach him, I'll just bust into practice and force him to leave, I guess.

Cassie: Emergency with Ralph. Call me back ASAP.

I hightail it across town and try not to think about the millions of scenarios Ralph could be finding himself in right now. A few minutes before I reach the practice rink, my phone buzzes.

"Hello?" I holler without even looking at who called.

"What's wrong?" asks Caleb.

Oh, thank god. He's done with practice.

"I'm still in practice," he says. "But I saw your text during a water break. What's going on?"

"Ralph didn't come home from school," I explain. "Hazel can't reach him, and she doesn't know where he is. I'm almost at your practice rink. Can you be ready in five minutes?"

There's a long pause and nothing but silence at the other end of the phone. I know what I'm asking. He has one of the most important games of his career tomorrow night. But he knows Ralph better than I do at this point, and as much as I'd hate to admit it, I need his help.

"Yes," he says finally. "I'll change now."

"Thank you," I say. "I'll be there soon."

The line goes dead as I speed through a yellow light. When I finally arrive outside the practice arena, I see Caleb running out of the front door covered in sweat, hair all spikey from his helmet. He'd look adorable if he didn't look so worried. I pull up next to him and unlock my car.

"Get in," I say as he opens the passenger door. "We'll start with Wash Park and go from there."

"Okay," he says, clicking his seatbelt as I drive off. "Let's go."

CHAPTER 48
CALEB

We don't find Ralph at Wash Park, and Cassie is panicking. I want to reach out and hold her hand. I want to reassure her that it will all be okay. But I don't actually know that it will be, and she seems singularly focused on Ralph right now, so I keep to myself as we drive to another arena in town that Ralph and I have met at a few times to practice.

He's not at the rink, but once I'm there, I'm reminded of something.

"Cassie," I start. "When did Ralph's dad die?"

"I think about a year ago, why?"

"About a year ago, or exactly a year ago?"

"Shit," she says.

"I think I know where he might be," I say.

We race back to the car, and Cassie guns until we reach the old beat-up arena I'm thinking of.

"Why would Ralph be here?" Cassie calls after me as I jump out of the car, take off, and run to the front door.

I don't reply; I just open the door, and I'm immediately met with hesitant relief. I can see a kid about Ralph's size through the windows overlooking the ice.

Cassie catches up with me and says, "Oh, thank god," when she sees him.

I walk into the rink and slowly approach the ice as if I could somehow startle Ralph. When he becomes clear, I can see he's firing pucks into the goal at rapid speed, wearing his dad's Team Fire jersey.

"This is where his dad used to play for the firefighters' hockey team," I whisper to Cassie. She nods with understanding. "Do you want to try?"

"I think he's more likely to listen to you," she says. "I'll call Hazel to let her know he's safe."

I nod and walk into his line of sight, careful not to put myself in a position of getting a puck to the face.

Ralph's eyes land on me as he fires another puck toward the goal. "Go away, Mack," he hollers.

I step out of his line of sight and move back toward Cassie.

"What are you doing?" she whispers. "You can't just give up."

"I'll be right back," I say as I take off jogging to the rink's skate rental station.

I haven't worn rental skates since I was five years old, but they'll do the trick. I ask to borrow a stick, noting that the attendant seems to be a bit starstruck about handing a hockey stick to me and run back into the arena.

Cassie's waiting for me just out of Ralph's view, and when she sees me, I know she understands.

"Good idea," she says.

Once I'm laced up, I walk around the edge of the arena so I'm behind Ralph when I enter the ice. I skate up behind him with more speed than I'd usually use with a kid and intercept the puck he just fired toward the net with ease. He comes chasing after me, but I'm a professional hockey player, for crying out loud. I take off and fire the puck straight into the opposite net from center ice.

"Fuck you," Ralph yells.

Well, okay then. I'm not sure what I expected by doing this, but it was not that.

I grab another puck, and this time, Ralph tries to block me. I weave around him, bringing myself closer to the net, and fire it off. I do it a third time just to really piss Ralph off because he can't keep up with my speed and agility. He is a kid, after all. Finally, he does what I've been expecting him to do since he cursed at me. He gives me a shove into the glass. I don't shove him back. I just maneuver around him. He grabs the back of my hoodie and pulls me backward, attempting to slam me into the glass again. But I'm over six feet tall, and according to Cassie, I'm made of muscle, so I only move an inch or two.

Ralph lets out a grunt and plops down on the ice. I lean over to help him back to his feet, ready to make a snide comment just to get him going again in the hope that it gets his anger out, but then I see the tears hitting the ice.

I sit down next to him and pull him into me. He sobs into my chest but doesn't say a word.

Eventually, he looks up at me, his cheeks still stained with tears. "I'm sorry," he whimpers.

"I know why you're being an a-hole," I say. "And it's okay."

"You know?"

"I figured it out. And I get it. But your last game of the season is tonight, and your team is counting on you, dude. And you scared the crap out of your mom."

He sighs. "I know. I just got overwhelmed, and I didn't know what to do."

"Hockey can be a safe place for you to go," I say. "But you need to communicate with your mom. If you can't explain how you're feeling, at least just tell her where you're going."

"Okay, I'll call her in a minute," he says.

"You can call her to apologize. I expect you to grovel. And I do mean grovel. But Cassie already called your mom so she wouldn't be worried."

"Ms. Flowers is here?"

I point over to where Cassie has been watching.

"Well, that's embarrassing. I promised her I wouldn't get in another fight."

I laugh. "It's cute that you think you can fight me."

He gives me a playful shove. Then he wipes the tears from his cheeks and starts to stand up.

"Come on," he says. "I have a game to get to."

CHAPTER 49
CASSIE

We arrive at Ralph's game with minutes to spare, but he doesn't head for the ice immediately. Instead, he finds his mom in the stands and gives her a big bear hug. She kisses his head as she holds him, and I can tell he feels awful for scaring her. After a few moments of what I assume is an apology, he heads toward the dressing room to get his gear on and get ready for the game.

Caleb and I take the two open seats next to Hazel, and she gives me a squeeze.

"Thank you," she whispers.

"It was all Caleb," I say. He offers a sheepish smile back before turning his attention to the ice where the boys are about to be announced.

Ralph and his team take the ice, and I recognize a number of the players. Some are from school, and others are from the game they attended back in the fall. I spot Henry; he's a forward, and he happens to be taking the first face-off. Ralph quickly points up at Caleb, and I can see the look of awe through his fellow player's masks.

I nudge Caleb, and he waves sheepishly as I yell, "Go, Ralph!"

Despite the afternoon we had, I can't help but laugh at the absurdity of it all. My hand is resting next to my thigh, and Caleb's fingers brush up against it when he shifts in his seat. He looks at me with a bit of hesitation before lacing his fingers through mine. I squeeze his hand, and we both turn our attention to the game. I want to tell him that it's more than okay. I've missed him so much over these past few days that I could barely breathe. But that feels too big and too honest, so I settle for watching kids play hockey for three hours.

I probably should have known that a bunch of twelve-year-olds would not be nearly as exciting as an NHL game, but I didn't really fully comprehend it. I'm bored out of my skull by the second period, but Caleb seems as enthusiastic as ever, commenting under his breath and even yelling when Henry gets his second goal. Caleb tells me that Ralph is playing really well, and I can see it. His size helps, but I notice he's also really fast, even for a kid.

In between the second and third periods, Caleb offers to get us snacks (he knows me so well).

Once he's out of sight, Hazel turns to me. "I know it's none of my business," she says, "but what's going on with you two?"

Well, now, that's an excellent question.

"I don't really know," I say. "We agreed to be together, but then I sort of panicked and shut down, and he's been so busy with the playoffs, and now I don't know where we stand."

"I'm sure it will be okay," Hazel says.

"How do you know? I mean, one bad day, and I completely freaked out. How will I ever be able to do this?"

"You just have to keep trying every day. Love isn't easy,

but he hasn't changed the way he looks at you when you aren't looking, so I doubt your little freakout shook him. Even if it did, he's still here, isn't he?"

I guess he is.

And I guess I know that love isn't supposed to be easy, but I didn't really expect it to be quite this hard, and I'm terrified. Terrified of losing myself, sure. But more than that, I'm terrified of losing Caleb. I'm not sure how to trust myself enough to let myself be with him. Won't I always be a little bit worried that I don't deserve him?

"How do I know that I'm worth it?" I ask Hazel quietly. It's raw and real, and I regret the moment it comes out of my mouth, but I can't take it back now.

"Oh honey," she says, wrapping an arm around me and giving me a squeeze. "I promise you, you're worth it. You're one of the best people I know, and you deserve to be happy. Does Caleb make you happy?"

More than I could ever express in words. So I just nod.

"That was a rhetorical question. It's obvious you two are made for each other."

She goes quiet, and I turn to see Caleb returning with my nachos and Hazel's pretzel.

"Thank you, baby," I say.

His shoulders immediately relax at the mention of the nickname. We still have some things to work out, but I feel so much better when he sits down next to me and wraps an arm around my waist. I know I can do this. He deserves for me to try.

"I know I said we should grab dinner," Caleb says as we're standing up after Ralph's team wins their game.

"You've got a huge game tomorrow, baby," I say. "You need to go to sleep. It's already late."

Part of me is sad because I was really looking forward to some one-on-one time with Caleb. But I know that I'll get it soon enough, and I'd hate for him not to play well tomorrow because he stayed up too late. Besides, this gives me a chance to get my shit together and figure out how to someday be the kind of partner he deserves. It'll take some time, but I think I might actually be able to get there.

I take my seat at what's now my regular bar to watch the away games with Stacey and Hazel. The Blizzards lost their game the other day, so they still have to win two more to win the Stanley Cup. Hazel and Stacey aren't here yet, so I pull out my phone. I have a text from Caleb, and my heart swells when I see his name on my screen.

Caleb: Hey baby. Missing you in Boston. Wish you were here.

I do too, I think. Since when did I become such a needy dork?

Cassie: I miss you too. Now go kick Boston's ass!

I've tried to keep Caleb's focus as much on hockey as possible over the past few days. It hasn't been easy, but I think he appreciates that I understand what his life is like during these intense times. It's one of the benefits of us having been friends for so long; I've already seen it all, which helps a lot.

Caleb: What do I get if I do?

He follows it up with a winking emoji. But I need his head in the game right now.

Cassie: You get the Stanley Cup…

Caleb: Ugh, fine. I'll focus. But once practice is over tomorrow, I'm coming over, and I plan to do very naughty things to you, baby.

I can't help but giggle a bit as I feel my cheeks flush with heat. Hazel and Stacey arrive a few minutes before the game starts, and about an hour after that, Hazel is drunk.

"I love hockey!" she yells at no one in particular. "And hockey players."

She giggles to herself under her breath. She's been throwing back drinks all night, and I've never seen her like this. She's usually the responsible mom. And while I generally don't love hanging out with drunk people when I'm completely sober, seeing Hazel let loose is actually sort of nice. She deserves a night off, and I'm glad she feels comfortable enough with me and Stacey to relax a bit. I wonder which hockey player she's talking about...

"Me too, unfortunately," Stacey says to herself. I choose to pretend I didn't hear her because I'm not about to open up the can of worms that is her and Greggs' weird relationship.

"Me three!" I say, confidently raising my Diet Coke in the air.

Before I can realize what I've done, Hazel and Stacey's eyes both go wide. "What?!" Hazel yells. "I thought you were still in freakout mode. Now you're saying you *loooooove him*?"

"I've moved on from freakout mode into missing him mode. I'm not sure which is worse."

At that moment, Caleb's face fills the screen. My heart swells in my chest, seeing his rosy cheeks and crooked smile after making a goal. He's been playing great tonight, and the commentators are talking about him as a possible MVP choice again. I'm sure he hates the attention, but deep down, he'd be honored to be chosen once the initial shock wore off.

I close my eyes and take a deep breath. God, I miss him. I miss the two of us just being in his condo. I know it was only a couple of weeks, but it was nice. Since moving back into my apartment, I've been feeling off, like maybe it isn't my home after all.

"So," the more sober Stacey starts. "You're in love with him?"

"Duh," I whisper, hoping Hazel doesn't hear me and make a scene.

"Oh my god, this is the best!" Hazel yells. So much for that plan. "And I'm only a teeny weenie bit jealous," she says.

"You're jealous?" I ask, suddenly feeling weirdly possessive of Caleb. I thought this feeling was reserved for dudes in romance novels.

"Not of Caleb!" she corrects. "I just really need to get laid."

Hazel sighs, zoning out into the distance.

This is the first time I've heard her talk about being with anyone but Eric. I'm glad she's doing well enough to consider hooking up with someone.

"Is there anyone we can set her up with?" I ask Stacey while Hazel looks out into the great beyond, now completely oblivious to our conversation.

"The only men I'm in regular contact with are your boyfriend and Greggs. And I wouldn't wish the latter on my worst enemy, so no. I've got nothing," Stacey says.

"Maybe an app?" I suggest.

"God, no. I definitely wouldn't wish that hellscape on my worst enemy either."

I groan. I want to help Hazel get back out there.

"What about King?" I ask.

"Nope!" Hazel is now back in our conversation, apparently having been listening the whole time. "No way, not going to happen."

I laugh at her quick reply, but I can't figure out why she had that reaction.

"Why do you say that?" I ask.

"Maybe because he's a massive playboy," Stacey says with an eye roll.

"Noooooo," Hazel whines. "He's too preeeetty."

I chuckle. "I don't see the problem here, Haze."

"Every time I'm around him, I get all weird and tongue-tied. I don't know what it is."

"It's because he's hot," I whisper. Stacey and Hazel both give me worried looks. "What? I may love Caleb, but I have eyes."

"There you go using the L word again," Stacey says.

"Why is this so shocking?" I ask.

"We know you love him, sweetheart. We're just surprised to hear you admit it," says Hazel.

"I'll bet she hasn't told him yet," Stacey says. "You haven't, have you?"

"Well… I, uh… No."

Hazel nods like she's realizing something. "This is making a lot more sense."

"What? I'm just waiting for the right time," I say. "I think."

"Nope. You're waiting because you're a chicken," says Stacey. "Don't make me cluck at you."

I sigh. I know they're right. I've been putting it off because, deep down, I'm still scared. I can't lose Caleb, and even though I know that won't happen, old habits die hard.

"I just want to think of a good way to do it," I say. "In a way, this has been a long time coming, and I really want to do it right."

"Are you sure you aren't hoping he'll say it first and let you off the hook?" Hazel asks.

I think about Hazel's question. She really gets deep when she's drunk, good lord.

"Maybe I was, but not anymore. I'm ready." I nod with commitment and slam my Diet Coke onto the bar. A little bit splashes out of the glass, and I can't help but giggle.

"Let's not get carried away here," says Stacey. "You can't tell him while he's in Boston."

I know she's right. But God, I want to. Now that I've admitted it to my friends, I just want to get this off my chest.

"We're FaceTiming tonight…" I start.

"No!" they both yell at the same time.

"Absolutely not," says Stacey.

"Don't you want this to be romantic?" asks Hazel. "You need to wait until after the season's over."

Hazel might be right, but I don't think I'll be able to wait another second after the winner of the Stanley Cup is announced. An idea is forming in my head, and I have these women to thank for it. I wrap my arms around them both and give them a squeeze. "You both are the best."

"We love you too, sweetheart," Hazel says.

Not one to show her feelings, which I can understand, Stacey nods and just says, "What Hazel said."

CHAPTER 50
CALEB

'm pretty sure Cassie has almost told me she's in love with me three times. But she keeps stopping herself. First, she almost said it on FaceTime, and then when we hung out a bit after training yesterday, it happened two other times. I don't know why she's hesitating, and it's freaking me out a little. I can understand that she's scared. I'll admit I'm a bit nervous about it too.

It's game day in Denver, and the air around the city is completely electric. I went on a run this morning, and I didn't even mind when two random people stopped me to wish me good luck tonight. I know if we lose tonight, we have one more chance to make it happen, but Cassie has parent-teacher conferences, so she can't be at the next game if we lose, and I refuse to win the Stanley Cup without her in the arena. Even if she is wearing her stupid Roy jersey.

My phone buzzes with an email notification. It's my building telling me I have a package, but I don't think I've ordered anything lately. I make my way downstairs and greet the guy who's at the front desk today.

"Hey, I think I have a package," I say.

"You do, but be careful, it's heavy."

He slides it across the desk toward me. I don't recognize the company it's from, but I pick it up, all forty pounds of it, and walk back to the elevator.

Once I'm back in my condo, I rip open the box. There's a note on the top.

In case I'm not here to squeeze you. Love, Cassie

I dig into the box and pull out a very large, very heavy blanket. It's a weighted blanket, I realize. I've been looking into getting one after my therapist suggested it, but I've been so busy I haven't had a chance. Cassie must have ordered this one after I had that panic attack. My heart swells at the thought of her picking it out, making sure it was the right size and that the color would work in my condo.

She really does love me, even if she can't say it yet. Maybe I need to stop waiting for her to do it. Maybe I can be the first to take the step, and it'll help her feel more comfortable. But it has to be perfect when I do. I can only do this once.

How am I supposed to do this?

I used the weighted blanket as part of my pre-game nap, and I've never been more relaxed. I even stopped to talk to a local podcast host that I actually sort of like on my way into the dressing room, and I agreed to do an interview later this week.

I still haven't figured out how I'm going to tell Cassie I'm in love with her. I know I have to at least wait until after the game, so I put on my headphones and do my best to tune in to my pre-game routine.

I'm stretching in the dressing room when Greggs and King both arrive.

"Ready for a great game, Mack?" asks King.

"You got it," I say. Greggs gives me a fist bump, and before I know it, the coach is rattling off last-minute details about Boston we can't forget tonight.

"Let's win this thing on our own turf," he says as he wraps things up. He's not exactly a pep-talker, so we all just nod and put our hands together in the center of the room. "Champions on three. One. Two. Three."

CHAPTER 51

CASSIE

hree.

Two.

One.

The puck drops, and the game is off. I'm so nervous I can barely think. I just watch the puck fly across the ice with Stacey on one side of me and Ralph and Hazel on the other. We have first-row seats near center ice, just like Caleb promised, and we can see the whole game perfectly.

I hold on to my sign for dear life, careful to make sure that it's facing the right direction. I know Caleb's seen it because a big grin spread across his face when he looked at me during warmups. It says "Go #8" in big block letters using Blizzards colors. I let my recess group help me decorate it with glitter today. Even though I historically hate glitter, it just felt right today. Ralph was especially proud of the little cut-out of Caleb he printed off and glued on.

What Caleb hasn't seen yet is my jersey. On our way into

the arena, I stopped in the team store and bought his. It might not be a WAG jacket, but I know it'll mean a lot to him to see me in it when I show him later.

My heart stutters as I think about what will happen after this game. If they win, Caleb will be a Stanley Cup Champion. He's worked so hard for this. I just hope they can make it happen.

I'm on my feet most of the first period because the team manages to keep control of the puck and gets three goals to Boston's one. It's going to be a high-scoring game, I think, because King hasn't even made a goal yet, which is virtually unheard of.

The second period went fairly well, although we gave up a goal and didn't manage to score ourselves. King still hasn't scored. He's had a few good chances, which I'm sure is driving him insane.

As Caleb leaves the bench after the second period, he searches the stands for me. I decide to turn around and show him my jersey. I figure he needs all the good vibes he can get tonight. When I turn back around, his cheeks are bright red, but his smile is huge. I give him a short wave before he heads into the dressing room one last time.

In the third period, Caleb takes a brutal hit from a Boston player right in front of us. His body slams into the glass, and he collapses onto the ground. My heart all but stops until he gets back up and slowly skates to the bench. I give Hazel a worried look, and she squeezes my hand. A few minutes later, he's back on the ice. He gets back at Boston by assisting a wild goal by King.

"Finally," sighs Hazel when King scores.

"What do you mean, Mom?" asks Ralph. "We've been winning the whole time?"

"Oh, nothing, honey. I'm just glad they're doing well," she says.

Stacey gives me a knowing look, and I try not to giggle too loudly.

There are two minutes left in the game, and Boston's goalie has left the net. Caleb, Greggs, and King are all on the ice. It's not unheard of for a team to score two points when they have an extra man on the ice, so the Blizzards need their best to make sure we win this thing.

Boston controls the puck for the first minute, but then Greggs gets possession and fires it off to Caleb, who's closer to Boston's empty net. Caleb fires it down the ice, and it smashes into the net. The team rushes Caleb and throws him into the air. Normally, he shies away from their hugs, but tonight, he's the one coming to them and giving them all a big embrace.

The final seconds go off without a hitch, and the announcer screams over the mic that the Blizzards won. *Caleb is a Stanley Cup champion.* My heart swells when I see the team rushing to hug him. King and Greggs even collapse onto the ground when they hug each other and just roll around for a second. Just when I think things couldn't get any better, Caleb searches the stands and points up at me. I'm screaming at the top of my lungs, and it's completely euphoric.

CHAPTER 52
CALEB

'm so overwhelmed by the entire experience that I don't hear them say my name. I'm just so happy to have been able to win a few minutes ago that the idea of maybe being MVP hasn't crossed my mind since before the game even started.

The announcer says my name again, and Greggs elbows me in the ribs.

I tentatively skate forward, unsure of what to do. They give me the trophy, and then there's a microphone in my face, and I start to panic a little because while I've gotten better at saying rehearsed lines, I really wasn't expecting this.

I search the stands for Cassie, hoping that seeing her will give me some courage. Seeing my name on her jersey brought me a weird amount of joy before the third period, so seeing her now should help too.

I find her face in the crowd, and she gives me a big thumbs-up. I'm brought back to the feeling of falling asleep under the weighted blanket earlier today, the feeling of her arms wrapped around me, giving me a squeeze.

The announcer repeats his question.

"Caleb Mack, you just won the Conn Smythe Trophy, making you the Stanley Cup MVP. What are you going to do now?"

At that moment, I know exactly what I'm going to do. It's so perfect, I can't even believe it.

"I'm going to tell my best friend I'm in love with her," I say.

Then I hand the trophy off and skate faster than I have in my entire life over to the glass where Cassie's sitting on the opposite side. As I approach her, a slight look of shock is painted across her face.

"Wisteria," I yell so she can hear me, and she giggles at the obscure flower. "I know you're scared. And I know this is still new. But I'm in love with you, and I can't wait to tell you any longer."

A smile spreads across her face and she picks up her sign, the one with my number on it. As cute as the sign is, I'm a bit confused until she turns it around.

I love you, Caleb Mack, it reads.

I let out a laugh because while I've seen signs like this before, none of them have ever been held by Cassie.

"I love you too," she yells.

She looks so stunning in my jersey with her hair back in a braid. I want to kiss her more than anything in the world. I need to feel her—*now*.

"Can we get her down here, please?" I say to one of the refs.

"I don't think it's time for that yet," he says.

As if I haven't watched every Stanley Cup final since I was three. I know what I'm asking is above and beyond, but if I don't get to hold Cassie in two seconds, I'm going to lose it.

The entire crowd seems to be chanting, *"Bring her down!"*

as the refs and security try to figure out what to do. I skate back to the team, where Greggs, King, and everyone else jump on top of me.

"I knew you could do it!" says Greggs.

"Nice work, buddy," says King.

And I know they aren't talking about the Conn Smythe.

All of a sudden, there's a feisty little woman jumping on my back. I almost lose my balance but manage to keep us both upright before turning around. Cassie looks up at me with her big eyes and freckled cheeks, and it takes my breath away. I close the space between us and give her a kiss that I hope shows her how much I love her. I let my lips tell her how incredible she is. I let my wandering hands show her how much she means to me.

"I wasn't expecting all of this," she says when we finally part. "I was just going to show you my sign afterward."

"I love your sign. I love your jersey. I love all of it." I pause and take both her hands in mine. "I love all of you."

We kiss again, and the entire arena erupts into cheers and applause. The noise is drowned out by Cassie's lips on mine, her hands in my hair. It's just us and a few thousand of our closest friends.

I know I took a risk telling her like this. Heck, I took a risk when I first asked to kiss her all those weeks ago. It was worth it. Loving Cassie is the single greatest thing I'll ever do. And even if it was scary to shoot my shot, even if letting myself fall for her was the biggest risk I could have taken, I'll never regret it. Because of all the shots I've taken, Cassie Flowers will always be the best one.

CALEB

ONE YEAR LATER

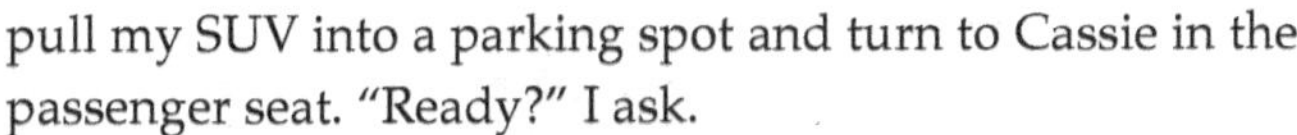

pull my SUV into a parking spot and turn to Cassie in the passenger seat. "Ready?" I ask.

"Ready," she says with a cute little nod.

I reach out and take her hand to give it a quick kiss before getting out of the car. It's these little moments that I love the most. Sure, our wedding was awesome, and the house together in our favorite neighborhood is nice, but there's nothing I love more than rocking out to music together in the car on the way to some mundane errand. Or, in today's case, on the way to the practice arena.

"It looks great," she says, surveying the sign-in table when we enter the lobby.

When I see the *Smashing Barriers* logo on the banner, my breath hitches in my chest a bit. This has grown to be so much bigger than I ever imagined and to be honest, I'm pretty anxious about it.

"It's going to be great," Cassie says, clearly able to tell I'm anxious. "They're going to love you. Just like I do."

I reach for her hand, and she gives mine a squeeze back. It started when we were friends, and it continued to be our little gesture. Something that we can use to silently say, *I've got you*, in tough moments. I used it for her when she had her second amateur fight last fall, and she used it for me when we lost in the third round of the playoffs this past year.

Through all of it, I've come to learn that I don't have to be with her 24/7 to be able to be the partner she deserves. I just have to have her back, especially in those harder times.

Ralph walks through the door a few minutes before the rest of the kids are set to arrive. He's going to be my assistant coach for the younger players, and I can't wait to see him grow into the role. I think he's going to be great.

"Hey, man," I say, offering him my fist for a bump.

"Hey," he says. "Everything looks great."

"That's what I was just telling Caleb," says Cassie. "Tell him he has nothing to worry about, Ralph."

"You have nothing to worry about, Coach." He laughs before walking toward the dressing room to get ready.

Coach.

Yikes.

I turn to Cassie and let her see the worried look I know is on my face right now. She says, "You've got this," before reaching out and giving my hand a squeeze again. *And I've got you*, it says.

I return the squeeze, mentally knowing that when push comes to shove, I've got her too. *Always.*

If you or someone you know is struggling with anxiety or another mental health concern, please know that you are not alone. **Text** the Crisis Text Line at **741741** for support, or **call 988** to reach the Suicide & Crisis Lifeline.

ACKNOWLEDGMENTS

Every time I get to the end of a book I'm reading, I love getting to read the author's acknowledgments. It's always given me a bit of inspiration to get to see a little behind their process and how many people it took to get their book into my hands. Part of me never thought I'd get this far, so this is going to be a bit long and a lot in my feels. You've been warned.

Writing a book is a wonderful, joyful, very difficult experience. There are so many people without whom this book would not exist, and I want to take a moment to thank just a few of them.

First and foremost, the woman to whom this book is dedicated, Jess. Something you said to me once about needing happy endings kept me going in the hardest moments of completing this book when I wanted to give up. Thank you for your friendship and for the big bright light you shine in this world.

Next, to my Alpha and Beta (and everything in between) readers, Taylor and Marissa. Thank you for not only providing such valuable feedback and for being my cheerleaders, but also for answering my 1:00 a.m. texts panicking about my ability to do this. You're truly the MVPs of this book and two of the best friends a gal could ask for.

To my husband, Brexton. From giving me my very own writing mascot to picking me up off of the metaphorical (and literal) floor on more than one occasion, thank you. This book would not exist without your support, and I truly would not exist without your love.

My family–immediate, extended, and in-law–has been so gosh-dang supportive of this dream of mine, and I'm truly so thankful to have the best support system around. I'd especially like to thank Mom, Dad, Andrea, Tina, Todd, Baylie, Jack, and Brett, for their endless support and love.

To Meika and Louise, thank you for randomly choosing to sit down at my table to eat your lunch. It changed the entire trajectory of my writing career, and I'm so unbelievably grateful for your continued support and mentorship.

To my writing teacher and general writing-life guru, Marcella, thank you, thank you, thank you. Your early words of encouragement are why I believed in myself enough to get after this dream.

I truly had the best team helping me pull this thing together. So to my cover artist, Anna, and my editors Sarah and Sherri, thank you. I'm so honored to have you on my team.

Lastly, every writer writes because a teacher once believed in them. Mr. Sniegowski and Dr. Shaw were mine.

Now that I'm nearing the end of this thing, I'm terrified that I've forgotten someone. BUT the one person I haven't forgotten is you, dear reader. Thank you for spending your precious time reading my book. I hope it brought you a little bit of hope and joy today.

ABOUT THE AUTHOR

Originally from Colorado, A.K. Isaacs (*she/her*) has lived in 12 states and Washington, D.C. Now an adoptee of the Midwest, she spends her days as a nonprofit fundraiser and her nights (and early mornings!) writing love stories. When not reading or writing, she can be found cheering on the Colorado Avalanche and painting with watercolor. She'd like to remind you that the world is a better place because you're in it.

Stay in touch by following @authorakisaacs on Instagram and TikTok!

www.ingramcontent.com/pod-product-compliance
Lightning Source LLC
Chambersburg PA
CBHW030428160726
47991CB00005B/1633